A Season of Angels

BY DEBBIE MACOMBER

Angels Everywhere

Christmas Angels

Mrs. Miracle

Sooner or Later

Someday Soon

The Trouble With Angels

One Night

A Season of Angels

Morning Comes Softly

And in Hardcover

Family Affair

A Season of Angels

Debbie Macomber

HARPER LUXE

An Imprint of HarperCollinsPublishers

HarperCollins books may be purchased for educational, business, or sales promotional use. For information please write: Special Markets Department, HarperCollins Publishers, 10 East 53rd Street, New York, NY 10022.

FIRST HARPERLUXE EDITION

HarperLuxe™ is a trademark of HarperCollins Publishers

ISBN: 978-0-06-206529-2

11 12 13 14   ID/RRD   10 9 8 7 6 5 4 3 2 1

To Lloyd Jassin,
my own personal Guardian Angel

Chapter 1

The manger was empty. Leah Lundberg walked past the nativity scene Providence Hospital put out every year, stopped, and stared. The north wind cut through her like a boning knife as Leah studied the ramshackle stable, her heart heavy, her life more so.

The blue of Mary's gown had long since faded, she noted. Joseph, leaning heavily against his staff, was slightly off-balance, and looked as if he'd topple in a stiff wind. There seemed to be one less lamb this year and one of the donkey's ears was missing. It was a small wonder the structure remained upright with the weight of the angel, yellow now instead of golden, nailed to the top. Triumphantly, she blew her chipped horn proclaiming the glorious news of the Savior's birth.

The hospital had reconstructed the Christmas scene every Advent for the last fifty years, long before Leah was born, long before she realized an entire lifetime of tears could be stored within a single tattered soul.

It was ironic that a woman who toiled as a nurse day after day on a maternity ward would be childless herself. Her work with laboring mothers was her gift, they said, her special talent. Women specifically requested that she be with them for the birthing of their children.

For whatever reason, Leah had been granted the touch, a gentle hand, and a sympathetic heart. Birthing mothers claimed she was inspiring, encouraging, and supportive. Labor didn't seem nearly as difficult when Leah was with a patient. She'd heard it all before, countless times, the praise, the gratitude. What most of Leah's patients didn't know was that she, who was an expert at labor and delivery, had never given birth herself.

Her patients left the hospital with their arms and their lives full. Each afternoon, Leah walked out of Providence alone. And empty.

Tears crowded her eyes and spilled unheeded down her cheeks. She bowed her head and closed her eyes in prayer. "Dear God," she whispered, choking down the emotion, "please give me a child." It was a plea she'd whispered innumerable times over the last ten years. So often that she was convinced God had long since given up hearing. Or caring.

Wiping the moisture from her face, she gathered her coat more closely around her thin shoulders and headed for the staff parking lot. She forced herself to smile. It upset Andrew that she continued to dwell on their inability to have children, and she didn't want him to know she'd been crying.

Her husband had accepted the news with little more than a shrug. He felt bad, knowing how desperately she longed for a baby, but it wasn't nearly as earth-shattering to him. If God saw fit to send children into their lives, then fine, if not, that was fine too.

It wasn't all right with Leah and she doubted that it ever would be.

Leah's prayer whistled in the breeze, up through the bare spindly arms of a lanky birch tree, winging its way higher and higher until it had ascended the clouds and drifted into the warm winds of heaven. It arrived fresh with the salt of her tears at the desk of the Archangel Gabriel. The very angel who'd announced the news of the virgin birth to Mary nearly two thousand years earlier. His responsibilities had been wide and varied through time, but he felt a certain tenderness for humans and their multiple problems. He found earth's population to be a curious lot. They were stubborn, rebellious, and arrogant. Their antics were a constant source of amusement to those behind the pearly gates. Who could help laughing at a group of people who heatedly declared that God was dead and clung to the belief that Elvis was alive?

"Leah Lundberg," Gabriel repeated softly, frowning. The name was vaguely familiar. He flipped the pages of a cumbersome book until he'd found what he was seeking. Sighing, he relaxed against the back of his chair and slowly shook his head. Leah was one of his most persistent cases. He'd heard her prayer often, had ushered it himself to the very feet of God.

Gabriel had sent countless couriers to intercede on Leah's behalf, but their efforts had been met with repeated failure. Time after time, their reports came back virtually the same. It was a familiar problem that blocked the answer to Leah's prayer. Herself.

It would have been much easier if Gabriel could sit down with Leah and talk out this matter face to face. Circumstances arose now and again when doing exactly what was required, but generally not when it came to answering prayer. Humans tended to believe all that was required of them was a few mumbled words, then they were utterly content to leave the matter in the hands of God.

Through the ages humans had yet to discover what should have been obvious. The answers to prayer required participation. The people of earth expected God to do it all. Only a shocking few realized they had their own role to perform.

A good example was a request that had come in earlier from Monica Fischer, a preacher's daughter. Monica had asked for a husband. Normally this wouldn't be a problem; she was twenty-five and strikingly attractive, or would be if she didn't choose to disguise her natural beauty. The whole process of attracting a young man was complicated by her self-righteous attitude. Few men, even devout servants of God, were willing to marry sanctimonious prudes.

Gabriel hadn't decided how he would handle Monica's request or the prayer that had come in the unusual form of a letter from Timmy Potter. Gabriel had a soft spot when it came to children's prayers. Timmy was nine, and had requested a father.

Gabriel shook his head, needing to clear his thoughts. He'd deal with one prayer at a time. For the moment Leah's request was the most pressing, and the most challenging. He'd figure out something for Monica and Timmy later.

He stood and walked around his desk. Gabriel thought best while on his feet. It didn't help matters that Leah chose Christmastime to issue her fervent prayer. The busiest time of year, no less. His best prayer ambassadors were already out on assignment and those who were left were young angels lacking in experience.

Of course there was always Mercy. She possessed a heart of pure gold and was especially patient with humans. But there was a small problem with this particular angel.

Mercy was enthralled with earthly things. Mechanical things. She seemed particularly fond of escalators and motor scooters and not even heaven knew what else. Reports of her escapades circulated in both spheres.

An angel, especially one under Gabriel's command, simply did not hijack meter maids' carts. That business with the forklift on the San Francisco waterfront . . . well, that didn't bear thinking about.

Gabriel's musings were interrupted by the whisper of rustling wings. Mercy appeared bright-eyed and hopeful before him, her hands clasped in prayerlike fashion. She was a dainty thing, petite in stature when compared to several of the other prayer ambassadors.

"You wanted to see me."

Gabriel grinned. He hadn't sent for Mercy, but apparently God had.

"I'd be happy to volunteer my services in any way I can," Mercy offered brightly, her wings fluttering slightly with anticipation. "I want to prove myself."

"Can you stay away from motor scooters?"

Mercy nodded eagerly. "And jet skis."

Jet skis. He hadn't heard about that one and it was best that he didn't, not now, at least. "I can't have you intercepting any more Boeing 747s."

"I've learned my lesson, Gabriel," she murmured, and smiled innocently, as if to suggest that these incidents were a series of minor misunderstandings. "I promise I won't get into any of the trouble I have before."

"I'm sure you won't," Gabriel muttered.

"Then you'll give me the assignment?"

Gabriel stood. His seven-foot stature was intimidating, he knew. Each time the heavenly Father had sent him on a mission to earth he'd been required to calm a multitude of fears before relaying his message.

"The prayer is from Leah Lundberg," Gabriel explained with a thoughtful frown. "For the past ten years she's been in constant communication with heaven. She longs for a child."

Compassion filled Mercy's deep blue eyes. "Her arms must feel empty."

"When Leah first married Andrew Lundberg the prayer request came now and again, but when she didn't become pregnant after repeated failure, well, let me put it like this. Leah had us in a tizzy for a good long while. At one point we had five angels assigned full-time to her prayers. A year later we reduced it to one, and now her prayers are infrequent, and her faith is weak."

Mercy blinked several times. "This is a problem case, isn't it?"

Gabriel nodded. Mercy had achieved some success in answering prayer, but her experience was limited. To assign her to Leah was an extreme measure. Gabriel regretted that, but he didn't have much choice.

"How often does she pray now?" Mercy asked, and her wings stilled.

"Once or twice a year. She's given up believing God listens to the concerns of His children. Unfortunately she's given up on her faith too," Gabriel explained with regret. "If that isn't tragic enough, she's walking straight towards the pit of despair."

"But that's not true about her prayers going un-heard," Mercy cried. "Someone should tell her, give her a message, offer her hope. Why, all that poor, dear woman needs is a bit of reassurance." Agitated, the petite angel paced the area in front of Gabriel's desk.

"Send me, please, Gabriel, I promise to stay out of trouble."

The archangel hesitated. He had the sinking feeling that Mercy's promise would quickly become famous last words.

He noticed that the tips of her wings feathered out and fluttered gently when he nodded. "I'll go with you and explain the circumstances. I can't afford to spare you much past Christmas."

"Just until Christmas," Mercy protested. "That doesn't give me much time."

"Do whatever you feel is necessary to help her," he said, granting her unprecedented powers.

Gabriel didn't want to say it, but when it came to Leah Lundberg, he felt her prayer had little likelihood of being answered. Over the last ten years the human had been given countless chances. Mercy was one of the least experienced angels in his task force. He didn't hold out much hope that she'd succeed when so many other far more accomplished ambassadors had failed.

"We should start right away, then, don't you think?" Mercy pressed, eager to begin.

Gabriel glanced at the stack of unanswered prayers piling up on his desk and nodded. "I can only spare a few moments."

"I'd appreciate whatever help you can give me."

Gabriel grumbled under his breath. This could be a waste of precious time, then again, it might well be the answer to a long-standing request. He'd witnessed far greater miracles.

"Come with me," the archangel instructed, and Mercy followed obediently behind him. He was fond of this prayer ambassador although he wasn't keen on admitting as much.

"I hope I can help her."

"I hope so too," Gabriel murmured. "Look with me and I'll introduce you to Leah and Andrew Lundberg.

Slowly he raised his massive arms and with one swift motion the thick white clouds parted into a gentle mist that slowly dissipated. The scene unfolded like the opening pages of a pop-up book as the majesty that surrounded Mercy evaporated into the midst of the mundane world. The archangel and Mercy stood on the sidelines as Leah Lundberg opened the front door of her house and walked inside.

"I'm home," Leah called out to her husband, removing her thick winter coat and hanging it in the hall closet. As always her house was spotless. Her furniture was polished, the latest in contemporary styling. The black-lacquer-on-silver dining table shone back at her like a mirror. Her gaze rested on a white lambskin sofa that had cost nearly four thousand dollars. Her home was expensive and ultramodern. A child would wreak havoc in her pristine domain.

Leah's friends envied her home. Their own were often a minefield of toys and other traps children left scattered about. Her friends' lives centered around feeding schedules, soccer practices, and flute lessons. Leah would gladly relinquish her grand piano for a crib and the Persian rug for a playpen. She would gladly trade her tidy existence for the chaos and joy a child would bring into her life and marriage.

"I've got dinner cooking," her husband announced from inside the kitchen. "How does marinated flank steak, new red potatoes, and fresh asparagus sound?"

"Excellent." She moved into the kitchen and wrapped her arms around Andrew's waist.

Their massive kitchen included every modern convenience imaginable. A large room for two people who dined out more often than they ate at home. Andrew, an architect, had designed her kitchen when they believed their future included children. She'd clung to the thread of that hope, but it had grown impossibly thin as the fiber of her dreams had worn away.

Leah's eyes rested on her shiny, clean cupboards and her waxed, spotless floor. Her heart moved into her throat with a sharp stab of unexpected pain. She longed for a refrigerator door smudged with jelly-coated fingerprints, and linoleum scuffed with marks made from walking shoes and toy trucks.

"Did you have a long day?" Andrew asked.

Leah nodded. She deeply loved her husband. Without him, she didn't know how she would have endured the last several years. "We delivered three babies before noon. Two boys and a girl." Leah had long since lost count of the number of births she'd assisted. Hundreds, she guessed. But it didn't matter how often or how commonplace it seemed, the miracle of birth hadn't lost its impact.

"What about you?" she asked.

"Same old grind as always," Andrew mumbled, preoccupied with their dinner preparations.

"We should have ordered out."

"I don't mind," he told her, and she could hear the warmth in his voice. "I talked to the decorator about a tree," he said, and turned to face Leah. He buried his face in her hair and breathed in deeply. "I thought we'd have the tree done in angels this year."

"Angels," Leah repeated softly. "That sounds nice."

"Mom phoned earlier," he continued. "She invited us over for Christmas Eve."

Leah nodded. Christmas was meant for children. Instead of stringing popcorn and cranberries on the tree with her toddlers, she was working with a decorator who would shape their Christmas tree into a work of art. She would have much preferred a work of love.

When, Leah asked herself, when, oh, when, would the raw edges of her pain go away? She'd be a good mother. Andrew would be a doting, loving father. That God in his almighty wisdom had not seen fit to give her a child was the cruelest of fates. Tears filled her eyes and she looked away, not wanting Andrew to see. He knew her so well it was difficult to hide anything from him.

"Leah?"

She snuggled closer in his arms, needing the warm security of his love.

"It's worse at Christmastime, isn't it?" he asked gently.

They'd had this same conversation a hundred times over the years. With nothing new to add, with nothing new to share, it was best shelved.

"When will dinner be ready?" she asked, easing herself from the comfort of Andrew's embrace. She managed a watery smile. "I'm starved."

"Have you seen enough?" Gabriel asked, standing directly behind Mercy.

She'd seen more than she wanted. Slowly, thoughtfully, Mercy dragged her gaze away from the scene below. Compassion swelled and throbbed within her. "Leah's hurting so terribly."

"She hasn't stopped and won't until . . ."

"Until when?" Mercy prompted.

"Until she's found her peace."

"Peace," Mercy cried, folding back her wings. "The poor dear's at war with herself."

Gabriel looked surprised by her insight. "Leah must fully accept her inability to bear a child before the invisible threads that bind her fall away," Gabriel explained. "Then and only then will she be ready."

"This is my mission, to show Leah the way to peace?" The tentacles of dread gripped Mercy's tender heart. Gabriel was seeking the impossible. She longed to help this woman of the earth, longed to ease the pain of her loneliness and the desolation of her soul. Slowly Mercy shook her head, wondering how she, an inexperienced prayer ambassador, would break through the barrier of Leah's misery and lead her to the warm, sandy shores of serenity.

"You may choose to refuse," Gabriel announced formally.

"I would never do that," Mercy said, surprising herself with the strength of her fervor. She didn't know how she'd manage but somehow, some way, she'd find a means of accomplishing her mission. One thing she'd learned since her appointment as a prayer ambassador. With God's help she could forge a path where there hadn't been one before. With God's help she would make a way where there was none.

"I can't spare you any longer than three weeks, earth time," Gabriel reminded her. "Not with the New Year coming on. You know what it's like around here when people start making resolutions. By the middle of January, earthlings decide to take one last-ditch effort and try prayer."

"Only three weeks," Mercy repeated slowly. Even now she was having a difficult time pulling her gaze away from the scene between Leah and her husband.

"You'll contact me with any problems?" Gabriel asked.

Mercy bristled. The archangel's offer insinuated that she'd encounter more than her share, which was an unfair assumption. It was true she'd had trouble with the last assignment, had gotten sidetracked a time or two, but she successfully managed to complete her mission.

"There's no physical reason why Leah can't become pregnant?" Mercy asked, wanting to be certain she had her facts straight. The last thing she wanted was to walk into the middle of a prayer request without adequate information.

"None whatsoever," Gabriel stated matter of factly. "Leah and Andrew have been to see every fertility specialist on the West Coast."

"What about adoption?"

"They applied five years ago, but the waiting list is several years long. They were chosen by a birth mother and then bitterly disappointed when she changed her mind at the last minute. They withdrew their name shortly afterwards."

"How very sad," Mercy said softly.

"The Lundbergs are deeply in love."

"That helps."

Gabriel's chuckle caught Mercy off guard. She swiveled her attention to the archangel, who was clearly amused.

"What's so funny?" Mercy demanded, irritated and not taking time to censure the thought. Gabriel, after all, was an archangel and she was in no position to be questioning him.

"Nothing," he said, smiling broadly.

Gabriel wasn't one to smile. He did so only rarely. Mercy wasn't convinced it was even in his personality profile.

"I'll give this prayer request my best effort," Mercy said, thinking it was important that Gabriel know that.

"I trust you will. Just promise me one thing."

IIere it came, the long list of offenses she'd managed to rack up in the short while she'd been serving as a prayer ambassador. "Yes?" she said, straightening for the coming lecture.

"Stay away from scooters and escalators this time."

Mercy grinned. "I will."

Chapter 2

It was a disgrace, a downright disgrace the way Providence Hospital continued to use the same weatherworn figures in their nativity scene, Monica Fischer mused. The colors had faded and the animals, why, it was a travesty how dilapidated they'd become. If the hospital insisted upon decorating the grounds for Christmas, then they should do so properly.

"Did you see the nativity scene at Providence Hospital?" she asked her father as she joined him and the other choir members outside Nordstrom department store, downtown Seattle.

"I adore the crèche," Lloyd Fischer said with a beaming smile. "Mary's seen better years, I know, but I can't help thinking that battered stable must be much closer to the way it actually was that night in Bethlehem than we realize."

Her father was right, Monica knew. He generally was. She tried to be as charitable in thought and deed as he was, but it seemed beyond her. That was the crux of her problem, Monica realized. Every man she met was measured against her father's goodness and none had withstood the evaluation. Not even Patrick, whom she'd dated off and on for the last two years. Apparently their relationship was more off than she realized. He'd phoned two weeks earlier to tell her he was engaged to someone else.

That hurt and it hurt deeply. Monica had been dating Patrick all this time and assumed they'd enjoyed one another's company. She hadn't a clue he was seeing anyone else. True, they hadn't spoken of love or commitment, but they'd shared something special, at least Monica had thought it was special.

To make matters worse Patrick had finished by saying he would always think of Monica as a special friend. Monica had wanted much more than his friendship. It was time for her to marry and start her own family, and she'd foolishly set her sights on the wrong man. Now she'd need to make up for lost time, but by heaven, she vowed she'd marry and soon. There was a man for her, she was convinced of that, and she fully intended to find him.

"Are you ready?" her father asked, cupping her elbow.

Monica nodded. She enjoyed these Christmas performances the church choir gave each December in the busy downtown streets. The harried shoppers would pause and listen to the joyous music, enjoying the short respite from the hectic holiday rush. For a few short moments peace would descend like a warm blanket upon the milling crowd.

Monica climbed to the soprano section on the back row of the risers. She was tall, nearly five-nine, and stood a full head above the majority of the sopranos. Unlike the others, she opted for sensible flats with her dark blue suit. Her hair, although shoulder length, was tucked into a tight bun at the base of her neck. She wore no cosmetics and frowned upon women who did.

This was the first year their music was provided by their own church band. To Monica's way of thinking they should have made a point of practicing more often. The band's mistakes stuck out in an otherwise flawless program.

She played the piano, and as a favor to the choir director, Michael Simpson, sat in for a couple of weeks in their practice sessions. She hoped her dedication and example would inspire the small group. Her plan hadn't worked and no one seemed to appreciate the rigorous practice schedule she set for herself and the others. Eventually she'd gone back to the choir, and was pleased she had. Michael, as a means of making amends, asked that she sing a short solo in one of her all-time favorite Christmas carols, "Silent Night."

When everyone was positioned on the risers, Michael raised his baton. The choir snapped to attention. Monica was proud of the professionalism of their small ensemble. Their voices rose in melodic harmony, blending smoothly. Monica's clear, high soprano voice escalated gloriously with the others. When she sang, she felt closer to heaven than at any other time, even when she prayed, which was something she'd been doing a good deal of lately. She needed a husband.

"Monica's the tall one on the top riser," Gabriel said, pointing out the earthling to Goodness. Like Mercy, Gabriel held a special fondness for this prayer ambassador, who, again like Mercy, possessed certain character traits that left him with misgivings. If it weren't for the business of the Christmas season, he wouldn't have assigned Goodness such a difficult case.

Unfortunately he had little choice and of those ambassadors left, Goodness was his best chance of seeing this prayer to fruition. If only he could guarantee that Goodness would stay away from television and movie screens. The incident of her showing up on an in-flight movie and using John Wayne's voice to warn everyone of approaching turbulence continued to rankle. He'd counseled her on a number of occasions, but to no avail.

"I know what you're thinking," Goodness said, looking up at him with eyes filled with innocent promise. "I won't pull any more stunts with humans. I've learned my lesson."

"You're sure this time?"

Goodness glanced toward Monica and nodded eagerly.

Gabriel wished he shared her confidence. His own gaze drifted toward Monica Fischer. Her name was a familiar one as her father, a man after God's own heart, often included her in his prayers. Monica came from a strong religious background. With her father serving as the pastor, Monica had been raised in the church. It was ironic that what the young woman lacked was faith when she was surrounded on all sides by it. Instead Monica was deeply religious and had yet to distinguish the differences between faith and religion.

"She's lovely," Goodness claimed, locking her wings together. "Finding Monica a husband won't be the least bit difficult, not when she's so outwardly beautiful. God must have a special man in mind for her."

"He does," Gabriel agreed with some reluctance, wondering just how much he should explain to this inexperienced ambassador. Goodness would learn everything she needed to know soon enough, he decided. The information he had would overwhelm her now. Soon enough Goodness would recognize exactly what God had planned for Monica Fischer.

The angel focused her attention on him, her eyes wide and questioning, awaiting an explanation. "What is it I must teach her?"

Gabriel drew in a deep breath and explained. "I fear Monica's steeped in the juices of her own self-righteousness. She struggles to be good under her own power and ignores all the help made available to her through faith."

Goodness sighed with heartfelt sympathy. "She must be miserable."

"No," Gabriel returned without hesitation, "she just makes everyone else feel that way. Monica's complicated her life with a long list of rights and wrongs and dos and don'ts. Her head's so clouded with matters unrelated to faith that she's lost sight of what it means to be a child of God. Her struggles are useless when everything has already been done for her. All she need do is ask." But Gabriel wasn't telling Goodness anything new. The earth was populated with those who looked for redemption through religion.

"The poor dear."

Gabriel didn't view Monica in those terms. It was her type that caused him the greatest concern. While Monica struggled to lead people to God, her sanctimonious ways often steered them in the opposite direction.

"She sings very well," Goodness commented.

Gabriel nodded. "She's gifted in several areas."

"I shouldn't have any trouble teaching what she needs to know before Christmas."

How confident Goodness sounded, Gabriel noticed. He sighed inwardly, wondering once more how much he should explain, then decided it would be best not to discourage Goodness's enthusiasm. She'd discover everything she needed to know soon enough.

"The man God has for her is ready for a wife?"

Gabriel was beginning to feel a twinge of guilt. "Yes, and eager. Very eager. Only he doesn't know it yet, but you won't have to worry about him. Monica's the one who needs you."

"Then I'll do everything within my power to help her."

"You're ready?" Gabriel asked, thinking he'd best send her soon before he said too much. This request would be a learning experience for this young prayer ambassador as well as for her charge. All he could do was hope for the best.

"Let's go," Goodness said, impatient to leave the splendor of heaven and walk incognito into a dull, sin-cloaked world.

Gabriel watched as Goodness floated down from heaven, thinking humans were right about one thing. God often did work in mysterious ways and never more so than in this instance. Gabriel was confident of one thing. Neither Goodness nor Monica Fischer would ever be the same again.

Monica looked out over the gathering crowd and was pleased at the attention their small choir had garnered. Shoppers stopped, their arms folded around packages and some of the tiredness left their eyes. A few joined in and sang themselves. Children were lifted in their fathers' arms for a better look. The transformation the singing group produced brought a small, satisfied smile in Monica's heart.

Then she noticed a man who stood head and shoulders above the others. He seemed to be trapped by the people around him, and was impatiently edging his way around the gathering.

Being on the top riser gave her an excellent view and she frowned at this intruder. He needed both a shave and a haircut. Even from this distance she noted his eyes, which were a cutting shade of cobalt blue. He seemed to need to get somewhere and was impatiently making his way through the crowd, scooting around one and then another with nary a word of pardon. He wore a beige trench coat and looked as if he'd slept in the bedraggled thing.

Monica's gaze followed him as long as she could, but he soon moved out of her peripheral vision. What an unpleasant man, she decided, annoyed at his intrusion into their performance. No doubt he was a modern-day Scrooge who resented every moment wasted on the celebration of the Savior's birth.

The small church band struck up the first chords of the next carol, "Silent Night." The highest notes were well within Monica's vocal range and her voice was strong enough to ring out loud and clear. When the moment arrived for her short solo performance she allowed her soul to soak up the music and fly free. Then unexpectedly, from out of nowhere, another voice joined and blended with hers.

Quickly Monica looked in both directions to see who had been so bold as to disrupt her one moment of glory. She knew she shouldn't be so concerned, but it bothered her, and yet as far as she could tell none of the other sopranos were singing.

She raised her voice a full octave, straining her vocal cords. The second voice followed her lead, angelic in its purity and so strong it all but drowned out her own. What perplexed Monica most was that no one else around her seemed to notice anything was amiss. Faces from the audience gazed on approvingly and even the choir director smiled, delighted by her performance.

As she drew to a close, the last of the notes fading into nothingness, the small crowd cheered and she was enthusiastically applauded. Annoyed that her one and only solo had been interrupted by an intruder, Monica twisted around to see if she could find the second voice.

She must have been more energetic in her efforts than she realized because she lost her balance. Her arms flew out in an effort to catch herself, but before she could alert anyone to her plight, she tumbled backward off the top step of the riser.

Crying out, her arms flapping in empty space, she was surprised to land in the unexpected cushion of a man's waiting arms.

"Well, well, what do we have here?"

It was him. The very man she'd noticed earlier, the one who'd cut his way through the crowd with such impatience.

"Ah . . ." For the life of her Monica couldn't make herself speak. All she could do was stare into his handsome features. On closer inspection his eyes were a deeper shade, a metallic blue, amused now, but dispassionate. The thick lines that fanned out from his eyes weren't from smiling. They spoke of experience, most of it harsh, and disenchantment, most of it warranted, she guessed. Lines bracketed his mouth as well, they deepened as he studied her with the same curiosity with which she regarded him.

"No need to take such a chance," he chided. "If you wanted an introduction all you needed to do was ask."

Gasping and breathless, Monica struggled until he slowly, reluctantly lowered her feet to the ground. He waited until she'd found her balance before he released her completely.

"You might want to thank me," he suggested lazily.

Flustered, Monica blinked several times, seldom at a loss for words as she was now. "Thank you," she managed, the words as stiff as starch, stuck in her dry throat. "I'm not sure what happened, but apparently I lost my balance."

His brazen grin broadened. "Was that you singing just now?"

She nodded, and the curiosity got the better of her. "Did you hear two voices or one?"

"One."

"But there were two. That's what flustered me so. Another voice blended with mine. A strong soprano. Surely you heard the other voice?"

"Listen, lady, all I heard was you and I'm not much for religious music, but from where I was standing you sounded real good."

She blushed with pleasure. Her voice was adequate and she did love to sing, but she didn't possess any great talent. To assume she did would have been vain on her part, and vanity was a greased track straight to the arms of the devil as far as Monica was concerned. "Thank you again."

"You need some help joining the others?"

Monica glanced toward the riser and shook her head. The ensemble was almost finished with their program and it would only disrupt the group to have her climb back into position now.

"Then I'll be on my way," he said. "I can hardly wait to tell Lou. It isn't often a beautiful woman throws herself into my arms."

"I didn't throw myself into your arms," she informed him primly, straightening the sleeves of her dark suit jacket.

"Not technically perhaps, but there you were, pretty as a picture gazing up at me, asking for a kiss."

Monica bristled. "I most certainly was not."

"It felt good to be in my arms too, didn't it?"

"I beg your pardon?" Monica stared at him in numb disbelief. Was the man so arrogant he actually assumed she'd hurl herself into open space on the off chance a man would catch her? He was being ridiculous and she took delight in telling him as much.

He was smiling when she finished, a cocky off-center smile that lifted the edges at one side of his mouth. "I'd say, from the look of you, having a man hold and kiss you is exactly what you need."

This sounded like a threat to Monica, and she pinched her lips together and retreated a step. "You're disgusting!"

He raised his hands, palms up. "I'm just an innocent bystander. I was minding my own business, looking for nothing better than to drown my sorrows in a cold beer when you catapulted into my arms. The way I look at it, you should be thanking your lucky stars I was here to catch you."

"You were headed toward the Blue Goose?" she asked, realizing now why he'd been so determined to cut through the crowd. He wanted a drink.

"Lady, after the day I've had, you'd need a beer too."

"Don't," she pleaded, urgently taking a step toward him.

He glared at her, and his beige trench coat fanned out at his sides. The cold cut through Monica, but it didn't seem to bother him. "Don't what?" he demanded impatiently.

"Drink. There are better ways of dealing with problems other than alcohol."

"Lady . . ."

"My name's Monica. Monica Fischer," she said, holding out her hand to him. He looked at it for a moment as if he were going to ignore it before reluctantly exchanging handshakes.

"And you're . . ."

"Sorry I ever met you," he muttered.

"Please, let my friends and me help you," she said, gesturing toward the ensemble standing on the risers, singing the last of the songs.

"Listen, all I want is a cold beer and some peace and quiet. I've been on a stakeout for the past twenty hours and I . . ."

"You're with the police?"

He hesitated, and it was evident by the way he glanced longingly toward the Blue Goose that he had other matters on his mind. "I'm a private detective," he admitted. "There, does that satisfy you?"

"You must be tired," she tried again, thinking fast, hoping to convince him of the error of his ways.

"And getting more so every minute. Good-bye, Marcia."

"Monica," she corrected. She hurried after him, convinced she owed him this much for having saved her from certain injury.

"Whatever," he said, without looking her way. "Have a good day."

"Has anyone ever talked to you about the direction your life is headed?" she asked, scurrying to keep pace with him. She was tall, but he was taller and it took two of her strides to equal one of his.

"Are you going to preach at me next? Trust me, the last thing I need now is a sermon."

"Not if you promise me you won't drink."

"Listen," he said, stopping abruptly, "I'm trying to be as polite as I can, but my patience for this malarkey is long gone. I'm a responsible adult and I don't have a problem with alcohol, so if you don't mind, I'd prefer to be left alone."

"You're drinking beer, aren't you, and it's barely afternoon," Monica insisted. "Anyone who needs alcohol this early in the day must be addicted."

"Fine, then, to satisfy you, I'll order coffee. There, are you happy?"

Monica knew a lie when she heard one. "Don't try to appease me with lies," she said, glaring at him.

They'd crossed the street by this time and he continued to ignore her as much as possible, but Monica was making that difficult. She didn't know what was driving her to behave so uncharacteristically. Normally she wasn't nearly as aggressive; she was weak on evangelism, but this man desperately needed help and she was returning a favor. He'd saved her and now it was her turn to do him a good deed and rescue him, although it was clear he didn't appreciate or welcome her efforts.

They'd reached the Blue Goose and Monica hurled herself against the thick wood door, flinging out her arms until she stood spread-eagled across the entrance.

"What the hell do you think you're doing?" he demanded, glaring at her.

"I'm saving you from yourself."

"Go save someone else, would you?" His eyes were formidable, cold and cutting, but Monica refused to back away.

"I'm doing this for your own good."

He clamped his mouth closed and appeared to be counting to ten. His head nodded with each number and by the time he reached eight, his patience had evaporated. "Either you move or I'll be forced to move you myself and I guarantee you won't approve of my methods."

Monica was saved from having to make a decision when the door opened and she was momentarily pushed to one side. By the time she'd turned around and recovered, her reluctant hero had disappeared. It didn't take her two seconds to know where he'd gone.

For half a heartbeat she toyed with the notion of going inside the Blue Goose after him.

Defeated and mildly discouraged, Monica trudged her way across the street. The other choir members were mingling with the crowd, passing out invitations for the Christmas Eve service. The idea had been her father's and although Monica feared they might attract riffraff from the streets, she hadn't said as much. It wouldn't do any good to argue with her father, not when he had such a soft spot in his heart for street people.

"Monica." Michael Simpson, the director, edged his way around two altos and moved toward her. "What happened?"

"I lost my balance and fell off the riser," she explained.

His eyes widened. "Are you all right?"

She nodded. "A . . . someone caught me."

"I'm glad you weren't hurt." His smile was shy as he gently patted her hand. "I wanted to congratulate you on your solo."

"But . . ."

"Your voice was never more pure."

Monica gestured weakly. To accept the credit would have been wrong. "But another voice joined mine. Didn't you hear it? I swear it came out of nowhere."

"Another voice?" Michael asked, frowning. "I only heard you, and you were magnificent. You really outdid yourself."

"Monica, Monica." The Reverend Fischer hurried to his daughter's side and clasped her hand between his. His eyes shone bright with tears. "I've never heard you sing more beautifully. You sounded so much like your mother. I'd almost forgotten what a stunning voice she had. This is God's gift to you, this voice."

"But, Dad . . ." She stopped, not knowing how to explain. There had been another voice that merged with hers. One that didn't happen to belong to anyone in the choir. It didn't belong to anyone she knew.

"Goodness, Goodness, Goodness," Mercy said in that small chiding tone Gabriel had used with her so often in the past. "You were the one singing, weren't you?"

Goodness did not attempt to deny it. "I couldn't help it. 'Silent Night' is one of my personal favorites."

"But she heard you."

"I know." That part had been unintentional. Simply put, Goodness had gotten carried away with herself. But she had used considerable restraint. No one, however, seemed to appreciate that part. She could have used Barbra Streisand's voice. Barbra could really belt out "Silent Night," or Judy Garland. Now, that would have caused a whole lot of comment. To her credit, Goodness had resisted, although on second thought, she did an excellent Carol Burnett.

"What if Gabriel hears about this?"

"Don't worry about it." The archangel would eventually find out, Goodness knew. There would be no keeping it from him, but even that hadn't been enough for her to resist singing with Monica.

"He might take you off the assignment."

"Not a chance. Gabriel's shorthanded as it is. If he was going to pull me off this prayer request it would be for something a whole lot more troublesome than singing." The prayer ambassador was far more concerned by the consequences of her folly. Monica had fallen into the arms of that hard-nosed, disgruntled private investigator. If anything unsavory had happened, Goodness would have held herself personally responsible.

Chapter 3

"Timmy," Jody Potter called from the compact kitchen. "Dinner's ready."

"In a minute." The nine-year-old kept his gaze level with the television as he worked the controls of the video game. "I'm just about to save the world."

"Timmy, please, we go through this every night." Jody's nerves were on edge and had been ever since she'd found the letter. The folded sheet of paper had slipped from Timmy's school binder when she'd set it on the kitchen counter the night before.

A letter to God, but this wasn't any ordinary letter. Timmy had asked for a father. Jody's first instinct had been to sit him down and explain that he already had a father. Only Timmy had no recollection of Jeff, who'd died when Timmy was barely ten months old.

Timmy had no way of knowing how proud Jeff had been of his son. How he'd insisted on holding him each night when he returned from the office and feeding him his last bottle. Timmy didn't remember that it was his father who'd sung him to sleep and then stood by his crib, gently patting his back. Her son couldn't possibly remember that Jeff had burst into tears of joy the night Timmy had been born.

What Timmy wanted now was a father who was alive. Someone who could throw a ball and catch better than she could, according to his letter. Someone who understood and enjoyed football. Someone who would be a friend.

What Timmy accepted far better than she did herself, Jody realized, was that Jeff was forever lost to them. Her son was looking for a replacement.

"I won," Timmy cried, leaping to his feet, holding his hands high above his head while he danced around the living room.

"I'm relieved to know the world is safe at last," Jody muttered, carrying the meat loaf over to the round oak table. "Can we eat now?"

"I guess." From habit, Timmy hurried into the bathroom and washed his hands, drying them against his thighs as he joined his mother moments later.

They sat down at the table together and Jody passed the vegetables.

Timmy stared down at the bowl and frowned. "I hate green beans."

"Take three." Jody didn't know why she chose three, but it seemed a reasonable number and she was hoping to have a heart-to-heart talk with her son. A confrontation over green beans would be detrimental to her plan.

Timmy judiciously sorted through the vegetables until he'd located three stubby green beans. Then he carefully placed them on the edge of his plate where they were in danger of slipping unnoticed onto the tablecloth. He paused and glanced up at Jody, who pretended not to notice.

She waited until he'd drowned his slice of meat loaf in catsup and loaded his plate with fruit salad and mashed potatoes before she broached the subject of his letter.

"We were supposed to write someone for Christmas," Timmy explained after she mentioned having found it. "I'm too old for this Santa Claus stuff so I went straight to the source. It was silly anyway, the post office won't mail a letter to God. The teacher made a fuss about it and now you are too. What's the big deal?"

"Nothing," Jody was quick to assure him. "It's just that I hadn't realized you wanted a father so badly."

"Every kid does," he said. "Don't they?"

"I guess." Jody's own father had died a year earlier and she missed him still. It had been a crushing emotional blow she hadn't expected. Her father's heart attack had taken the family by surprise. Just a week earlier, he'd been in for his yearly physical and was given a clean bill of health. Both Jody and her mother had been rocked by shock and grief. She'd assumed because her father had lived a long, full life that death would be easier to accept. That hadn't been the case any more than it had been with Jeff, whose death had come without warning.

"I don't mean to be rude, Mom," Timmy continued, burying a green bean deep in his pile of mashed potatoes, "but you can't throw a ball worth a darn and I need to practice. Mr. Dillard said I had a chance of being a really good player someday."

"I see."

"You're not ugly either. I bet there's some man out there who'd be willing to marry you."

Jody had to stop and think about that one. Her son wasn't intentionally insulting her. In his eyes, he'd paid her a high compliment. "I'm sure there is someone who'd be willing to take a chance and marry me," she said after a moment.

"You think so?" How eager he sounded. He scooted to the edge of his seat, propped his elbows against the table, and looked solidly at her. "Could you find and marry him before Christmas?"

"Timmy, be serious, Christmas is less than a month away."

"You mean it'll take longer than that to get me a dad?"

"Yes, I'm sure it will."

"How much longer?"

Jody shrugged, not knowing how to answer. "I . . . I don't know if I'm ready to be married again."

"Why not?" Timmy asked, his eyes wide and innocent. "Rick Trenton told me his mom's been married three times. You've only been married once. I was thinking about that and it doesn't seem right. You're a lot prettier than Rick's mom and she's already had two more husbands than you."

"It doesn't have to do with how pretty a woman is."

"Then what does it have to do with?" He cocked his head to one side, awaiting her answer.

Jody wished she knew. "Marriage is a complicated business." Much more complex than she could adequately explain to a nine-year-old boy who seemed to think she could find a husband on a grocery store shelf. She was about to suggest signing him up for Big Brothers when Timmy buried his fork in his meat and added, "Besides, I was thinking about you having a baby. I've decided I wouldn't mind if I had to share my bedroom. Rick's mom just had another baby and she let me hold him, and you know what, I kinda liked it."

"How does Rick feel about having a little brother?"

"He thinks it's cool, especially since he's got two little sisters. Rick said you don't get a choice if it's a boy or a girl when babies are born. I don't know how I'll feel about a sister instead of a brother, but I decided I'd do what Rick does."

"And what's that?"

"Take what he gets."

Jody set her fork aside, her appetite gone. "That's a mature attitude," she murmured, wondering what she was going to do next. Timmy was serious. He wanted a father. Now he was talking about a brother or sister too.

"Then you'll start looking for a new dad for me?" His big brown eyes studied her carefully as if her decision was a momentous one.

"I'll think about it," Jody said thoughtfully. "Now eat your green beans."

"I already did."

"They're buried in your mashed potatoes," she said, waving her fork at him. "Now eat."

"Aw, Mom."

It wasn't until after nine that night, when Timmy was sound asleep in his bed, that Jody walked over to the bookcase and took out the bulky photo album. She sat in the overstuffed chair that had been Jeff's favorite and held the book against her breast in the dim light.

For several moments she closed her eyes. It had been almost a year since she'd last looked at the pictures. Twelve long months since she'd tortured herself with the memories. Timmy was right. It was way past the time for her to pick up the pieces of her life instead of dwelling in the past. A sob swelled in her throat as she tried to figure out how she was ever going to give up loving Jeff.

"That's Timmy's mother," Gabriel said in quiet, somber tones.

Shirley looked down upon the young mother and her heart ached. "She seems to be crying. What's happened to make her so sad?"

"She's thinking about Jeff, her husband who died," the archangel explained.

"Why does she torture herself this way?" It made no sense to Shirley that this young woman would continue to torment herself with memories.

"Jody is the problem," Gabriel continued. "She continues to hold onto her husband. Before you can answer Timmy's prayer you've got to deal with Jody. She must learn to trust enough to willingly let go of the past and reach toward the future. If she doesn't, she'll never be ready for the man God has for her."

"But it's been over eight years, doesn't she realize what she's doing to herself and to her son?"

"No, all she knows is the pain. Your assignment is to gently guide her toward the joy that awaits her and Timmy."

"And you expect me to accomplish this before Christmas?"

Gabriel didn't look any more pleased about this time restraint than Shirley. "I can't spare you any longer."

Shirley's wings stretched to their full reach, then folded over themselves once more. She'd assumed this would be a cushy assignment. After all, she'd only been serving as a prayer ambassador for a short while. The other cases she'd been given had been far less complicated.

"I . . . might not be able to help her," Shirley murmured.

"Apparently God the Father feels otherwise, or He wouldn't have personally requested you for Timmy's prayer."

"But how can I reach Jody when others have failed? How can I show her she doesn't have to stop loving Jeff, only open up her heart and her life to the love God has ready and waiting for her?"

"You'll think of something, only . . ." Gabriel hesitated and leveled his strict gaze on her. "You're not to pull the tricks you have in the past, understand?"

"Yes," Shirley agreed. "I won't misplace a single thing," she promised.

"That's what Goodness and Mercy told me earlier. I don't know what it is about you three, but you worry me more than all the other prayer ambassadors combined." He wiped his hand across his face, and briefly closed his eyes. "Just do your level best to stay out of trouble."

Chet Costello sat down at the bar in the Blue Goose and ordered a cold draft beer. He glanced over his shoulder to be sure that pesky little missionary hadn't decided to follow him inside. Seldom had he met a more aggravating woman.

"What's plaguing you?" Lou asked from the other side of the bar. He polished the mahogany surface with a clean rag, his hand making wide circular movements as he studied Chet. "You look like you've lost your best friend."

"You would too if you'd sat up all night in the cold."

"You were on a case?"

"No," Chet returned sarcastically, "I enjoy spending my nights in a freezing car peeking at a couple through binoculars. These infidelity cases have always thrilled me."

"No need to bite my head off."

"Then don't ask stupid questions." His little run-in with the do-gooder hadn't done anything to improve his mood. He'd encountered a hundred pious souls just like her over the years, each one convinced he needed to be saved from himself. He'd had it with that religious garbage years ago, and hadn't darkened the door of a church since his mother had died ten years earlier. He had no intention of changing his ways now.

He laughed out loud, the sound echoing like a sonic boom around the almost empty bar.

"What's so funny?" Lou asked, eager to share in the humor.

Chet paused, the beer bottle poised in front of his mouth. "She said there were better ways of settling problems than booze."

"Who?" Lou asked, bracing both hands against the edge of the bar and grinning, waiting for an explanation.

"Never mind." Chet wasn't in the mood to talk. She'd gotten under his skin, he realized, somewhat surprised. What was her name again? Marcia, no Monica. With her clear, dark eyes and her prim and proper ways, she was desperate to save him from the clutches of demon alcohol.

Part of the problem was how good she'd felt in his arms, all soft and feminine. The last time he'd held a woman had been . . . longer than he cared to think about, Chet realized. It was this job, he decided, that soured him on relationships. No one was faithful anymore, not according to the statistics he'd collected. The child custody cases were the worst and he'd sworn off those. After he'd left the police department years earlier, he'd floundered for a bit before deciding to work as a private investigator. What a crock of bull this had turned out to be. The time was fast approaching when he'd need to find something else. He wouldn't go back to the force, not after Tom's death. He didn't trust himself, not anymore. His partner had gotten killed, and Chet had accepted responsibility for the loss of his friend. The incident continued to haunt him. There were certain things in life a man didn't put behind him, and this was one.

For reasons he couldn't explain, the erstwhile missionary drifted back into his mind, with her warm, pleading gaze and her soft, sweet mouth.

"You know, what she really needs is to be kissed," he said aloud. "None of this pansy stuff of holding hands and gazing longingly into each other's eyes either."

Lou glanced his way and without comment continued to polish the sleek wooden surface of the bar. After
a moment, he paused and scratched his head. "You
looking to talk?" he asked.

"Hell, no."

"That's what I thought." The bartender resumed his
task.

Remembering the way she'd flung herself against the
tavern door produced another burst of laughter. The
buttons of her jacket had strained with the effort until
she resembled a martyr tied to the stake. She had nice,
full breasts, although heaven knew she did everything
she could to disguise the fact that she was a woman. If
he ever did have the opportunity to kiss her, which was
highly unlikely, the first thing he'd do was pull the pins
from her hair. It was a travesty to keep it twisted away
from her face that way. She'd have thick, luxuriant hair
and he'd run his fingers through it. He imagined she'd
put up a fuss at that. Anything remotely related to sensual
pleasure was sure to be sin, pure, unadulterated sin.

Chet knew her type. The mission house down the
street from his office was filled with do-gooders thinking their efforts with the derelicts and vagrants was
going to make a difference. Chet felt sorry for them
more than he did the street people they struggled to
reach with their message.

Then why couldn't he stop thinking about her? The hell if he knew. The hell if he cared. One consolation, he wasn't likely to run into her again.

"Of course I remember you, Mr. Lundberg," Mrs. Burchell, the caseworker from New Life Adoption Agency, assured him over the telephone. "It's good to hear from you again."

Andrew rolled the mechanical pencil between his palms, praying he was doing the right thing. "I'd like to know how difficult it would be for my wife and me to resubmit our application." He leaned against the back of his chair. Leah had been on his mind all day and he was worried about her.

It was so unfair that they couldn't have children. What troubled him most was that there didn't seem to be any physical reason. They'd spent years, and thousands of dollars, working with fertility specialists. Leah's life was governed by that ridiculous book she kept. He swore she'd documented her temperature every morning for the last seven years.

Perhaps if they'd been able to pinpoint the problem as his, Leah might have been able to accept their situation.

"I have your file right here," the caseworker went on to say. "I know you and your wife were terribly disappointed when Melinda Phillips decided to rescind the adoption of her infant son. It doesn't happen often, but unfortunately these girls do change their minds."

"I understand," Andrew said, not wanting to rehash the details. Having the birth mother change her mind had been much harder on Leah than on him. They'd gone to the hospital, their hearts filled with joy, only to return empty-handed an hour later. Afterward Leah had sat for hours alone in the nursery they'd so lovingly prepared. Nothing Andrew could say reached her. He'd been disappointed too and for a while there'd been a strain between them. Then one day he returned home from the office and discovered that Leah had dismantled the nursery. She calmly announced that she'd withdrawn their application from New Life and that they'd simply wait for her to become pregnant and bear a child of their own. She refused to subject them to that kind of torment again.

"I'll be happy to resubmit your names," Mrs. Burchell said, "but I must warn you there are fewer babies available for adoption now than before."

"How long would you predict?"

The caseworker hesitated. "I can't really say. It's different with every couple."

"What about the Watcombs?" Andrew asked. "We went through the orientation classes with them three years ago."

"Ah, yes, the Watcombs. Jessie and Ken, am I right?"

"Yes. Has their adoption gone through?"

"Not yet, but we're hopeful we'll have an infant for them soon."

Andrew's hopes plummeted. The Watcombs were special people and he couldn't imagine any young mother not choosing them to rear her child.

"You were in the same orientation class as the Sterlings, weren't you?"

Andrew allowed the name to filter through his mind. "He was a fireman as I recall."

"That's the couple. They adopted a baby girl last October."

"That's wonderful."

"I thought you'd be pleased."

He was, of course, but a small part of him couldn't help being envious. Leah desperately wanted a child, and in an effort to reassure her he'd downplayed his own desire for a family. He loved his wife and would give anything for them to have a child.

"Do you still want me to resubmit your name?" Mrs. Burchell asked after a moment's silence.

"Please," he said, his hand tightening around the receiver. If it took another five years or more, then that was just how long they'd need to wait. That he was doing this behind Leah's back didn't sit well with him, but some action needed to be taken, and this seemed the most logical choice. If they were chosen by a birth mother again, then they'd make the necessary adjustments. A child was welcome into their lives at any time. Love guaranteed.

For the life of her, Monica hadn't been able to forget the private investigator. Heaven knew she'd tried. He was little better than an alcoholic, drinking beer in the middle of the day. Not only that, he'd been arrogant, rude, and curt with her. He'd treated her as if she were a senseless child when she'd tried to help him.

Monica didn't understand what it was about this one man that intrigued her so. She'd gone to bed that night and dreamed of him. She'd woken breathless, her heart pounding double time. A woman had no control over her dreams, Monica assured herself. If she had, Monica certainly wouldn't have allowed that . . . man to touch her. The very idea was appalling. No, Monica corrected, closing her eyes and shaking her head, that wasn't the truth. It was the problem. She had thought about him touching her, kissing her. Her untamed imagination had taken over and she'd allowed it to happen in her dreams.

"There you are," her father said, strolling into the living room. "I've been looking for you." He settled down in the leather chair by the fireplace and reached for the evening paper. "I'm afraid I'm going to need you tomorrow afternoon."

"For what?" He seemed to forget she had a job and even if she did work as the church secretary it was a demanding position. Her father would cover for her if necessary, but she would rather he asked first instead of volunteering her services, which was something he often did.

"Mrs. Ferdnand just phoned and she can't be a bell ringer for the shift she signed up to take last Sunday."

"But, Dad." Standing on a cold street corner and collecting charitable donations was the last way Monica wished to spend an afternoon. An hour never lasted so long and by the end of her shift she'd be frozen solid.

"I wouldn't ask if it wasn't necessary."

"I know." It was useless to argue with him. The man had the patience of Job and an answer for every argument.

"It's downtown so you'll be sure to get plenty of traffic," her father added, reaching for the sports section of the newspaper and folding it open.

"Great." She stabbed the needle into the fabric and set aside her needlepoint. After working on this Ten Commandment project for weeks she was only on the fourth commandment, which meant she hadn't a prayer of finishing before Christmas. She studied the tiny stitches. Ironically the one she was currently stitching stated Honor Thy Father and Thy Mother. God must have worked it out that way, sealing any argument she might have given.

"Are you all right?" her father asked her unexpectedly, momentarily setting the paper aside.

"I'm fine," she said, then amended, "a little tired perhaps."

"I thought as much. You don't seem to be yourself lately."

"Oh?"

"I know this thing with Patrick hurt you and . . ."

"Patrick is a friend, Dad. He was never anything more. I don't know why you insist upon dragging his name into every conversation." It was a white lie to suggest she hadn't cared about Patrick, but sometimes she found those necessary, although she was never comfortable stretching the truth.

"I noticed Michael talking to you the other day. He's a very nice young man." He eyed her speculatively as if waiting for her to comment.

"Very nice," she agreed. But Michael didn't stir her blood, he didn't make her heart throb and the thought of him kissing her produced not so must as a whit of excitement.

Her father was right, there was definitely something wrong with her.

The following afternoon, Monica was dressed in her dark blue suit, standing on the corner of Fifth and University, ringing her little heart out. Surely there was a reward awaiting her in heaven for this.

A man dressed in leather and wearing enough gold to strangle himself stopped and inserted a ten-dollar bill in the bright red pot. When Monica thanked him, he insisted upon "giving her five." It took her a good three minutes to realize what he intended. He was simply looking to slap her hand. He ambled away, suggesting she get with it, whatever or whomever "it" was.

Okay, so she wasn't cool, if that was the current vernacular. Nor was she hip or groovy or several other words that came to mind. She was God's willing servant. All right, she wasn't so willing just then, but she was doing her part and that was all that mattered.

Her ears were cold and her fingers had lost their feeling and she had another half hour to go when it happened.

It was him.

The man who'd caught her in his arms three days earlier, the one she'd attempted to restrain from entering the Blue Goose. He was standing on the other side of the street waiting for the traffic to pass so he could cross. Everyone else would wait for the green light and the walk sign, but not him. Oh, no, he was too impatient for that.

She stopped ringing the bell, then started again with a vengeance, closing her eyes, hoping with everything in her that he'd simply walk past and not notice it was her.

Monica should have realized that would have been asking too much.

"Well, well, well," he said, strolling all the way around her. "And who do we have here? Monica, am I right?"

She ignored him and stared straight ahead, jerking the small bell back and forth for all she was worth, her shoulders so stiff they ached.

"It's mighty cold to be standing outside for any length of time, isn't it?"

Monica didn't deign to answer him. A lady in a fur coat walked past and dropped a few coins into the red kettle. "Merry Christmas," Monica said from pure habit.

"The same to you," the private investigator answered.

"Please leave me alone," she whispered.

"It seems to me I asked the same thing of you recently and did it help? Oh, no, you were convinced I needed to be saved." He flung his hands into the air. "Hallelujah, brother."

"Please." She tried again.

"Not on your life, sister," he responded.

"If you continue to pester me you'll leave me no choice but to contact the police and have you forcibly removed."

"Threats?" He folded his arms over his broad chest and arched both brows in mock terror. "So you want to involve the authorities. Fine. Good luck finding a cop walking his beat. In case you weren't aware, the city's seriously understaffed, and this time of year is busier than most."

Monica knew God was looking out for her when a city cop turned the corner just then, casually sauntering down the sidewalk. "Officer, Officer," she called, wasting no time. "This man is bothering me."

The policeman, who was tall and burly beneath his thick coat and cap, was casually swinging his billy club. "You troubling this young lady, Chet?"

It was just her luck that they knew each other.

"Bothering this woman? Me? You know me better than that," Chet answered, beaming Monica a cocky smile. "I've got more important things to do."

"That's what I thought."

"He refuses to leave," Monica supplied huffily.

"Now, listen, miss, I know Chet's a sorry-looking alley cat, but he's harmless. Let me assure you, you're in no danger from him."

"Thanks, Dennis," Chet said and dipped his head slightly.

"That's simply not true," Monica tried again, more adamantly this time. "I politely asked him to leave and he refused."

Dennis bounced the billy club against his open palm a couple of times. "Chet, stop pestering this pretty young lady."

"Sure thing."

Dennis touched the tip of his hat. "He'll leave you alone now, miss." With that he strolled away.

"You aren't going to leave, are you?"

"Trust me, sweetheart, he's got better things to do than listen to you making a fuss over nothing. This is a public sidewalk, there's nothing Dennis can do but ask me to move on, which he's already done."

"Why do you insist upon doing this?" Monica demanded, straightening her shoulders. She forced herself to look directly ahead and away from him, because looking at Chet caused her stomach to flutter as if she were coming down with the flu.

"Hey," he said, raising both hands, "I'm paying you back for what you did the other day."

"I was trying to help you."

"You were a major pest. Now you know how it feels."

"If you're looking for me to apologize, then—"

"No, thanks." He walked all the way around her once more, then stood directly in front of her, hands on his hips. "You know, you might really be something in the looks department if you ever decided to wear makeup."

Monica ignored the comment.

"A little blush and eye liner aren't tools of the devil, you know."

She pursed her lips to restrain herself from chastising him the way he deserved.

"My, oh, my, look at that sour puss. I was right the first time."

"About what?" she demanded before she could stop herself.

"What you really need is to be kissed, and sweetheart, I'm the man to do it."

Chapter 4

C het never intended to kiss Monica. He'd taken delight in teasing her and she was easy game. Her face flushed with color, brightening her cheeks, and her eyes snapped with outrage, challenging him. Chet was ready to laugh and walk away when a Metro bus came rushing down the street, the thick tires spraying the sidewalk with a shower of icy, muddy water.

Monica, standing as close to the curb as she was, would receive the brunt of the spray. Thinking quickly, Chet caught her by the shoulders and whirled her around. The bus passed and the muddy water sprayed him against the back of his legs. He grimaced as the icy liquid soaked through his trousers at his calves.

"What are you doing?" Monica demanded.

Her back was against the brick building and she was breathing hard. Her breasts rose up and down and her hands clenched at the lapels of his trench coat as though to push him away. When she moistened her lips as if she fully expected him to follow through with his threat, it was his undoing. He felt as if a fist had been plowed into his gut. He didn't want to kiss her any longer, he *needed* to.

"No, please," she blurted out, sounding as if she were near panic.

"Relax," he whispered coaxingly. "This isn't going to hurt in the least."

She jerked her head to one side but he caught her by the chin. By all that was right he should have released her then, but the temptation was too strong, too sweet and piercing to ignore.

Slowly he lowered his mouth to hers with the confidence of years of experience. His lips cut off her gasp of protest, and the strong pressure of his mouth opened hers to him. She tasted good, damn good, a hell of a lot better than he expected. When his tongue entered her mouth, her nails dug into his coat, and then she amazed him and quite possibly herself with a soft, womanly sigh of pleasure. Chet slanted his head and kissed her with months of pent-up passion.

He didn't mean to be so demanding, but he couldn't stop himself.

With effort, Chet forced himself to break off the intensity of the kiss and wean himself away from her with a series of short, nibbling ones. With a reluctance he didn't dare question, he lifted his mouth from hers. He would have enjoyed continuing this experiment and given the opportunity, a hell of a lot more.

Monica's chest was heaving and her eyes were closed. Her head was slightly lowered but not enough to disguise the soft, feminine look about her. He noticed that half the pins were missing from her hair so that it fell haphazardly over one shoulder. Hell, he didn't even remember doing anything more than plowing his hands into the thick fullness and positioning her head so he could kiss her properly.

Her eyes slowly opened and she looked slightly dazed and definitely pale. She gazed at him steadily for just a moment and then quickly lowered her eyes. Her slender throat moved up and down as she swallowed and it seemed that she was getting ready to speak.

"I . . . wish you hadn't done that."

"No, you don't," he returned, sounding far more cocky than he intended. Insolence was part and parcel of his job. He didn't like it in himself, but he didn't know how to stop.

"Please, will you leave me alone now?"

"Is that what you really want?"

She nodded, but refused to meet his eyes.

He stepped away from her and she immediately went about tucking her hair back into place, her hands trembling so badly that Chet had to resist offering to help.

"It was just a kiss," he said in a weak effort to comfort her, although he was beginning to feel he was the one who needed reassurance. This woman was completely unaware of what a powerful punch she packed. She'd felt good in his arms, as if that was where she was supposed to be. The thought didn't sit well with Chet. Nor was he keen on admitting how difficult it was to walk away from her.

"I . . . think it would be best if you left," she said, struggling valiantly to compose herself. She refused to look up at him.

Chet's mind was sluggish and his pulse still hadn't returned to normal. He nodded, unable to think of anything more to say. As he moved away from her, he found the small, silver bell she'd dropped on the sidewalk. Stooping, he retrieved it for her.

"Thank you," she whispered.

"You're sure you're all right?"

She nodded and Chet stepped away from her, walking backward. He bumped into a lamp post, his shoulder hitting it hard enough against the steel column to jar him. Sucking in a deep breath, he rubbed his hand over the tender spot, turned, and walked away.

He didn't want to think about what had just happened. He'd kissed a woman who, for all intents and purposes, was living the life of a nun. It shouldn't have been this good. One kiss should have been enough to cure him of ever thinking about her again. He could tell right now that it wasn't going to happen that way.

By the time Chet returned to his office, he discovered he was shaking like a leaf. He'd faced danger a dozen times, hell, more than that, but no encounter with life or death had left him so jittery that he needed to sit down. It took a morally uptight missionary intent on saving the world to reduce him to this.

"Oh, Leah, look," Pam Hewitt said, holding up a thick cable-knit sweater the color of winter wheat. "Doug would love this." She checked the price tag and then slowly shook her head. "Unfortunately I can't afford two hundred bucks for a sweater."

"I thought we were shopping for a party dress for you," Leah reminded her friend. They'd known each other since university days and kept in close contact although they weren't able to get together often. Pam had temporarily traded in her nurse's uniform to be a

full-time housewife and mother to her three young-
sters. Leah loved each one, but Scotty, the just-turned
three-year-old, held a special place in her heart. The
baby Andrew and she were to have adopted had been
born around the same time. Somehow Leah had transferred to Scotty all the love she had for the child that
was to have been hers. She gave Pam's three children
gifts every Christmas and invented excuses for outings
with them, but it was Scotty who ruled her heart.

"I hate Christmas parties," Pam muttered, folding
the sweater and setting it back on the table. She ran
her hand over the top and sighed expressively. "I was
thinking I'd cut down the fancy maternity dress I wore
a couple of years ago and—"

"Absolutely not," Leah insisted. "We're going to
find you a dress that will make you feel like a queen for
Doug's Christmas party."

"That will take some doing," Pam muttered. "Two
years at home with the kids and I'm afraid I've lost it."

"Lost what?"

"I don't know how to explain it," Pam admitted
slowly. "I think a part of the brain starts to deteriorate
after so many years of dealing with diapers, bottles,
and potty training. It's like you're on the children's
level for so much of the day that you lose the ability to
communicate with other adults."

"All this tells me is that you need to get away more often."

"That's probably true," Pam agreed, "but you wouldn't believe the trouble it is to find a baby-sitter, especially on weekdays."

"What about taking some time for yourself while the kids go down for their naps?"

Pam laughed softly as they headed toward the escalator. "Nap time is like an oasis in the middle of the day. I treasure every moment of that hour, but lately even that time's been robbed from me. I'm sewing Scotty and Jason Batman pajamas and that's the only free time I have to do it."

"Batman pajamas?"

"They're crazy about him and Spider-Man."

"Why don't you sew in the evenings?" Leah suggested. It made perfect sense to her since the three were generally in bed by eight.

Pam laughed and shook her head. "Because, my dear friend, I'm too pooped. Honestly, I head for bed no more than an hour after the kids. I never dreamed I'd be in bed before nine. Remember me, the original night owl? Trust me, kids will do that to you."

A pang of envy struck Leah at the thought of her life being dominated by the demands of a houseful of children. Then again, the grass always appeared greener on the other side of the fence. More than once, Pam had said how much she envied Leah her freedom.

Freedom. True, she often had time on her hands, but for what?

"I'm on a budget, you know," Pam complained when they reached Nordstrom's second floor.

"Would you stop?" Leah demanded, laughing. "We haven't even gotten to the women's section yet and already you're convinced you aren't going to find anything."

"My old maternity dress isn't all that bad."

"Pam!" Leah braced her hands against her hips and glared at her friend. "Now I understand why Doug insisted I go shopping with you. He knew darn good and well that you'd end up buying something for everyone else and nothing for yourself."

"Did you see that darling pinafore," Pam said, pointing toward the children's section. "Diane would look like an angel dressed in that."

Leah looped her arm through Pam's and steered her in the opposite direction. "I'll tell you what I'm going to do."

"What? Hog-tie me and force me to try on several dresses?"

"Close. I'm taking you directly to the dressing room and bringing the party dresses in to you."

Pam's shoulders sagged with defeat as they entered the dressing room area. "All right, just try to find something reasonably priced, will you?" Leah opened the white louvered door and gently pushed her friend inside.

Pam stuck out her hand and waved her index finger. "Check on the sale rack first. I'll feel better about spending so much money on myself if the dress is discounted."

"Never you mind," Leah argued. "I'm not even going to let you look at the price tag."

"But, Leah—"

"Don't even try to argue with me. I'd have thought you'd know better by now." Smiling to herself, Leah left the dressing room.

"My hips aren't nearly as slender as they used to be either," Pam called after her. "You'd better start with a size twelve instead of a ten . . . better make that a fourteen."

Leah stopped long enough to roll her eyes, then headed for a rack of newly arrived fashions. It took less than five minutes to find a wide selection that would suit her friend.

"Mercy, where are you?" Goodness called, frantically circling Nordstrom's like the second hand of a clock gone berserk.

Mercy turned around to find Goodness, her wings all aflutter, breezing six feet off the ground, close to a state of panic.

"I need to talk to you right away," Goodness said breathlessly.

"Over here," Mercy called, wondering what could possibly have gone wrong so quickly. "I'm on the light fixture."

Goodness soared to her side, rustling the dress display and toppling a mannequin. Apparently feeling guilty, she scooped up the lifeless form and set it back into place to the horror of a sales clerk who gasped and placed her hand over her heart to watch a lifeless form right itself.

"Goodness," Mercy shouted. "Would you stop before you get us both into trouble?"

"I need help," Goodness blurted out for the second time, joining Mercy who was dangling from the light fixture.

"So soon? You just received the assignment. What could have possibly gone wrong?"

Goodness, who was easily flustered, looked helpless and confused. She cast a pleading look at Mercy. "I knew I was in way over my head when Gabriel first gave me this assignment, but I wanted to help Monica Fischer. You know I'm a sucker for romance, and finding her a husband didn't sound as if it would be the least bit difficult." She stopped long enough to draw in another deep breath. "Now the poor girl's more confused than ever and I'm afraid it's all my fault."

"What happened?"

"Nothing . . . well, obviously it's something, but . . . oh, dear, I'm afraid I've made a terrible mistake."

"I take it this has something to do with finding Monica a husband?"

Goodness nodded energetically. "I found the most suitable young man who has a wonderful heart for God. He directs the choir and he's half in love with her already."

"Then what's the problem?"

"Monica isn't the least bit excited about him. She has this dangerous attraction for that . . . that private eye. They're completely incompatible. Why, a union between the two of them will never do, and I fear I'm the one responsible for them meeting."

Mercy frowned. "Goodness, when will you ever learn?"

"Me!" Flustered, she wrung her hands and eyed her fellow angel. "You don't think I know that was you riding up and down the escalator just now?"

"You couldn't have known that was me."

"Let's just say I made an educated guess," Goodness said confidently. "A woman's being treated with smelling salts and two kids are telling everyone what they saw, and it sounds to me as if they were describing you. Who else do you know with long, blond hair, deep blue eyes, and magnificent wings? You know better than most that children's spiritual eyes have yet to close. You were taking a terrible chance."

"Ah . . ."

"Just as I thought. Mercy, what are you going to do if Gabriel hears about this? You know he will eventually. Why, he could pull you off of this assignment in nothing flat and with good reason."

"But he won't," Mercy said with utter confidence.

"How can you be so sure?"

"Because he'd never have assigned me to this prayer request if he had anyone else to send. We both know that."

"But he might never give you another assignment if you continue to do crazy stunts like that."

"Sure he will. Gabriel has a soft spot in his heart for the three of us. I venture to say we're his favorites, although he'd never let us know that."

Goodness stared at her with round, disbelieving eyes.

"He'll forgive me just about anything," Mercy continued, undaunted, "because I'm going to find a way to teach Leah what she must learn and as soon as she does, she'll become pregnant."

"Mercy, have you been sniffing the eggnog again?"

"Don't be ridiculous."

"But you've got the most difficult assignment by far. How can you be so confident Leah's ever going to learn what she must when so many others have failed?"

"Simple," Mercy said with a cocky tilt to her head, "I'm going to teach her. Now stop worrying about me. Let's concentrate on what's happening with you and Monica Fischer."

Goodness adjusted her wings around the troublesome light fixture. "I hate to admit it, but I'm worried. She really likes this Chet fellow."

"Chet who?"

"Chet Costello. He's a private investigator and from what I've managed to learn of him . . . let me just say this, Gabriel would need to assign a legion of angels to work with him."

"You're sure Monica's infatuated with him?"

Goodness nodded. "I read her journal this morning and it was full of all the things she felt while he kissed her. She said she never knew that kissing could be this good or that a woman felt those kinds of things when a man touched her."

"Oh, my." Mercy waved her hand in front of her heated face.

"And that's not the half of it."

"You mean there's more?"

"She wrote that she felt herself responding to him even when she promised herself she wouldn't and how disappointed she was when he stopped."

"Do you think Michael knows about Chet?"

"No one knows, not even her father. She raced home afterwards and went directly to her room where she wrote everything down. When her father came to ask if she wanted dinner, Monica claimed she wasn't hungry."

"Kissing is better than food?" This was a whole new thought to Mercy.

"Apparently so."

Goodness wrung her hands once more, then blurted out, "Say something. Anything. I need help."

Mercy slowly shook her head back and forth. "You've got trouble."

"I know that, otherwise I wouldn't be here. What do you suggest?"

Mercy thought long and hard. "We both need to talk to Shirley. She's much better at deciphering these matters than we are."

"Let's meet at Reverend Fischer's church at midnight in the choir loft," Goodness suggested as she elegantly slid off the dangling fixture. "I'll see you then."

Mercy nodded.

Goodness fully intended to leave the shopping mall right then and return to Monica, who was sitting in the church office typing up the bulletin for the Sunday morning worship service. But when she shot past a video store, she skidded to a stop. Mercy seemed confident that Gabriel would leave them on their assignments because he was so shorthanded. Maybe she should test her friend's theory, and have a little fun herself.

Row upon row of television screens faced her. There must have been over fifty in various sizes and shapes, all tuned to the same channel. The temptation was too much to resist.

She hesitated and laughed silently at the thought of her face showing up on all fifty screens at once. The mere suggestion was her downfall. If Mercy could ride up and down the escalator then she should be able to enjoy a few short moments of notoriety.

"This is our best model," the salesman was saying, stepping over to the wide twenty-five-inch screen. The salesman was busily showing an older couple the capabilities of the remote control when Goodness popped onto the screen.

"What's that?" The grandmotherly woman pointed to the television.

"It seems to be a . . . woman with wings," the man with her added.

"Wings?" The salesman quickly adjusted the buttons. "We had it tuned to a game show earlier. It's nothing to worry about, folks, this happens sometimes. I'll just change the channel."

"The same woman appears to be on that channel as well," the woman said. "If I didn't know better I'd say it was an . . . angel. Do you think she's trying to tell us something, Delbert?"

"She sure is," the man grumbled. "She's saying we shouldn't be buying this fancy new television when the one we've got is perfectly fine."

"Don't be ridiculous. This is the punishment you get for skipping mass last Sunday. God's sent this angel to show you the error of your ways. Then again"—she hesitated while Goodness adjusted her wings for show—"she might be telling us we should pick up some lottery tickets on our way home."

The salesman was becoming more and more agitated as he punched a variety of buttons on the remote control. "I'm sure there's been some mistake." He looked around and shouted, "Harry! I think it might be a good idea if I have the manager take a look at this."

"I've seen enough," the older man said, reaching for his wife's arm. "Let's get out of here."

"It has to do with you missing church, I'm sure of it."

"Don't be ridiculous," her husband said with annoyance.

"We are going to stop for lottery tickets, aren't we?"

"We don't do this nearly enough." Jody's mother set the pot of tea on the oak kitchen table.

"I agree," Jody said, slipping into the chair across from her mother. She didn't drop by to visit her mother as often as she had before her father's death earlier in the year. Her childhood home stirred far too many memories. Privately Jody wondered how her mother managed. Perhaps it wasn't so difficult to understand. Jody continued to live in the tiny two-bedroom house she and Jeff had purchased when she'd first learned she was pregnant with Timmy. Giving up even this small part of her life with her late husband was more than she could have borne.

"Where's Timmy this evening?" Helen Chandler wanted to know.

Jody smiled although she knew her mother didn't understand her amusement. "He's spending the night with Rick Trenton."

"I thought it was Ricky."

"They're in the fourth grade this year and suddenly Ricky is Rick. Timmy is Tim to all his friends now too. He's growing up more and more."

"I didn't think that sort of thing happened until junior high."

Jody had been amazed herself. "Kids mature much faster these days. Generally Rick spends the night with us, but his mother just had a baby and Timmy's enthralled with the little tyke. He . . . he went so far as to suggest that I remarry so he could have a brother."

"He said that, did he?"

"I don't mind telling you, Mom, it threw me for a loop. I found a letter in Timmy's binder. His class was assigned to write a letter and he opted to address his to God."

"That grandson of mine is one smart cookie. What did he have to say?"

Jody stirred a spoonful of sugar into her tea with enough energy for some to slosh over the rim of the delicate china cup. "He wrote about needing a dad."

Helen Chandler grew quiet at that. Jody expected her mother to laugh or perhaps lecture, but she hadn't expected her to say nothing.

"You don't have any comment to make?" she asked, eyeing her mother speculatively.

"Of course I do, but I'm not so sure you want to hear it."

At this point Jody was more than willing to listen to words of wisdom. She'd thought of little else but the letter from the moment it had slipped from Timmy's binder. The conversation with her son had served to disconcert her even more. This hadn't been an impulse; he'd been serious.

"Go ahead, Mom, say what you want and I'll listen."

Her mother smiled and reached for Jody's hand, squeezing it gently. "I don't think I fully appreciated your grief when Jeff died. I ached for you and would have given anything to bring Jeff back, but the depth of your pain escaped me until . . . until this past year." She paused as if she needed to steel herself. "After Ralph died I knew what you'd endured. The death of a loved one is the sharpest pain a human can experience. I felt like a piece of myself had died with your father."

"Oh, Mom." Jody's grip on her mother's hand tightened, to let the gesture say what she couldn't because of the huge constriction blocking her throat. They were close, had always been close. Jody had been an only child and the bond had been firm and strong between her and her parents.

"I can appreciate far more the agony you endured when you lost Jeff. I understand why your grief has lingered all these years, but I also know Timmy is right. The time is long past due for you to get on with your life."

"But—"

"Listen, please, and when I've finished you can say what you wish.

"Take the love you and Jeff shared and place it in the most tender part of your heart. Treasure the few short years you had together as a precious gift God gave you and then offer it back to Him in gratitude that you found such a special man to love."

Tears rolled unchecked down Jody's cheeks. She'd assumed the well was dry after spending the night looking through the photo album, but they returned fresh and hot, streaming down her face.

"In my heart I know Jeff wouldn't have wanted you to grieve this way."

"I know that too," Jody whispered, struggling to check the emotion. She'd wanted to be strong when she spoke to her mother, but it took only a few words for her to realize how weak she actually was.

"Meeting other men, even marrying again, doesn't mean you have to stop loving Jeff," her mother continued.

"I don't think I could ever stop loving him."

"I understand that. It would be impossible for me to stop loving your father."

"It is time for me to start dating again, isn't it?" Even as Jody made the suggestion, she couldn't help wondering if she was doing the right thing. It didn't feel right, but then nothing had from the moment she'd received word Jeff was gone. It seemed as if her world had been knocked off its orbit and would never right itself. Now her mother and her son were saying different. There was a new life waiting for her and the possibility of finding love again, if she were willing to put the past behind her and march forward.

"It's past time," her mother told her gently. "I'm sure you've been asked out over the years. You're a beautiful young woman."

Jody nodded, twisting a tissue with her hands. "Glen Richardson surprised me last week with an invitation to dinner. I was so shocked I didn't know what to tell him."

"I don't believe I've heard you mention his name before."

"He's one of the attorneys at the firm. I don't work directly with him, but it seems we continually bump into each other at the copy machine. It's become something of a joke."

"What did you tell him?"

"Heavens, Mother, I don't remember. I made up some ridiculous excuse, but he said he'd ask again and he probably will."

"And when he does?" her mother prompted.

"When he does," Jody said, clenching the tissue in both hands, "I'll . . . I'll promise to think about it."

"Jody Marie Potter!"

Jody laughed and relaxed against the back of her chair. "Oh, all right. One date, just to test the waters."

Her mother smiled broadly, looking downright pleased with herself.

The phone was ringing when Jody let herself into her house later that same night. Setting down her purse, she hurried into the kitchen and caught it on the fourth ring, just before the answering machine took over.

"Hello," she said, her voice shaking with breathlessness.

"Jody?"

The voice was strangely familiar. "Yes?"

"This is Glen . . . Glen Richardson. I hope I didn't catch you at an inconvenient time."

Jody's shoulders sagged against the wall. "No. I just unlocked the door and had to run to catch the phone."

"The funniest thing just happened. I was thinking of calling you and for the life of me, I couldn't find your number. Then I walked into the kitchen and found it attached to the phone. Heaven only knows how it got there. It seemed fate was telling me to give you a jingle," Glen said, sounding confused even now. "And to think I caught you just as you walked in the door."

"I just got back from visiting my mother."

"I suppose you've already had dinner."

"I'm sorry, Glen, but we ordered Chinese take-out." He sounded so bewildered that she almost felt sorry for him. "What are you doing, sitting home alone on a Friday night?"

"My best gal turned me down for a date."

It took Jody a moment to realize he was talking about her, leading her to wonder what excuse she'd given him earlier.

"I was thinking I should suggest a deli sandwich and a couple of sodas for the next time we meet at the copy machine. Larry Williams warned me that you don't date often."

Often. The last time she'd gone out with a man, she'd ended up marrying him. Jeff had been persistent too, she remembered, unwilling to take no for an answer. He'd wooed her carefully and when they'd fallen in love, it was the kind of love that was meant to last a lifetime. She might marry again, even give birth to another child, but she'd never stop loving Jeff. This was her vow, to his memory and to the extraordinary love they shared.

"Jody?" Glen said, interrupting her thoughts.

"I'm sorry, I got distracted."

"I know it's short notice and all, but how about a movie? I understand there're several good ones playing.

How would you feel about that? I could meet you at the theater if that'd make you more comfortable," he added, rushing the words together in his eagerness.

So soon. It was happening so fast, much faster than she'd expected. Much too soon, long before she was ready. Then she remembered her mother's words about placing the love she shared with Jeff in the most tender part of her heart. She didn't know what to make of him finding her number pasted on his telephone.

"A movie," she repeated. There was a six-plex less than a mile from her house. "Ah, all right."

"Great," Glen said, sounding a little like Timmy when she'd given in on something he'd really wanted. "This is just great. I promise you, you won't be sorry. Just you wait and see."

Jody wondered if that were possible.

Chapter 5

S hirley loved old white churches with tall steeples and huge bells. In the Reverend Lloyd Fischer's church she felt a certain kinship with this righteous man of God. She was waiting for her two compatriots in the choir loft, which was situated up the winding stairway in the back of the old church. The freshly polished pews gleamed in the moonlight and the scent of lemon oil wafted toward her.

She frowned as she viewed the magnificent old organ. It would take a minor miracle to keep Mercy away from this. The public address system didn't bear thinking about.

"Shirley?" Goodness arrived first, agitated and impatient, racing up and down the center aisle.

"Up here."

Goodness joined her, hurling herself over the wooden railing of the choir loft. "Where's Mercy? She should have been here by now."

"I'm sure she will be soon."

No sooner had Shirley spoken than Mercy appeared. "I'm up here. No one bothered to tell me Leah Lundberg's a night owl." She sagged into one of the choir chairs and tilted back her head. "I'm bushed. Leah had me running from one end of the shopping mall to the next. After she found her friend an absolutely delightful party dress, she took off on her own and shopped for hours. I didn't know a single human being possessed so much energy."

"We're all learning lessons about earthlings," Shirley maintained. Her own experiences had been exhausting as well.

"You're telling me," Goodness joined in. "All Monica's done since Chet kissed her is stew in the juices of her self-righteousness. She's convinced God never intended a good Christian woman to experience desire. I think it must be the first time she was ever kissed, I mean really kissed. I don't mind telling you, this whole situation has got me plenty worried."

"You?" Mercy cried, and a look of frustration and bewilderment marked her face. "How am I supposed to help Leah when she crams every spare minute of the day with mindless activity? It isn't any wonder the woman has no peace. She doesn't take time to listen to herself, let alone anyone else."

"This must be a common trait with humans," Shirley added thoughtfully. "Have you seen Jody's yard? Why, it's meticulous. The woman must spend every available minute maintaining those flower beds."

"I'd hoped to make a real difference in Leah's life," Mercy continued, "and now I wonder if that's possible."

Shirley surveyed the small group of prayer ambassadors. She was new at this and uncertain herself, but then they were all relatively inexperienced and it made sense that they help each other.

"What about you, Shirley?" Mercy asked, her gaze skittering past the organ and then drifting lazily toward the huge pipes. Shirley could all but see Mercy's mind feverishly devising ways of getting at that organ.

"As it happens, things are developing nicely with Jody and her son, Timmy," Shirley said, walking directly in front of the organ, cutting off Mercy's view. "Jody went out on her first date in years this evening and afterwards Glen asked her out for dinner and she agreed."

"Glen? Who's Glen?"

"An attorney. They work for the same law firm. Glen's hardworking and sincere. From what I was able to learn about him, he's interested in settling down and starting a family. I'm sure once Timmy meets him everything will fall neatly into place."

Goodness slapped one disgruntled wing against her side. "I'm going to do my very best to remain angelic here, but it seems to me you received a cushy assignment while Mercy and I are at our wits end."

Mercy chimed in in agreement. "In case you haven't guessed, Goodness and I are experiencing some minor difficulties."

"It might help," Shirley said in gentle, forgiving tones, "if you stayed away from escalators and television screens."

"You heard?" Goodness ventured.

Shirley nodded. "And so has Gabriel."

Mercy closed her eyes. "Is he furious?"

"He hasn't pulled you off the assignment, has he?" Shirley asked. "I heard what you said this afternoon, and you're right. Gabriel doesn't have the angel-power to replace you just now and I'm sure all will be forgiven if, and it's a big if, Mercy is able to help Leah find her peace. Goodness, you've got to help Monica find a decent husband."

"I thought it'd be easier than it is," Goodness confessed in a small voice.

Mercy joined her friend, sagging defeatedly into a chair. "We could both do with some suggestions. This prayer business is difficult work."

Goodness agreed with a sharp nod. "Being around humans for any length of time is enough to make any angel go stir-crazy."

Shirley did a poor job of containing a smile. How well she understood her friends' frustrations. Most of her career had been spent working with humans. "Just don't ever volunteer to work as a guardian then," she suggested. The stories she could tell!

"Can you help us, Shirley?" Mercy asked.

Her friends' faces were both tired and gloomy, and Shirley didn't know if she had any words of wisdom to offer them. "I can try. Tell me what's happening."

Mercy and Goodness exchanged glances. "You go first," Goodness suggested.

"I've already told you about Leah's day. I've spent most of my time observing her, and frankly, I haven't gained a lot of insight into her personality. She holds her pain deep inside herself, unwilling to give up even the smallest portion of it, as if it were something of value."

Shirley thoughtfully mulled over this information. "If that's the case, it seems to me she must find joy before she finds peace."

Stubbornly Mercy folded her arms and frowned and her chest lifted with a gigantic sigh. "Gabriel didn't say anything about joy. All he mentioned was peace. Who exactly does he think I am, St. Peter?"

"Perhaps that was the problem with the other prayer ambassadors. They were looking for shortcuts as well."

"Oh, all right," Mercy said ungraciously. "But how am I supposed to teach her about joy? Joy, peace, what's the difference?"

"What are Leah's favorite things?"

Mercy frowned. "It's difficult to tell. She enjoys her home, but she'd gladly relinquish it for the chance to be a mother. While she was with her friend this afternoon, they talked quite a bit about Pam's kids. A spark shone from Leah as they discussed the children, especially her friend's three-year-old. I think she said his name was Scotty."

"Children," Shirley repeated, her thoughts deep and grave.

"But that's the crux of the problem, don't you see," Mercy said, and the expression in her eyes changed, becoming more intent. "She doesn't have a child so she holds fast to her disappointment. The child will bring her the true joy, and I doubt that anything else will."

Goodness had grown especially quiet. "What if you brought a child into her life for a short time, like a weekend or something? You could manage that, couldn't you?"

"I suppose." But Mercy didn't sound overly enthusiastic.

"If she had a taste of deep inner happiness, she might be willing to release a portion of her pain," Goodness added. "It seems to me what Shirley's saying is that what Leah really needs isn't an absence of sorrow, or a feeling of gladness. Earthly joy wouldn't accomplish your purpose. Leah needs a connection with heaven."

"Yes," Shirley shouted with her excitement. She couldn't have said it better herself. "That's exactly what I mean."

"In other words," Mercy said slowly, thoughtfully, "if Leah would be willing to take hold of a . . . higher level of joy, then she might be willing to release her disappointments and frustrations."

"Exactly," Shirley said and Goodness echoed, "Exactly."

Shirley realized they made it sound simple, but she didn't envy Mercy her task. It was little wonder so many other prayer ambassadors had been defeated by Leah's problem.

Mercy stood and was pacing in front of the huge church organ, sending longing looks toward the antique instrument. "Anyone have any other suggestions how I'm supposed to accomplish this?"

Shirley was silent and so was Goodness.

"Don't worry, I'll think of something," she offered brightly. "I always do."

"Let me tell you what's going on with Monica," Goodness said next, looping her legs over the arm of the chair and tilting her head back with a dramatic flair. She sighed and placed the back of her hand against her brow. "She's enthralled with this . . . this private investigator. The choir director might as well not exist, and Michael's perfect for her, just perfect."

"What about Chet?" Mercy asked. "He might not be as bad as you think."

"He's not for Monica," Goodness said firmly, brooking no argument. "I was able to check into his past and believe me, it isn't a pretty picture. He's lied, he's stolen and been in trouble with the law, although he once worked for them. He's not exactly what I'd call an upstanding prospective husband for a minister's daughter."

"Oh, my," Mercy mumbled.

Shirley mulled over the situation, tapping her fingers against the top of the railing, her thoughts moving in several different directions at once.

"Furthermore," Goodness added seriously, "he's egotistical, chauvinistic, and he hasn't darkened the door of a church in more than ten years. The last time he prayed he was in his early teens."

"He doesn't sound like the man for Monica," Mercy agreed.

Shirley hesitated, then decided she might as well speak her mind. "I don't think we should be so hasty here. Isn't your mission to teach Monica to be more flexible and accepting of others? From what I understand she's caught in a trap of following a list of rules and regulations."

"Yes, but any lessons I have to teach her don't include Chet."

Shirley wasn't convinced of that. "From what you've told me, she views everything as black and white, with little room for compromise."

"True," Goodness was willing to admit, "but don't you see? The two are completely incompatible. Gabriel wanted me to get her feet wet, not throw her off the Freemont Bridge."

"All I can suggest is that you be patient with Monica."

"One thing's in my favor," Goodness said, sounding encouraged. "They aren't likely to meet again."

"Then there's nothing to worry about," Mercy said, slipping onto the bench in front of the massive organ.

"Mercy," Shirley warned, knowing her friend well enough to recognize the movement was anything but casual. The organ was too big a challenge to ignore.

"Don't worry," Mercy reassured her, "I'm going to be good."

Shirley wasn't the least bit convinced, and she was right. As she winged her way out of the church and back to her charge, a blast of organ music crescendoed into the night. Groaning aloud, Shirley recognized the opening bars from *Phantom of the Opera* and knew exactly where they'd come from.

"Dinner was lovely," Jody said, slipping out of the rich velvet booth in the luxurious downtown restaurant. Glen had been a wonderful dinner companion. Although Jody had been nervous when he'd come to pick her up at the house, he'd quickly put her at ease.

"It's still early," Glen was saying as he helped her with her full-length wool coat. "I can take you back to the house, if you want, but I was hoping you'd consider taking a ferry ride with me."

It had been a year or more since Jody had last been on any of the Washington State ferries. After she'd received the word of Jeff's death, she'd come down to the waterfront often. She found a peace, a solace here that escaped her otherwise. On more than one occasion she'd whiled away an hour or more riding the ferry, standing on the deck facing the wind, letting it batter her. She'd close her eyes and pretend Jeff was with her. She'd breathe in the scent of sea and salt while the birds screeched overhead. Each time she came away rejuvenated.

"Where do you want to go?" she asked, reluctant for reasons she didn't care to explain. The ferry ride had been her own private haven, and she wasn't entirely sure she wanted to share this.

"Anywhere you like. The Bainbridge run is a half hour each way. We could get a caffé latte and look at the city lights. The Bremerton run is an hour each way."

"All right," Jody surprised herself by saying. It was easy to be with Glen. He was friendly and undemanding, allowing her to set the course of their evening, deciding even if there was to be a relationship. Jody found the lack of pressure necessary and reassuring.

He kept his hand at her elbow as they walked along the waterfront. The scent of Puget Sound mingled with that of fried fish from the takeout booths in the crisp night air. The cold nipped at Jody's cheeks and she buried her hands deep within the silk lining of her coat pockets.

"Here," Glen said, wrapping the muffler her mother had knit for her around her face, covering her mouth and ears. "I can't have you catching a chill."

How thoughtful he was, she noted. This was exactly the type of thing Jeff would have done. Jody forced all thoughts of her dead husband from her mind. It was time to let go, time to put the past behind her and look forward, not back.

Remember Lot's wife.

Jody didn't know where the thought came from, it was as if someone had whispered it into her ear. Lot's wife? Why she would even think of the Biblical character was beyond her. All Jody could remember was that Lot's wife had turned into a pillar of salt when she fled Sodom and Gomorrah. Against the angel's command, she'd stopped and looked back.

That was it, Jody realized with a sudden burst of insight. Instead of setting her course for the future, Lot's wife had looked back over the life that she'd once had. In many ways Jody had been doing the same thing, and in the process she'd become frozen, unable to move forward to whatever awaited her.

They arrived at the ferry terminal minutes before the ferry pulled away from the huge dock, headed toward Bainbridge Island. Holding hands and laughing, Jody and Glen raced through the terminal and onto the ferry, their steps echoing like ricocheting bullets in the stillness of the night.

While Jody found them a table in the small cafeteria section, Glen ordered their caffé lattes. She was lucky enough to find a booth by the window. Surprisingly, there didn't seem to be many passengers. The majority of the commuters remained in their cars for the short crossing.

"Here we go," Glen said, slipping into the seat across from her and handing her the thick paper cup.

Jody trained her gaze out of the window, watching the city lights grow smaller as the huge boat effortlessly glided its way across Puget Sound. She lowered her gaze to the hot drink cradled in her hands. The time had come for her to be forthright with Glen.

"You mentioned the other night that you'd learned I don't date much."

"That's the scuttlebutt," Glen agreed.

"I'm a widow."

"I know that too, with a nine-year-old son. I was sorry to have missed meeting him."

"Timmy and my mother went to McDonald's for dinner. I'm sure he'll still be awake when we get back." She didn't mention that he'd probably give Glen the third degree, asking him about baseball and other sports. To be fair she should warn Glen about her son's inquisitiveness, but before she could he spoke again.

"No one seems to know much more about you."

"I . . . generally don't combine my home life with business."

"I understand," Glen was quick to assure her. "If you'd rather not talk about yourself, that's fine. I don't want you to think I'm pressuring you."

"You aren't," she said, touched by his gentleness and how hard he worked to please her. "It's only fair that I tell you about Jeff . . . he was my husband."

"Only if you want," he said and sipped from his coffee. As he did, Jody noticed what nice hands he had. Large, but gentle. They were the kind of hands that comforted a child, that shook on fair deals, and were rarely clenched in anger.

"I met Jeff shortly after he graduated from college," Jody continued. "I was going into my junior year and we fell deeply in love. We dated for several months and talked about marriage. The next thing I knew Jeff had sold his car so he could buy me an engagement ring." She paused as she remembered how she'd wept with joy the night he'd given it to her. For weeks afterward he took a bus to job interviews. "To make a long story short," she continued when she could, "he got a job with Boeing and shortly after that we were married. Timmy wasn't a planned pregnancy, but I've thanked God for my son every night since I lost Jeff. I . . . I don't know what I would have done if it hadn't been for Timmy. He . . . he gave me a reason to live."

She paused, needing a moment to collect herself.

"Jeff's job entailed a lot of traveling. He was always very good about keeping in touch with me. Timmy was only ten months old when Jeff was sent on assignment to Berlin. We set a convenient time for him to phone me each day. When he didn't call one evening I knew immediately that something was dreadfully wrong. I tried his hotel room several times, but there wasn't any answer."

Her voice wobbled and Glen reached for her hand.

"A week passed with no word. Nothing. I was frantic and so was Jeff's mother. Together we traveled to Germany. We stayed there nearly a month, in an effort to learn what we could."

"You mean he just disappeared into thin air?" Glen asked as they pulled into Winslow, the dock on Bainbridge Island. The sound of the cars driving off the ferry was followed by those boarding. The activity in the cafeteria increased.

"It seemed that way. We did everything we could, pulled every string, made a nuisance of ourselves at the police station and the American embassy. The best we could figure then was that Jeff had gone for a walk along the Spree River, which was close to the hotel. There'd been a string of muggings and beatings that year. The only scenario the authorities could give was that Jeff had been the victim of such a crime and either been thrown or had fallen into the river. I toured every hospital in the city. Gloria, Jeff's mother, did as well. She insisted Jeff was alive, and refused to give up hope."

"And you?"

"I held on to the belief as well because the alternative didn't bear thinking about. Soon there was nowhere else for us to look, no one for us to see. We didn't have anywhere else to turn, and had no choice but to return to the States. Gloria lives on the East Coast and after I returned to Seattle, she continued to pressure the powers that be."

"Did she learn anything?"

"Nothing . . . but I did." Those early months had been a living nightmare to Jody. "As much as I believed in Jeff's love for me and Timmy, I couldn't help wondering if this disappearance was planned. I know it sounds ridiculous now, but you have to understand my mental state at the time. I . . . had him investigated. If there was another woman in his life, I needed to know about her. I had to find out if this was some kind of cruel hoax."

"What did you learn?"

Jody focused her gaze on the caffé latte. "Very little. The only remote possibility came from a background check and I discovered Jeff had been approached by a government agency, the CIA, I believe—one of those—while he was in college. He turned down the offer. My father had a good friend in government who did some discreet checking and they reported back that what I'd found out was true. Jeff had been recruited, but declined, and that was the end of it."

"How'd you manage to live?"

"It wasn't easy because I wasn't working at the time. Within a few months my finances were a nightmare. My parents helped me out as much as they could, but I didn't want to live off their generosity. I couldn't. Jeff had disappeared, but because there wasn't a body I couldn't collect his insurance or any of the other benefits that would normally be available to a widow. Somehow I managed to hold on for nine months, with the help of my family and a few good friends. Eventually I was forced into filing for a divorce in order to sell some property. That gave me income to return to school and live on until I could get a job."

"They never found a body?"

Jody looked out the window, the night was inky and thick, and her heart felt more so. "Yes, eventually they did, but it took nearly three years."

"My God, what happened?"

A tingling sensation roved up and down her spine even now, after all this time. "I . . . received word from the German police that they'd found a body caught in the cable beneath a bridge. They believed it was Jeff. They needed me to provide dental X rays and claim the body."

"It must have come as a terrible shock."

Jody managed a nod. "It was. As best the authorities could figure, Jeff was mugged, beaten, and knocked into the river and left for dead. The body was so badly decomposed that there wasn't any real way of telling us much more than that. The news came at a bad time. Timmy had the chicken pox and I don't think I could have borne returning to Germany. Those weeks in Berlin three years earlier had been the most painful of my life. I thought to ask Jeff's mother to go, but she was always a bit eccentric and after Jeff's death she became more so."

"How do you mean?"

"She continually insisted Jeff was alive and was furious with me when I divorced him. Our relationship was strained afterwards. She claimed she'd talked to spirits in a séance, and Jeff had sent a message to her. He wanted Gloria to tell me how terribly disappointed he was in me because I'd divorced him. I didn't talk to her much after that."

"She insisted he was alive and that she'd been able to talk to him in a séance? It sounds like she had a rough time of it."

"She has. I don't know that she'll ever fully recover." Then again, Jody didn't know if she would either. "My father, bless his heart, volunteered to make the trip.

The dental X rays matched and that's the end of it. That was nearly five years ago now. Jeff's been gone a total of eight years."

"I'm sorry, Jody, I really am. Jeff must have loved you and Timmy very much."

"I know he did. I get angry with myself that I doubted him even for that little bit."

"Anyone would have." Glen took their empty cups and deposited them in the garbage. He slipped into the seat and seemed unnaturally quiet. "I don't pretend to understand the grief you experienced, but I was in a relationship that lasted for three years. Breaking it off was one of the most emotionally difficult times of my life."

"Would you think I was prying if I asked you what went wrong?"

His mouth moved into a half smile. "Not at all. You were frank with me and deserve the same consideration. I loved Maryann and wanted to marry her, but she's a successful attorney and, well, I'll simplify it by explaining that her career is more important to her than marriage. Somehow or another we got involved in a game of ultimatums. I wanted a wife and children. Maryann claimed she wasn't ready for either. In the end she suggested a compromise. She thought it was a good idea for us to move in together. I wasn't willing to fall into that trap, and that was more or less the end of it."

"You still love her, don't you?"

Glen lowered his gaze. "I think it's very much like you and Jeff, I don't think I'll ever stop loving her. It's been several months now and nothing's going to change. I've accepted that and apparently so has she. We still bump into each other in court occasionally, and it's awkward, but there's nothing left for either of us to say."

"Then it doesn't bother you that I have a child?"

Glen straightened in his seat. "Bother me? I consider your son a bonus."

"Don't say that until you meet him. He's quite a character."

"I'm looking forward to doing exactly that."

They were nearing the Seattle dock and Glen stood, eager for them to be on their way. He glanced at the gold watch on his wrist. "You think Timmy might still be awake?"

Jody laughed and nodded. "I'm sure of it. He's anxious to meet you too and please don't hold it against me if he asks you a lot of personal questions."

"Does Timmy like sports?"

"He loves them. According to his coach, he's going to be a dynamite pitcher someday."

"Really." Glen actually beamed. "I was the pitcher for our high school team."

"You were?" This was like a match made in heaven. Almost too good to be true. "If you mention that to my son, he'll be your friend for life."

Their pace was fast as they headed toward the car. Glen's hand was at Jody's elbow and although they were walking up a steep hill, it didn't seem to thwart their enthusiasm.

As Jody suspected, Timmy was dressed in his pajamas waiting for her return. The instant he heard the front door open, he raced from the family room like pistons firing awake an engine. He stopped abruptly in front of Glen and threw back his head to look up at him.

"How tall are you?"

"Six-two. Is that tall enough?" Glen asked, crouching down so that they met eye to eye.

"That depends."

"Timmy, where are your manners?" Jody reminded her son.

"I've got to check him out, don't I?"

"Let me introduce you before you bombard him with questions," she said.

Timmy held out his hand. "I'm Timothy Jeffery Potter."

Glen stuck out his much larger hand. "Glen Francis Richardson, but don't tell anyone my middle name's Francis, all right?" The two exchanged enthusiastic handshakes.

"I won't tell a soul." Timmy spit on his two fingers and crossed his heart. "I promise and you can zap me with a laser gun if you find out that I have."

Just then Helen Chandler came out of the family room, which was situated off the kitchen, and Jody made the introductions. "If you don't mind, I'm heading home. My favorite television program's about to start and I don't want to miss it."

"I'll see you to the door," Jody said. She needn't have worried about Glen. Timmy led him back into the family room, insisting that he show Glen his baseball card collection. At this rate her dinner date would be there for hours.

"How'd it go?" her mother whispered loud enough to be heard into the next county and certainly the family room.

"Very well," Jody said, opening the door. She didn't want to stand in the doorway and carry on a conversation when it was likely Glen could hear every word they were saying.

"Do you like him?"

"Mother."

"Well, do you?" Helen pressed.

"Yes."

Her mother threw back her head and shocked Jody out of five years of her life by shouting, "Hallelujah!"

"Mom," Timmy called from the other room. "Are you coming? Did you know Glen has a signed Ken Griffey, Jr. baseball card?"

"I have to go," Jody said, grateful to her son for the convenient excuse. This was neither the time nor the place for this intimate conversation with her mother. "I promise I'll call you after church tomorrow morning."

"Mom," Timmy shouted again, "can Glen go to church with us?"

"Ah . . ." Jody glanced from her mother to the other room, not knowing which way to turn.

"Go and talk to Glen and Timmy. We can chat later." Before Jody could turn away, her mother impulsively reached for her and hugged her. "Everything's going to be just fine. I can feel it. I've waited a good long time for this," she said and kissed Jody on the cheek with a loud smack.

"Mom." Timmy raced into the room and grabbed her by the hand, dragging her into the other room. "If Glen comes to church with us, you'll cook breakfast for him, won't you? Make something really good, though, okay, because I told him you're a really fabulous cook."

He lowered his voice substantially, to a soft whisper. "Just don't serve that liver sausage stuff you did at Christmas, it was yucky."

"All right, all right," Jody said, walking into the room. It amazed her how easily Timmy had accepted Glen. Her eyes met Glen's and he smiled at her. "You've got yourself quite a son, Jody. He's everything you said and more."

"I like Glen, too," Timmy announced. "I bet he'd make me a great dad."

Chapter 6

"You're up bright and early," Lloyd Fischer said when Monica came down the stairs early Sunday morning. It was still pitch dark and although Monica had tried countless times, she hadn't been able to get back to sleep. Every time she closed her eyes, Chet Costello drifted, unbidden and unwelcome, into her thoughts, planting himself in her mind and refusing to go away.

If that wasn't bad enough, Monica was scheduled to sing with the choir that afternoon in downtown Seattle. She'd be near the Westlake Mall where she'd first met Chet. The tantalizing threat of bumping into him a third time had plagued her like an overdue mortgage payment.

"I couldn't sleep," Monica mumbled, helping herself to a cup of coffee. She kept her back to her father, letting him know she wasn't interested in conversation. She didn't mean to be rude, but she didn't feel up to her usual cheerful chatter.

Her father generally woke around four on Sunday mornings, enthusiastic and eager to review his sermon and make any last-minute changes. He was the first one at the church, turning on the furnace so the building would be warm when the congregation arrived. He was a gentle spirit, her father, a man who brought joy to God's heart. His tendency to look at the bright side of an issue was often a source of contention between them, but it was a minor fault.

One of them had to maintain a realistic outlook on life and it was the role she'd chosen. Because of this, others tended to view her in a less than favorable light. Her father, on the other hand, was loved by all. He was a good shepherd to his flock, sensitive and gentle, steering them toward a deeper understanding of God's word.

Monica sluggishly stirred a teaspoon of sugar into the coffee. She wasn't looking forward to the outing with the choir, and had toyed with the idea of digging up a plausible excuse not to go. Knowing it would have caused a hardship for the others was her only hesitation.

No, she corrected, striving for honesty, that wasn't entirely true.

Some small, dark part of herself hungered to see Chet again. It pained and troubled her to admit that. The man had taken advantage of her, threatened her, and then, against her will, had blatantly kissed her. The mere thought of their last encounter brought a flash of heated color to her cheeks.

It mortified her to recall the way she'd responded to him, the way she encouraged his advance, the way her body had reacted to his. No decent woman would feel the things she had, Monica was convinced of that. Patrick had kissed her several times early on in their relationship, and what she'd experienced with him had been a small spark of tenderness. When Chet had kissed her, she'd felt as if she were standing in the middle of a forest fire.

"Are you feeling all right?" her father asked, studying her closely as she sat down at the kitchen table across from him.

Now was the perfect time to say she wasn't up to par. *That* was all she need do. Her father would be the one to suggest she not participate in the choir's performance that afternoon. Naturally she'd put up a token fuss, but he'd be adamant, insisting her health was more important, and the choir could make do without her.

"I'm fine, Dad," she murmured. She braced her elbows against the edge of the table and sipped from the thick ceramic cup, wondering what it was about Chet that caused her to be so weak willed. It was unlikely that she would run into him, although, as luck would have it—not that she believed in such matters—she'd encountered Chet twice now within the same week.

Her father left and returned to the kitchen a moment later, dressed in his thick winter coat. He wrapped a wool scarf around his neck, slipped his hands into leather gloves, and announced, "I'm going over to the church."

She acknowledged him with a nod, grateful she'd be alone for the next several minutes. Instead of worrying about the possibility of seeing Chet, she should be praying for him. The man was clearly in need of divine intervention. One look at him told her everything she needed to know about his shabby life and immoral habits. Their all-too-brief conversations had reinforced her suspicions. He was cynical, irrational, stubborn, and only heaven knew what else.

"Then why won't he leave me alone?" she asked out loud, surprising herself with the shrill sound of her own voice.

She leaped from her chair and paced the compact kitchen. Absorbed in her thoughts, Monica continued walking about the room, circling the wooden table a number of times. She'd prayed long and hard for God to send a man into her life, but she hadn't asked how she was supposed to recognize him.

How she wished her mother were alive. Esther Fischer had always seemed to know what to do even in the most awkward of situations.

Her father looked surprised to see her when he returned fifteen minutes later. His nose was red and his cheeks bright with color from the short walk from the church to the parsonage.

"It's a beautiful morning," he announced cheerfully, removing his gloves, one finger at a time.

It could be blizzard conditions and her father would say the same thing. Sundays were beautiful to him no matter what the weather, because he was leading his flock in worship.

"Dad," Monica said, walking over to the refrigerator and taking out a carton of eggs and a package of bacon. She set them on the counter and then purposely turned around to face him. "When you met Mom, how did you feel? I mean did you have an inkling that this was the woman you'd eventually love and marry?"

If her father thought her question was out of the ordinary, he gave no indication. "I saw your mother for the first time in church."

"I know." She loved the story of how her parents had met while in the college-age Sunday school class. Her mother's family had recently moved into the area and Esther had felt shy and awkward that first Sunday.

Her father had been captivated by the beautiful young woman and had wanted to claim the empty seat beside her. Unfortunately several of the other young men had shared the same idea. While they were arguing about it, Esther had quietly stood and moved over to the chair and sat next to Lloyd. It wasn't a wildly romantic story, but Monica had enjoyed hearing it again and again as a young girl. It had deeply impressed her that her mother, although she was only nineteen at the time, had the presence of mind to choose such a wonderful man as Monica's father.

Monica doubted that she had such finely tuned discrimination herself, and after meeting Chet she was convinced of it.

"Did I know that first Sunday I was going to love your mother?" her father repeated her question slowly, his look thoughtful. "It's funny you should ask about her. I was just thinking about her myself and how she loved cold, crisp mornings such as this."

"How soon after you met did you realize you were going to love her?" Monica pressed, anxious now.

Her father poured himself a fresh cup of coffee. "It would sound romantic if I said I did that first Sunday, wouldn't it? Don't get me wrong, I was attracted to Esther from the moment I laid eyes on her. Any young man with a lick of sense would have been. She was lovely then and more so as the years progressed."

"You dated for several years, didn't you?"

"Yes, those were difficult times. We weren't married until four years later, after I'd completed seminary."

"I know that. What I want to know is when you realized you were in love with her."

He sat down at the table and rubbed his hand over his face.

Monica laughed. "It shouldn't be this hard, Daddy."

He nodded, his dark eyes intense. "I was trying to think back and it's been more years than I care to count. As best as I can remember, falling in love was a gradual process for me. Your mother and I saw a good deal of one another and I always enjoyed her company. It just seemed to me that she'd make a good pastor's wife and so I asked her to marry me."

"I see." Monica didn't bother to hide her disappointment. She'd been looking for something that hadn't been there. Her parents, while deeply in love, hadn't shared any great passion for each other. To the best of her memory she couldn't remember them doing more than holding hands in public.

Her disappointment must have shown because her father looked at her and asked, "This troubles you?"

"Oh, no. I . . . I was just wondering, is all. It isn't important." Only it was.

Even when they were young and in love her parents had been sensible and prudent when it came to choosing their life's partners. There hadn't been any explosion of—she hated to even say the word—*passion* between them. They'd drifted into marriage as a natural conclusion to a long-standing relationship.

It was the way her romance had started with Patrick, but their relationship had fizzled out and died without Monica even realizing what had happened. What she'd hoped to hear had been a confirmation of the feelings she'd experienced since meeting Chet. Not that she'd ever consider marrying anyone like him.

"I deeply loved your mother."

"I know that, Dad."

"I understand you're impatient to be a wife yourself, and all I can say is that God will bring a man into your life in His own time."

Monica nodded and, returning to the stove, placed an iron skillet on the stove. "I'm in no rush," she said, and even as she spoke, Monica knew that wasn't true.

"Remember what happened when Sarah decided to take matters into her own hands by giving Abraham her servant girl?"

"I remember."

"Don't make this a do-it-yourself project."

Monica laughed. "I won't."

Her father was silent for a moment, then asked, "Michael's certainly a nice-looking young man, don't you think?"

Monica resisted the urge to laugh outright. Her father couldn't have been less subtle. The choir director was a couple of years younger than Monica, not that it mattered. He was reserved and quiet, and frankly, she couldn't imagine spending the rest of her life with him. She liked Michael, and appreciated his efforts with the choir, but when she looked at him there wasn't any spark, any sizzling attraction. She felt nothing.

How she wished she could say the same for Chet. What she felt for him had to be immoral. It *was* immoral. Only that morning, when she was trying desperately to sleep, her thoughts had been full of Chet and the kiss they'd shared. The mere memory had turned her body into a traitor. Monica was convinced those feelings were ones godly women were never meant to experience.

"Ah, yes," her father continued, blithely unaware of the route her unruly thoughts had taken. "Michael would make you a good husband. I'm an old man, and I don't know much about romance, but my guess is that he'd very much like to get to know you better."

"He's a good man," Monica agreed, unwilling to say anything more.

"You could do far worse."

Her father hadn't a clue how true those words were. He approved of Michael, but she had no doubts of what the good reverend would think should she introduce him to Chet. Monica could well imagine the look of alarm that would come into his eyes. Naturally, he'd be gentle with his concern, but his response would be impossible to conceal.

After she'd finished frying the bacon and eggs, Monica set the plate on the table and said, "I'm going upstairs to change."

Her father tossed a surprised look her way. "You're not eating?"

She shook her head.

"You're sure you're feeling all right?"

At the moment Monica wasn't sure of anything.

"Come sit with me," Andrew invited. Leah's husband was relaxing on the white leather sofa, his feet stretched out and propped against the end of the glass coffee table. He set aside the morning paper and held out his arms coaxingly to her.

"I was going to wash the breakfast dishes," Leah said, and hesitated.

"Do them later."

"Andrew!" Her husband had the look about him that was unmistakable. He wanted her the way a man wants his wife and he wasn't willing to wait much longer.

"Yes?" she asked, poising her hand against her hip and shifting her weight to one foot. "It's barely ten o'clock in the morning." She didn't know why she was making excuses, she was as eager for him as he was for her. This was a good time of the month as well, her temperature would confirm that, but she hadn't taken it yet that morning.

"So? Who cares about the time?" he asked, holding his arm out to her. "Does the clock have to chime a certain number of times before I'm allowed to make love to my wife?"

"No." She walked toward him, her steps slow and provocative. When she was close, Andrew gripped hold of her waist, and gently lowered her onto his lap.

"Have I told you how beautiful you are lately?"

Leah smiled and shook her head. "Not since yesterday morning."

His hands stroked the length of her arms, his touch light and gentle. "Then I need to make up for lost time, don't I?"

"By all that's right, you should do penance."

"Oh?"

She looped her arms around his neck and pressed her forehead to his. Andrew's hands were busily working open the fastenings of her robe. After ten years of married life, Leah's body was well acquainted with that of her husband's.

Their kiss was slow, sultry, and thorough. She was breathless and panting by the time Andrew dragged his mouth from hers.

"You taste good."

"So do you," she whispered, her eyes closed.

His hands left her breasts and eased aside the elastic of the silk bottoms of her pajamas to stroke her flat stomach sensuously.

Andrew groaned as she moved against him, and kissed her again and then again, each one growing more intense in length and need.

"You know what I want?" he whispered hoarsely close to her ear, panting.

"Let's go in the bedroom."

"Why?" He kissed her neck and his hands sought her breasts. "You're my wife, I can make love to you any place I please, can't I?"

"I should take my temperature first. This might not be the best time of the month for us to be doing this. If we're going to make love let's do it when there's a chance I could get pregnant."

The silence that followed her words was filled with tension. Leah didn't know what she'd said that was so terrible. Their lovemaking had always been arranged according to her menstrual cycle and her temperature, which signaled ovulation.

"Andrew?" she asked, not understanding.

He moved away from her and straightened his clothes. She noticed that his hands were shaking. The anger came off him in waves like heat shimmering off concrete in the hottest days of summer.

"It'll only take a moment," she promised.

He kept his back to her. Still not understanding what she'd said, Monica sat up herself and straightened her own pajamas.

"It . . . it only makes sense if we're going to make love to do it at a time when I could get pregnant."

At her words, Andrew vaulted off the sofa and stormed into their bedroom. It was rare for him to act this way and she instinctively followed, wanting to right the wrong.

"Don't you agree?" she asked softly, placing her hand on his arm.

He whirled on her then, eyes flashing with anger, his teeth clenched. "No, Leah, I don't agree."

The force of his anger took her by surprise and she gasped and automatically stepped away from him. She couldn't remember him ever looking at her this way.

"I . . . I assumed you want a baby too," she offered weakly.

"I do." The words were hurled at her like sharp knives. "But not at the expense of everything else. It might come as a shock to you, but I'd appreciate being treated more like a husband and less like a robot. Every time we make love, all you can think about is making a baby. Did you ever stop to consider why we make love less and less often? Have you?" he shouted.

Leah had backed all the way across the room. Her backside was flattened against the wall. "I . . . I didn't notice we made love less often."

"For the last seven years it's been sex on demand. Our entire love life is centered on what time of the month it is. If Mars is lined up with Jupiter or some such stuff."

"That's ridiculous," she said, wanting to defend herself.

"My thoughts exactly. We make love when you want, when you think there's a remote possibility you might become pregnant. It isn't love any longer, it's sex, and if that was all I wanted, I could get it on the street."

Leah felt the color drain from her face. "You . . . you don't mean that." It was a fear she'd lived with from the moment she realized she might never bear a child, that Andrew would eventually leave her. That he'd find another woman who could give him the family he wanted.

He tore out of his pajamas, dressing quickly. "I can't remember the last time we made love," he said, jerking a shirt from the closet. The hanger swung with the force of his action. "Really made love," he amended. "It isn't me you want, it's what I can give you, and if I can't, then I'm no use to you."

"That's not true."

Andrew didn't answer. He yanked on a pair of pants, then sat on the end of the mattress to pull on his socks and shoes. His shirt wasn't buttoned as he stalked past her, toward the door.

"Where are you going?" Leah asked, running after him. Tears blurred her eyes and it was difficult to speak normally.

"Out."

"Andrew," she cried, "please wait."

His hand was on the door, his back to her.

"Don't go. You're right. I'm sorry, so sorry. Please."

His shoulders rose and then relaxed. For the longest time he didn't move. She wasn't entirely sure he was breathing—she knew she wasn't. The only sound in the room was her soft whimper as she struggled not to weep.

"I won't be gone long," he said, opening the door and walking out.

Leah flinched when the door closed, the sound exploding in the otherwise quiet room. She pressed a hand to her flat stomach and for a moment she thought she was going to be physically sick.

How long she stood there, paralyzed with pain, she didn't know. She couldn't guess. After a while she turned and headed for their bedroom. Slumping onto the edge of her mattress, she opened the drawer of her night stand and reached for the temperature chart she faithfully kept. Staring at them, her eyes filled with tears. After a moment, she walked into the kitchen. Her feet felt heavy and made small scuffing sounds against the floor as she listlessly made her way across the other room.

She opened the garbage compactor and tossed it inside. Along with the spiral pad, Leah felt as if she were throwing away her dreams.

It took her a moment to compose herself before she drew in a deep, stabilizing breath and reached for a dirty plate from their breakfast. She rinsed it off and blindly stacked it into the dishwasher.

Chet wasn't anywhere in the audience, at least not where Monica could see him. Relief swept through her as she looked out over the crowd of Christmas shoppers from her stance on the top riser. She hadn't approved of this Sunday afternoon outing. To her way of thinking a performance on Sunday wasn't proper for Christians. The way she interpreted the Bible, the Sabbath was a day of rest. Those who opted to spend their time shopping were breaking the observance of the Lord's day. She'd tried to reason with her father and Michael when they'd first planned this performance weeks earlier, but her objection had been overridden. Her father had claimed their singing was a way of spreading the message of love and joy. As usual, Monica had no argument.

Now she was pleased it had been overridden because it gave her an opportunity to see Chet again—if she did. It didn't feel good to admit that, but Monica was tired of fooling herself. She needed to see him again, just once more, to banish him from her mind, to prove there could never be anything between them.

The performance went well, although Monica was preoccupied searching the sea of faces for Chet's.

No doubt he was entertaining himself in the Blue Goose, the bar he chose to frequent. It would serve him right if she walked right in there and demanded to talk to him. She could embarrass him the way he had her.

Sneaking away from the others, however, proved to be more difficult than she anticipated.

"Are you coming?" Michael asked her. He was tall and so thin the first thing she thought of whenever they met was that someone should feed him.

Monica looked up at him, her mind a blank. She hadn't been listening to the conversation and hadn't a clue what he was talking about.

"To Sherry's," he elaborated when she didn't respond right away. "She's invited the ensemble over for hot cider and cookies."

"I . . ." Her gaze darted to the Blue Goose. "I have an errand to run first, but I'll be there shortly."

"An errand," Michael repeated. "Downtown?"

She said in a no-nonsense tone, grateful he didn't quiz her about what she was doing, especially in light of her earlier protests about abusing the Lord's day. "I won't be long . . . you go on ahead with the others. I'll be at Sherry's within the hour."

"You mean you aren't going back with everyone else?"

The man seemed to have a comprehension problem. "Yes," she said forcefully. "I already explained I have an errand I need to run." Then feeling mildly guilty for the outburst, she added, "I won't be long."

"Perhaps we should wait for you."

"No," she said quickly. She could well imagine what the others would think if they saw her walking into a tavern. "I appreciate the offer, but that isn't necessary."

Michael looked as if he weren't sure what he should do, which only served to irritate her further. "Perhaps I should stay with you."

"Michael, please, that isn't necessary." The man seemed intent on thwarting her, which aggravated her so much she was barely civil. "I'll see you within the hour." Not waiting for any further arguments, she turned and abruptly walked across the street to the Westlake Mall.

The crowds were thick and the moment she was free to leave, she escaped the shopping mall and hurried across the street. Making certain none of the other choir members had lingered, she walked purposefully toward the Blue Goose.

Her hand was on the door when she realized what she was doing. She was willing to walk into an establishment that practiced iniquity in the lowest form, in order to locate Chet. A man who plagued her thoughts from the moment they'd met. Something was dreadfully wrong with her.

She turned, practically running in her eagerness to escape, stopping only when she came to the street. She felt someone move behind her.

"I thought as much. You were looking for me, weren't you?"

There could be no mistaking the voice. It belonged to Chet Costello.

Chapter 7

It must have taken Jody forty-five minutes to persuade Timmy to go to bed, and then only after Glen agreed to help her tuck him in.

"I'm not tired," Timmy insisted as Jody pulled back the sheets of his twin bed. "I want to talk to Glen."

"About what?" Jody knew the instant the words escaped her lips that she'd walked right into that with both feet.

"All kinds of stuff. I need to know what kind of dad he's going to be. After all, God sent him, didn't He?"

A gigantic hole for her to fall in would have been welcome just then. Her son had a knack of knowing exactly what to say that would embarrass her the most. "Timmy, please."

"I don't really need to be tucked in," Timmy told Glen, sounding mature for his years. "I just wanted to show you my stuff." Something that he'd spent every available moment doing since Glen had arrived. Timmy had dragged out his baseball mitt and bat and his beloved baseball card collection for Glen to inspect. The poor man hadn't had a moment's peace in over an hour.

"Good night, Tim," Jody said sternly, standing in the doorway, her hand on the light switch.

" 'Night, Mom. 'Night, Glen."

Jody felt as though her cheeks were red enough to guide ships lost in the fog. She barely knew Glen and already her son was announcing what a great father he'd make. There was no help for it, she was forced to explain.

"I'll get you that coffee now," she said, leading the way into the compact kitchen and reaching for a mug. Her back ached from holding it so straight and stiff. She didn't know how she could possibly explain. "I apologize for what Timmy said earlier."

"About what?"

"You know, about you making him a great father. He's at the age now where he misses a man in his life."

"I imagine his friends talk about their dads."

Jody nodded. "Recently Timmy wrote a letter in school to God asking for a father. Apparently he looks at you as the answer to his prayer because . . . well, because you're the first man I've dated in a long while and . . ."

"That explains the comment about God sending me," Glen said as he carried the two steaming coffee mugs to the table.

"I suppose." Jody reluctantly admitted that much. "I didn't want you to feel pressure because of what he'd said and I certainly didn't want you to think that . . . that I'd put him up to it."

"I didn't." Glen sat down and crossed his legs, relaxing against the chair. He appeared more amused than concerned. "He's a wonderful boy. You've done a good job raising him."

"Thank you." His words made her proud, but at the same time she realized that she'd failed her son in some way, otherwise she would have recognized his need for a man in his life. Her father had served that purpose for Timmy until his death and the void had been deeply felt by her young son.

"I'm honored that Timmy thinks I'm good father material," Glen added between sips of coffee.

"It helped that you had a signed Ken Griffey, Jr. baseball card," Jody teased, then grew serious. "I thought I should explain why Timmy's so eager for us to get to know each other better."

The lines that fanned out from Glen's eyes relaxed as he set aside his mug and reached for her hand. "I'm just as eager to know you and Timmy better, but I'm an adult and it wouldn't be considered cool to let it show. I realize we've only been acquainted a short while, and it's much too soon to be thinking along the lines Timmy is, but . . ." He hesitated and his eyes studied hers, his look intense. He seemed to be weighing his words carefully, then shrugged and added, "Oh, what the hell, you can think what you want, but I like you, Jody, I like you a lot, and I think Timmy's a great kid. I haven't made it a secret that I'm strongly attracted to you.

"As far as I'm concerned the fact that you have a son who's looking for a father is an added bonus. I want a family, and have for some time. I'd be pleased if we both started thinking along those lines.

"There, I've said it and I've probably shocked you, but we're both mature adults, capable of handling the truth, don't you think?"

Jody didn't know what to say. She felt overwhelmed and apprehensive. She stood abruptly, nearly toppling her chair in her haste. "I'm flattered, really flattered, but . . . it's too soon, much too soon for us to be thinking along those lines."

"Of course it is," Glen agreed patiently. "I'm sorry, Jody, I didn't mean to upset you. You're right, of course, I got caught up in Timmy's enthusiasm. Forgive me."

"There's nothing to forgive."

Glen hadn't done anything more than sample his coffee, but he stood and carried the mug to the sink. "I should be going."

Jody nodded, but immediately felt guilty. Glen looked a little like Timmy after she'd had to tell him no when it was something he really wanted.

"Would you be willing to see me again, or have I completely terrified you?" he asked when he reached the front door.

Jody couldn't see how she could refuse. "I'd enjoy going out with you again."

The defeated puppy-dog look was replaced with a wide smile. "I'll give you a call some time tomorrow, then."

"That'd be fine."

Glen opened the door and paused. "Would you be willing to see me if it weren't for Timmy?"

Jody laughed softly. "Probably."

She was rewarded with another warm grin that lit up his eyes. He took a small step toward her and then stopped abruptly and exhaled a long, deep breath. "I'd very much like to kiss you, but I'm afraid that might be pushing matters. We'll do this your way, Jody. I'm a patient man, especially when the prize is one of such value. Good night and thank you for one of the most enjoyable evenings of my life."

" 'Night." She stood at the door and waited until he'd reached his car. Once he pulled away, his headlights illuminating the dark street, Jody closed the door and leaned against the heavy wood.

Glen had nice eyes, she decided. The eyes of a man she could trust, who wouldn't rush her into something she wasn't ready for. The eyes of a man who was well acquainted with pain and disappointment himself.

After a few moments she walked over to the mantel in the family room where Jeff's picture rested. She stared at his familiar features, the features she loved so dearly. Even after all these years, he had the power to stir her.

Reaching out, she traced her fingers over the outline of his jaw, waiting for the swell of emotion that generally accompanied such moments. To her surprise none came. Not guilt. Nor doubt. Jeff smiled benignly out at her and perhaps it was her imagination, she was sure it must be, but he seemed to approve of Glen, approve of the job she'd done raising Timmy. It seemed he was telling her that even in death he would always love her.

Leah heard the door shut. Andrew had returned after being away most of the day. She closed her eyes, and took a moment to compose herself before she faced her husband. He was right and she knew it. Having a child had become an obsession with her, so much so that she was systematically destroying the most important relationship in her life.

Stepping out of the kitchen, she watched as Andrew sat down in front of the television and reached for the remote control.

"I . . . I thought that must be you," she said, which sounded silly since it couldn't have been anyone else.

"As you can see, it's me." His words were as stark and cold as they had been earlier. It wasn't a good sign.

"Can we talk?" she asked, tentatively stepping into the room.

"I don't know that there's anything more to say."

The fact that they were having this conversation with his back to her said far more than any words they might have spoken.

"I'm sorry, Andrew," she whispered, struggling not to break into tears. She hated any kind of discord between them. They'd always been so close, she didn't think anything could destroy their love. She feared now that she might be wrong.

"You've already apologized, you don't need to do it again." The newsclips from the game between the Seattle Seahawks and the San Diego Chargers were playing and the noise of the game filled the room.

Leah, who was wearing jeans and a sweatshirt, wiped her hands against her thighs. "I was hoping we could talk," she said, lowering herself onto the far side of the sofa across from him.

"Leah, listen," Andrew said sharply, "I'm not good company at the moment. If we're going to talk it should be when we're both in the right frame of mind."

She could never remember Andrew being like this. They rarely disagreed and when they did, both were eager to resolve their differences.

"When do you think you'll be in the right frame of mind?" she asked, swallowing her pride.

"I don't know. I just need some time to put my thoughts together. I probably shouldn't have come back to the house, but it's cold and I wasn't keen about spending the rest of the day and evening sitting in my car."

"Of course you should have come back here. I'm glad you did. Do you want me to get you a cup of coffee? Some dinner?"

He shook his head. "What I'd appreciate more than anything is some time to myself."

"Sure," she said, scooting off the leather sofa, "whatever you want. Take all the time you need. I was thinking of going out anyway."

He acknowledged her with an abrupt nod and continued to stare at the television screen. "That sounds like a good idea."

So he wanted her to leave, was willing for her to go. Leah hadn't realized how deeply she'd injured Andrew's pride or how she'd weakened the foundation of their marriage. It came as a painful shock.

He didn't say anything more to her when she left. Leah went about gathering her coat and purse as if she were going on an outing she'd looked forward to for weeks. Humming softly she called out cheerfully, "I won't be late."

Not knowing where to go, Leah drove around for an hour before heading toward Pam's house. Her college friend knew there was something wrong the minute she opened the door. Not that Leah would have been able to hide it.

"Leah," Pam said, alarm filling her eyes. "What happened?"

Unable to speak, Leah shook her head from side to side.

"Come inside. I'm sure it's nothing a long talk and a strong cup of tea can't help."

This was what Leah loved about Pam—the ability to solve any problem with a cup of tea and a stiff upper lip. Now that she was here, she wasn't keen on talking. What she really needed was a friend, not a counselor.

"It's not all that bad," Leah said, making light of her troubles as she followed Pam into the kitchen. The sink was stacked with dirty dishes and the cupboards were smeared with miniature fingerprints, a stark contrast to her own spotless kitchen.

"Auntie Leah?" Scotty raced into the kitchen, clutching his stuffed dinosaur, the one she'd given him for his birthday a month earlier.

"Scotty, you're supposed to be asleep!" Pam said, hands on her hips.

Leah scooped the three-year-old into her arms and hugged him close while he pressed happy kisses over her face. He was a sweet boy with deep blue eyes and a froth of unmanageable curls and Leah loved him as much as if he were her own.

"How's my darling?" she asked, setting him on the countertop and brushing the curls away from his forehead.

"Look!" he said, proudly holding up his thumb.

"It's dry," Pam explained. "Scotty has given up sucking his thumb, isn't that right?"

Scotty nodded eagerly and Leah carried him back into the bedroom he shared with his younger brother. Thirteen-month-old Jason was sound asleep, his knees tucked under his stomach, his small buttocks thrust into the air.

"Shhh," Scotty said in a loud whisper as Leah set him back in his bed, after maneuvering around a stack of plastic building blocks and several wooden puzzles. Pieces were scattered all about the area.

"I'm very proud of you for not sucking your thumb," she whispered.

Scotty beamed with the praise. She kissed his forehead and tiptoed out of the room.

Pam had the tea brewed by the time Leah returned. "Where's Diane?" she asked about her friend's oldest child.

"Doug had to run an errand and she wanted to go with him. As you can see I haven't gotten around to the dinner dishes. Sit down and tell me what's upset you so much."

Leah didn't know where to start, or if she should. It wasn't easy to admit her failings. "Andrew and I had a spat, is all. We both needed some time to think matters through so I left."

"It's nothing serious, is it?"

Leah shook her head, discounting her concern. "I . . . I don't think so. We'll be fine."

Pam brought the china teapot to the table. "You're sure?"

"We rarely squabble and it upsets me when we do."

A series of short horn blasts interrupted their conversation. Although the sound was irritating there seemed to be a certain rhythm to it. Leah closed her eyes and listened carefully. If she hadn't known better she'd swear it sounded like someone was tapping out "Hit the Road, Jack."

Pam sent a curious look Leah's way. "Doug must need my help," she said, "he's certainly being clever about getting it."

"It sounds like . . ."

" 'Hit the Road, Jack,' " Pam finished for her, snapping her fingers as she walked toward the door. She stopped abruptly and turned around, looking puzzled.

"Is it Doug?" Leah asked.

Pam shook her head. "It's coming from your car."

This had to be some kind of joke. She set aside her tea and followed Pam. "Are you telling me my car's making that weird sound?"

"It's your horn," Pam insisted. "Just listen."

"My horn!" She joined her friend at the doorway.

"This is the weirdest thing I've ever seen in my life."

"You?" Leah laughed. "I better find out what's going on here." She grabbed her car keys and hurried across the yard.

"**Mercy, stop** that right this minute."

Mercy whirled around to find Shirley hovering over the trunk of Leah's car, her hands braced against her hips. Knowing she'd overstepped her authority, Mercy reluctantly complied. No doubt she'd done it this time and the archangel had dispatched Shirley to send her home.

"Did Gabriel send you?" Mercy demanded defiantly. If she was going to crash, she was going down in flames.

"No, I'm here to stop you before you get yourself into even bigger trouble."

"I had to do something fast," Mercy cried. "Andrew's worried because he can't find Leah."

"What?"

Mercy should have known she'd need to explain. "Leah and Andrew argued this morning and now he feels terrible. He wants to talk to Leah but he doesn't know where she is."

"We're not to get involved in any human's life," Shirley chastised. "By the way, what's with that ridiculous song?"

"It was popular several years back, one Leah would recognize. I'm trying to tell her to hightail it home."

Shirley folded her arms over her chest and impatiently tapped her foot. "You're courting trouble with
this one. By heaven, Gabriel's going to be furious. Sec-
ular music, no less. You couldn't have come up with
something more . . . spiritual?"

" 'Swing Low Sweet Chariot' just didn't hack it. I
was desperate. It worked, didn't it? Look, Leah's leaving now and two to one she's headed home."

"You're placing bets now too?" Shirley said behind
a smile. It wasn't unheard-of for a prayer ambassador
on earth assignment to return home with a few minor
bad habits. Some angels were known to have found
gambling appealing.

"Are you with the God Squad Police Patrol or something?" Mercy blurted out impatiently. Shirley had
the luxury of having everything falling neatly into
place with her prayer assignment. The last she'd heard,
Timmy's mother had agreed to date a fine, upstanding
young man who'd make Timmy a great father.

She and Goodness should have it so easy. As for
herself, Mercy was batting zero when it came to helping Leah, and from what she heard, Goodness wasn't
in much better shape. If anything, matters had gotten
progressively worse. In the last report from Goodness,
Mercy had learned that Monica Fischer had stretched
the truth in an effort to seek out Chet Costello. For a

woman who prided herself on rigid honesty this was not an encouraging sign.

"I don't mean to sound so bossy," Shirley explained, looking apologetic, "but Gabriel could have your wings for this."

"My wings! I don't think so." It would take a whole lot more than tapping out "Hit the Road, Jack" on a car horn for that to happen.

"I'm only trying to help you."

"I know, but . . ."

A whoosh of warm wind accompanied Goodness, who arrived breathless and impatient, with her feathers ruffled with indignation. "What is going on with you two?" she demanded.

"Shirley decided to appoint herself as my guardian and—"

"I was watching out for your best interests."

"Stop! Both of you!" Goodness cried, tossing her arms in the air. "I had to leave Monica and Chet at the worst possible moment for this."

"Not really, we were—"

Goodness cut her off by stamping her foot. "Shall we all get back to our jobs? Humans are trouble enough without the three of us squabbling."

"I was only looking to help," Shirley offered with an injured look.

When Leah pulled into her driveway, she wasn't sure what to expect. The business with her horn had ceased the moment she started the engine. Since Andrew took care of the maintenance on their vehicles it was something she should tell him. But how could she explain her horn going all weird on her?

The front door to the house opened even before she had a chance to climb out of the car. Andrew's large frame filled the doorway as he rushed out to meet her.

"Where were you?" he asked, his face tight with concern. "I must have made a dozen phone calls and sounded like a complete idiot looking for my wife."

"I . . . I drove over to Pam and Doug's."

"Pam and Doug," Andrew repeated and stabbed his fingers into his hair as if to punish himself. "I should have tried them first—it makes perfect sense, the way you love those kids," he said, steering her toward the house. He closed the door, shutting out the cold.

"You weren't ready to talk, remember?" Leah said. "You were preoccupied with the sports news and needed time to sort through your feelings. Or so you said."

Andrew nodded. "I behaved like a fool. I'm sorry, Leah."

"You? I was the one who owed you an apology."

"You gave it," Andrew reminded her, and something she couldn't read flared in his eyes, "Hell, I don't know what was wrong with me."

"You needed your space," Leah supplied, removing her coat and hanging it in the hall closet. "We all do at one time or another. I understand."

"I should never have let you go. You wanted to settle matters then and there. I was the one who made everything so difficult." He brought her into the circle of his arms and sighed as she relaxed against him. "I love you so damn much," he said.

"I know," she whispered. His fingers lovingly worked through the tangles in her hair. "I love you too. You're right, Andrew, I realize that now and I'm so sorry for the way I've treated you—"

"Hush," he whispered, gently kissing her. "It's forgotten."

"You're the most important person in my life."

"I found the record book in the garbage. Do you mean it, honey? Can we stop worrying about a pregnancy and concentrate on each other?"

Leah understood what he was asking. He wanted her to let go of the frantic need she had for a child, to stop looking for a pregnancy to fulfill her as a woman.

She'd cheatcd her husband out of far more than she realized. All these years she'd been subtly and not so subtly telling him his love wasn't enough. Every time she'd dragged him to another doctor, to another fertility clinic, through another series of tests, she in essence said she found him lacking and that she needed something more. She tagged a condition onto her happiness, insisting she needed a child, the child he should give her.

Wrapping her arms around Andrew's neck, Leah slowly nodded. The dream was dead. It had been from the moment she realized what she'd done to him.

"Mom." Timmy greeted Jody at the door the minute she walked into the house after work Monday morning. "A package came for me from Grandma Potter. Can I open it?" He was hopping up and down like a pogo stick, following her from one room to the next. "It's addressed to me."

"A package?"

"It's probably for Christmas. You're not going to make me wait, are you?"

Jody moved into the family room and stopped short. Timmy hadn't exaggerated, the package was huge. She was curious herself. Gloria was very good at remembering Timmy on his birthday and Christmas, but she generally sent a check, claiming he should save for his college education.

"I don't think it'd do any harm to open it up," Jody said, curious herself.

"I've got the scissors all ready," Timmy said, racing into the kitchen.

"Don't run with scissors in your hand," she warned.

"I'm not a kid!" Timmy chided, walking back with exaggeratedly slow steps.

"Sorry," Jody said, smiling to herself.

The box had been carefully packaged, as if it contained something of exceptional value. Once the tape had been cut away they were able to peel back the cardboard lid. Timmy immediately starting digging when they discovered the box was filled with Styrofoam packing balls. The material flew in every direction. She laughed, watching her son virtually attack the present.

He bent over the top, his feet six inches off the ground. "There are a bunch of smaller boxes inside," he called, lifting out the first of what proved to be several.

Jody lined them up on the coffee table and Timmy opened the largest one first. "What's this?" he asked, bringing out a trophy.

Jody was puzzled herself.

"Look, there's a letter in here for you."

Jody took the envelope and ripped it open.

Dearest Jody and Timmy,

You're were right, Jody. Jeff is dead and it's time I accepted as much. Forgive an old woman who can't bear to believe that her only son is gone. The truth was too painful to accept. Painful for you and Timmy too, I realize.

It came to me the other day that now Timmy's growing up, he might be interested in having the things that once belonged to his father. Jeff's childhood treasures are his now and don't belong to a grieving mother. Take them, and treasure them, but most of all, remember Jeff.

"What's the trophy for?" Timmy asked, turning it upside down and examining the bottom. "This is weird, the way they put it together."

Jody could barely speak for the tears in her throat. "Your father won that when he was twelve," she said, holding onto the statue with both hands. "For soccer."

"My dad played soccer?"

Jody nodded.

"I didn't know that."

Jeff was wonderfully athletic, the same way Timmy was, but he'd concentrated on football and track in high school and college.

"Wow," Timmy said, "look at this. It's really old."

"It's your dad's report card from when he was in the first grade."

"He was smart, wasn't he?"

"Very smart."

"You were too, weren't you, Mom?"

She nodded.

Timmy was hurriedly opening one box and then the next. "This stuff is really neat. I can keep it, can't I, forever and ever?"

"Of course."

"I'm never going to forget my dad. Never," he vowed, sitting back on his legs and releasing a slow, uneven sigh. "You know, Mom, it might not be such a good idea for you to get me another dad. Not when I already have one. It was just that until now he was a face in a picture you keep by the fireplace. But he was really a neat guy, wasn't he?"

"Yes, sweetheart," she agreed, "he was someone very special."

Timmy's eyes grew serious. "Then it'd be wrong to look for another dad."

Chapter 8

Monica was in a tizzy. Chet had seen her standing outside of the Blue Goose, and knew she'd sought him out. Her first thought was that she should adamantly deny everything. That, however, would be a lie and she prided herself on her honesty.

"Couldn't stay away, could you?" he said in that impertinent way of his.

"I'm sure you're mistaken," she snapped. The buzz of traffic zoomed past her as she stiffly stood on the curb, waiting for the light to change.

Chet laughed, the sound mingling with those from the street and the busy holiday shoppers. The signal changed and she remained frozen, unable to move with the others.

"I imagine that's as close to the truth as I'm likely to get from you," he said, and gripping hold of her elbow, escorted her across the street. He didn't tell her where he was taking her and she didn't ask. Although she had long legs, she had trouble keeping up with his brisk pace.

He steered her into Woolworth's and over to the lunch counter.

"What are we doing here?" she demanded, disliking the assumptions he was making.

He ignored her and slipped into a booth. She would have brought attention to herself if she'd continued standing so she uneasily claimed the seat across from him.

"You hungry?" he asked nonchalantly, reaching for the yellowed plastic-coated menu tucked behind the silver napkin dispenser.

"I . . . as a matter of fact I am, but . . ."

"The steak sandwich is excellent and they don't do a bad chicken-fried steak."

"I'll just have coffee," she told him. By all that was right she shouldn't be sitting with him. She barely knew the man and what she did know was a cause for a twenty-four-hour prayer vigil.

"Suit yourself."

The waitress came, an older woman with gray hair in a pale pink uniform. She chewed gum and looked more worn than the linoleum in Monica's kitchen.

"I'll have a BLT on wheat, with coffee," Chet ordered.

The waitress wrote down the order and looked to Monica expectantly.

"The same, only put mine on a separate ticket."

The woman left, jotting down Monica's order as she went.

"I saw you outside the Blue Goose," Chet announced casually.

It was all Monica could do not to cover her face with her hands. It mortified her to know he'd seen her standing outside the tavern, debating whether she should go inside or not.

"I know why you were there too."

"You do?" Her rebellious gaze shot to his. She was certain he could see her pulse beating in the vein in her neck, the sound echoing in her ear like thunder.

Chet set the menu back in place and waited for the waitress to finish pouring their coffee before he continued. "You're curious about the same thing as me."

"Which is?"

He smiled without humor, "I don't know if you have enough courage or honesty to admit it so I'll say it. We're both trying to figure out if what happened between us was real."

Monica had entertained a whole spectrum of possibilities of what had happened when Chet had kissed her. She blamed him, then herself, and eventually her upbringing. Having lived a sheltered, protected life hadn't prepared her for the sensual magnetism she experienced at his touch.

"I certainly don't have any intention of allowing you to kiss me again," she told him, the words ringing with disdain. It was important he understood this right now.

"Not to worry, I'm not exactly thrilled with the prospect myself. I'm curious, and you have to admit you are too, otherwise you wouldn't be here. Frankly, I can't figure out what it is about you that intrigues me so much."

"I . . . I was wondering the same thing myself. You won't leave me alone either."

Their sandwiches arrived and Chet tore into his as if he hadn't eaten in a week. Monica glared at him and pointedly reached for her napkin and spread it evenly across her lap. Bowing her head, she murmured a simple prayer of thanksgiving. When she'd finished, she lifted half the sandwich from her plate, holding it daintily in both hands. Chet had started on the second half of his before she'd taken the first bite.

When he finished, Chet reached inside his pocket and brought out a small spiral pad. He flipped through several pages until he found what he was looking for.

"Your father's name is Lloyd Fischer, the Reverend Lloyd Fischer. You're an only child and your mother died when you were in your teens. Currently the church employs you as a full-time secretary. You play the piano on Sunday mornings and teach a Sunday school class. Your two best friends are married and live in another state. It's said that you miss them dearly and write often."

Monica was so shocked it took an effort for her to disguise her distress. "How . . . how do you know all that?"

Chet grinned suspiciously. "I have my ways. I'm a private investigator, remember? Don't tell me you didn't find out what you could about me."

"I most certainly did not." She snapped her mouth closed before she added to the lie. She had looked up his name in the business directory and noted the address. His office was close to the Westlake Mall on First Avenue in a dingy part of town. The mission was situated on the same street and she'd mentally calculated which building was his. She'd looked his name up in the white pages as well and learned that his apartment was in the same building.

"So," he said, pushing the empty plate aside and reaching for his coffee. "Do you have any suggestions?"

"For what?" She wasn't sure where he was leading, but she had no intention of continuing with this farce. Having lunch with him was about as far as she intended to go.

"Figuring out what's going on between us," he said loudly as if she were hard of hearing.

"Keep your voice down," she pleaded.

"The thing is," Chet continued, "I'm not sure I like you. You annoy the hell out of me and at the same time I can't help thinking you could be a real woman if you'd let yourself go a little bit."

Monica jerked her shoulders back and scowled at him. "You haven't exactly endeared yourself to me either, Mr. Costello. You're everything I *don't* want in a man."

Instead of insulting him, her words appeared to do just the opposite. He grinned as if she'd stroked his ego with compliments. "Ain't it a bitch?"

Her head snapped back at the use of vulgarity. "Kindly watch your language."

His grin was cocky in the extreme. "You want me so much you're practically frothing at the mouth."

Monica's hands were shaking so badly she could barely open her purse zipper. She removed her wallet and carefully extracted a ten-dollar bill, which she set next to her plate.

"I don't believe there's anything more for us to say," she said crisply.

Chet held up his hand. "Don't be so hasty. We've got several matters to discuss."

Monica slipped out of the booth and dramatically tossed her purse strap over her shoulder. "I won't say it's been a pleasure," she said, taking her gloves from her coat pockets. "Good-bye, Mr. Costello."

She heard him swear and winced at his words as she walked away. His hurried footsteps sounded behind her before she left the store and reached the sidewalk.

"All right, I apologize," Chet murmured impatiently, "I shouldn't have said that."

The man was full of surprises. She certainly hadn't counted on him making amends any more than she'd expected him to chase after her. Monica wasn't sure how to react, or what she should do. She was more comfortable believing him to be a hopeless Neanderthal. His sincerity went against the assumptions she'd made about him.

"You want to go for a walk?" Chet asked before she had time to sort through her feelings. "It'll be a test of our control to see how long we can go without finding something to argue about."

"Where do you suggest we walk?" Monica asked, as if that were her only concern. She looked up at him and found his deep, blue eyes intently studying her.

"The waterfront's as good a place as any. There're always lots of things going on down there."

"All right." Her words were little more than wisps of sound. She hurriedly looked away because she found his gaze mesmerizing and buried her hands in her pockets. Chet followed suit, his own hands waist deep in the pockets of his beige coat.

"You seem to know a lot about me," she said as a means of opening the conversation, "it only seems fair for you to tell me something about yourself." She wasn't sure, but this sounded like a good place for them to start. Her only concern was in knowing exactly what they were starting. She didn't know if she could be friends with this man, and anything else was impossible.

"I'm thirty-three and have never been married," Chet said, cutting into her thoughts.

"Why not?"

"You're twenty-five and I didn't ask you that," he barked, then seemed to regret his tart remark. "I never found a woman who'd be willing to put up with me."

Monica smiled to herself. "I guess you could say the same thing about me. I don't seem to communicate very well with men. I thought I did, but I was wrong."

"That sounds like you're speaking from experience. I take it someone's hurt you."

She shook her head. "We're talking about you, remember?"

He frowned as if he found the subject boring and was much more interested in her. "What do you want to know about me?"

She shrugged, not knowing what to say. "Where'd you go to school, that sort of thing, and how you got into the detective business."

"All right," he said, releasing a beleaguered sigh. He seemed eager to get this part over so he could learn what he wanted to know about her. "I graduated from the University of Washington with a degree in criminology and took a job with the local police force. After a few years I decided I'd rather strike out on my own."

Monica speculated that there was a great deal missing in this story, but she didn't feel she should pressure him for details, not when she was unwilling to supply the missing pieces of her own story.

"Did you enjoy police work?"

"Yes and no. When I was shot—"

"You were shot?" Monica couldn't hide her alarm. She studied him for any evidence of permanent injury, and her heart raced at a furious pace.

"It was little more than a flesh wound, nothing to worry about physically, at any rate." He hesitated as if he'd said more than he intended, more than he wanted her to know.

"What do you mean?" she probed, not willing to drop the subject.

"Nothing. We'll leave it at that, all right?" The way he said it told her she wouldn't get any more information out of him. Knowing that he'd been physically injured had a curious effect on Monica. A strange sick feeling attacked her. Knowing he'd suffered terrible pain greatly distressed her.

They reached the waterfront, the day was cold and gray, and the angry sky reflected on the waters of Puget Sound. The sidewalks were crowded with the heavy tourist and Christmas traffic.

"What made you decide to become a private investigator?" she asked as they stood at the end of the pier. The wind buffeted her and she turned her back on its force. Chet, however, leaned against the rough wood railing, his hands clenched.

Chet glanced her way. "You aren't going to like the answer to this one."

"I asked the question, didn't I?" His attitude irked her.

"All right, since you asked, I'll tell you. A shapely blonde with loose morals and legs that reached all the way to her neck—"

"You're right," Monica cut him off, "I don't want to hear the rest."

"That's what I thought."

They strolled back to the sidewalk and turned into a small shop that specialized in seashells, tacky souvenirs, and gaudy jewelry. Curious, Monica moved to a crowded aisle, no particular destination in mind. She found a paper Japanese fan with a brightly painted dragon and spread it open, fluttering it in front of her face.

Chet grinned and she lowered the fan. Slowly the amusement drained from his eyes and darkened to a shade as deep and dark as a moonless night. His sudden enmity unnerved her and she quickly snapped the fan closed and returned it to the table, wondering what she'd done that had displeased him so.

His hand stopped her. "You're beautiful when you choose to be," he said.

His words confused her as much as his look.

She turned hurriedly up another aisle and paused at a rack of necklaces. Taking one, she slid the chain against the palm of her hand until she reached the pendant. A mustard seed was framed in a glass teardrop. The scripture verse about faith the size of a mustard seed leaped into her mind.

"Faith is an amazing thing," Chet surprised her by saying.

That he'd know the verse shocked her. "You've read the Bible."

He made a gallant effort not to laugh and failed. "I'm not a heathen, Monica, even if I've been known to frequent seedy bars and sleep with immoral women."

"I see." Embarrassed now by his honesty and her assumptions, she started to leave the shop. To her surprise, Chet took the necklace from her hand and carried it to the front of the store.

"What do you believe in?" she asked as they waited to make the purchase.

"Do I need to believe in anything?"

She could tell that the question made him uncomfortable. "Everyone has a belief system, whether he acknowledges it or not." She sounded far more versed in the subject than she was. Her own had been so clearly defined for her from the time she was a child.

He didn't answer her for a long, silent moment. "I believe life's a bitch," he said as he paid for the necklace.

Monica bristled, but then she'd asked and he'd told her.

He moved behind her and put the necklace around her neck. The glass teardrop felt cool against her skin. "Thank you," she whispered, touched that he'd bought it for her.

"Don't make a big deal out of a few bucks," he said as if he regretted the purchase.

When they came out of the store, Monica was surprised to find that it was snowing. She couldn't remember the weatherman mentioning snow. The fat flakes came down fast and furious and had already covered the sidewalk.

"I'd better hurry to the bus stop," she said, anxious to get home before the weather made it impossible. She was already an hour later than she said she'd be.

By the time they'd climbed the steep hill to the bus stop, Monica was breathless. It seemed that everyone in town had decided to head for home at the same time. Within minutes it became clear she was in for a long wait.

"You go on," she urged Chet. "I'll be fine." But he refused to leave her and after waiting a half hour, Chet shook his head.

"This is ridiculous," he said, "I'll drive you home myself."

"But it's snowing, and the road conditions might make that impossible."

"We'll wait out the craziness and once everything settles down I'll get my car out of the parking garage."

He didn't leave room for her to argue, and she doubted he would have listened if she had. Chet steered her toward the exit and reached for her hand when it looked as if they might be separated in the crowd.

"Where are we going?" she asked while they were making their way down the street. The conditions were blizzardlike. They were bent nearly in half as they walked against the brunt of the storm.

Chet didn't bother to answer until they entered a redbrick building. In the foyer, he stamped the snow from his shoes and led the way to the elevator.

"Where are we?" she asked, obediently following him.

"My building, and before you get that outraged virgin look I promise I won't so much as touch you."

"I'd better call my father or else he'll worry." Monica sincerely doubted that he'd ever dated a woman who needed to check in with her family. She was pleased she couldn't read his thoughts.

"No problem," Chet said. At his floor, he took her down a narrow, dark hallway. His office had his name painted on a milky white door. Chet inserted the key and opened it for her, letting her precede him.

The first thing Monica noticed was the calendar with a naked blond woman sprawled out on a blanket of black velvet. The year 1963 was printed in bold letters down the side. His desk looked as if it had weathered a war on the losing side. It was scarred and battered and so cluttered it was impossible to see any part of the surface. His chair came straight out of the 1920s. A row of antique slot machines lined one wall.

Chet made his way around her and Monica realized she'd been blocking the doorway. "This is my office," he explained.

"Your calendar's for the wrong year," she said, her voice little more than a whisper.

He laughed. "Only a woman would notice that." He walked over to the other door and opened it. "Home, sweet home," he said, gesturing for her to go before him.

Monica was just getting accustomed to the disarray in his office. She held her breath as she stepped into his living quarters, preparing herself for the worst.

She hesitated in the doorway. "It's not so bad," she said, then realized she'd verbalized the thought. There appeared to be some order to his studio apartment, compared to the chaos of his office.

Dishes were washed and stacked on the drainboard and the only food on the counter was a bowl with three overripe bananas. The sofa was a large overstuffed one with a stack of laundry—she couldn't tell if it was clean or dirty—piled in one corner.

"The phone's by the television," Chet said. "I'll make us some coffee."

"All right," she said, taking several tentative steps into the room and reaching for the phone. Her father answered on the second ring.

"I got caught in the snow," she explained.

"I don't understand why you didn't leave with the others." Her father was rarely angry, but he was close to being so now. "Just how do you propose to get home?"

"I'm an adult, Dad, I can take care of myself. Stop worrying. I'll call again if I run into any problems." Rather than get into discourse that required explanations, she quickly ended the conversation. When she'd finished, Chet brought her a steaming mug of coffee.

"It's instant," he said, and with one sweeping motion of his hand, he cleared the surface of the sofa.

Monica sat close to the edge of the cushions, cradling the mug with both hands, her back straight, her knees together. Rarely had she felt more out of place. She'd never been alone with a man in an apartment before and her sensibilities were badly shaken. Chet had promised to be a gentleman, and to her dismay she was sadly disappointed by his assurance.

"Relax," Chet said, sounding irritated. "You look like you're waiting for me to pounce on you. I said I wouldn't touch you."

She decided to ignore the comment. "Do you have any idea of how much snow is forecast?" she asked, looking for a means of light conversation. She wished now that she'd stayed and waited for a bus. No matter how tardy the transportation it would have saved them both this awkwardness.

"Sweetheart, the weatherman didn't know about this. You don't honestly expect me to figure it out, do you?"

She didn't like the way he said sweetheart. He made the term of affection sound like an insult. "I'd rather you didn't call me that."

"What?"

"Sweetheart."

"Why not?"

"Listen here, honeybunch," she murmured sarcastically, "I'm not your sweetheart or anything else."

"I didn't say you were. Let's just forget it, all right?" He stalked over to the sink and dumped what was left of his coffee. "I'll see about getting you home now."

One look out the window told her the snow hadn't let up in the least; if anything, it was coming down heavier. Chet wanted to be rid of her and she was just as eager to go. She didn't know what she was doing with a man who hung a picture of a naked woman in his office. She was out of her element and eager to get back where she belonged.

"I can take the bus." She felt obliged to volunteer, but it was doubtful how much longer the transit would continue to run in the heavy snow.

Chet cast her a look that told her what he thought of that idea. "Come on, this might take a while."

Monica bundled her coat around her and hurried after him. The wind was bitterly cold as it sliced through the open garage. Chet drove a battered Chevy Impala with a tail pipe that hung so low she wondered if he could make it over a speed bump. She couldn't imagine that the faded green was a factory color.

"My Mercedes is in the shop," he said, unlocking the passenger door for her.

Monica let herself inside and searched until she found the seat belt, clicking it into place. Chet started the engine, which came to life with the roar of a lion, and pulled out of the parking space.

The streets were terrible, and the traffic was a nightmare, but Chet was an excellent driver and managed to avoid the worst of it. Monica breathed a sigh of relief as they left the congested downtown area.

Both were quiet for several minutes, and as they neared her neighborhood, Monica tensed. "It might be a good idea if you dropped me off a block or so before the house."

"Why? You aren't wearing boots—your feet would be drenched within minutes."

"I know, it's just that . . ."

"It'll save you having to make explanations if your father happens to see me."

"Yes," she murmured, appreciating that he'd said it for her. He drove a few more blocks, before pulling over to the side of the road. The church and parsonage were within sight, but it wasn't likely that her father would notice her with Chet.

Now that she was near home, Monica wasn't eager for her time with Chet to end. She clenched her purse in her lap with both hands. "Thank you," she whispered, fingering the mustard-seed necklace. "For everything."

"Think nothing of it."

"I mean it," she said, more adamant this time. "You didn't need to do this and I appreciate everything you went through . . . even when it didn't seem like it." Only heaven knew how long it would take him to drive back into the city. The streets were difficult enough as it was.

Chet's hands were braced against the steering wheel, his gaze focused straight ahead. "I don't know that we solved anything."

"You're not the monster I assumed," she said, making light of her prejudices. Honesty, however, could be a burden. Now that she'd admitted as much, she wasn't sure where that left them. Monica didn't know and she doubted that Chet did either.

"You're not quite as prudish as I believed."

They looked toward each other and a smile blossomed between them, slow and sweet. Time stood perfectly still, but it seemed impatient as if waiting for them to act. The stillness swelled around them, cutting off sound except the silent wonder of the falling snow.

Monica didn't know who moved first. It didn't seem that either of them had, when she found her mouth inches from his. Chet was motionless. She could barely feel his breath, barely feel her own. She should move, should turn away from him and flee while she could, but she couldn't make herself do it. Enthralled, she raised her hands and placed them on his shoulders. He felt solid and strong. Her touch was all Chet needed. He bent forward and claimed her mouth in a slow, leisurely exercise.

This wasn't the way it was before. It was much better . . . much worse. She dragged her mouth from his, frustration close to the surface, but she wasn't allowed to vent that or anything else. Before she could so much as draw in a stabilizing breath, Chet caught her face and brought her mouth back to his.

His need was urgent now and he kissed her again and again as waves of confusion assaulted her. A warm, dizzy feeling began to build within her, spreading throughout her body. The sensation flooded every cell. She was aware of everything about Chet, the taste, the feel, the masculine scent of him.

When they did finally ease away from each other, neither of them seemed to know what to say.

Slowly, Monica raised her eyes to his. His gaze revealed the extent of his confusion. The same bewilderment, the same questions, the same doubts.

Monica had no idea how long they stared. The air crackled with static electricity, with sexual tension.

"You better get inside," he said, and his voice sounded as if it were coming from the bottom of a deep well.

She nodded and turned away from him. Her hand was on the car door when he spoke again.

"Will the choir be downtown again any time soon?" he asked brusquely.

Monica wasn't so dense not to know what he wanted. He was asking to see her again. She shook her head and not daring to look at him, she said, "I was planning to do some Christmas shopping though."

"When?"

The question shouldn't have been so difficult. Her plans had been nebulous at best. Sometime over the next weekend, but that seemed far too long to wait to see Chet again. A whole week was out of the question.

"Monday night," she said, still not looking at him. "Around six." Not waiting for a sign of confirmation from him, she hurriedly climbed out of the car. Walking as fast as she could, she rushed toward the house, not looking back until she reached her front porch. Only then did she chance a look over her shoulder.

Chet was parked in the same spot, she noted, waiting for her to make it safely inside the house.

Chapter 9

J ust when everything was straight in her mind, this had to happen, Jody mused as she drove home from work Tuesday afternoon. The snow that had taken Seattle by surprise on Sunday had melted away Monday morning to a dirty slush that filled the side streets.

Jody's route from the house to the office had been traveled so often she could almost do it blind. She avoided the busy intersections by taking a side street that led her past Providence Hospital.

For reasons she couldn't explain even to herself, she pulled into the hospital parking lot and climbed out of her car. Glen had asked to take Timmy and her out for pizza Thursday evening, and she'd put him off, claiming she had to check her schedule. He'd seemed surprised and disappointed, but he hadn't questioned her further.

Timmy claimed he didn't want another father, not now, not after he'd carefully gone through Jeff's items. For the first time his natural father was real to him. It didn't seem right to start another relationship now.

The nativity scene had been up for several days and she'd driven past it for the last seven years without ever stopping. Now seemed the perfect time. Now seemed the worst possible moment.

She walked over and stood before the manger scene, and breathed in the serenity.

"Jeff," she whispered, "help me." She didn't honestly expect him to hear her, nor did she believe it was possible for him to respond to her despondent prayer. Yet she reached out to him, because she wasn't sure which way to turn.

"You'd like Glen," she whispered. "He's the kind of man you would have called a friend."

The only sounds that returned to her were from the traffic in the streets.

This wasn't helping, Jody realized. Nor was it hurting. She took a few more minutes to soak in whatever comfort she could before returning to the car.

Timmy was waiting for her. Every day she called the babysitter when she left the office and Timmy walked down the block, unlocked the house, and was there when she arrived home a few minutes later. It made him feel less of a kid and more of a young adult. Less of a Timmy and more of a Tim.

The lights shone from the windows as she pulled into the driveway. Timmy was in the family room, the football video game blaring from the television screen.

"Glen called," he told her when she joined him.

"Did you bring in the mail?"

"It's on the counter. Nothing interesting, just bills."

Jody sorted through the small stack, disappointed not to receive so much as a single Christmas card. Her own had yet to be mailed.

"Are you going to call Glen back?" Timmy wanted to know as he expertly manipulated the game control.

"In a minute." She scooted the ottoman over to her son, who was kneeling on the floor, intent on his game. "Can we talk?"

"In a minute, Mom, I'm just to the good part."

"Are you ready to save the world again?"

He broke his concentration long enough to cast her a disgruntled look. "You can't do that with football."

"Oh."

Apparently having lost, he groaned and set aside the controller. "Okay," he said, looking at her expectantly. "I'm ready."

"Glen wanted to take us out to dinner one day this week. What do you think?"

Timmy's eyes brightened with enthusiasm before his gaze slid to the row of trophies he'd set out the night before on the fireplace mantel.

"I don't need another dad."

"I remember you said that earlier, I just wanted to be sure you meant it."

Although he looked disappointed, Timmy said, "I meant it. You'd better call Glen back and tell him no."

Timmy was unusually quiet during dinner, but Jody wasn't up to much conversation herself. After she'd finished the dishes, she phoned Glen, and was grateful when his answering machine came on. It was a cowardly thing to do, but she left a message on his recorder declining his offer to take Timmy and her to dinner.

Timmy was sound asleep when the doorbell chimed. Jody glanced at her watch, wondering who'd be dropping by unannounced at this late hour. She hesitated, then realized anyone who intended to do her harm wasn't likely to ring the doorbell first.

Glen stood on the other side of the door.

"Glen."

"I know it's late, but do you have a moment?"

"Of course," she said, stepping aside.

A blast of cold air accompanied him as he stepped into her house. He rubbed his hands together and cast her an apologetic look.

"Would you like a cup of coffee?"

"If you don't mind," he said, continuing to look uneasy. "I shouldn't have come."

Jody felt a twinge of guilt over the way she'd rejected his offer to take Timmy and her out for pizza. It had been a cowardly thing to do.

"Please, sit down," she said, motioning toward the kitchen table while she assembled a pot of coffee and waited for the liquid to drain through.

Glen stood until she'd finished with the coffee before he took a seat himself. Jody guessed that this didn't have anything to do with manners. He seemed preoccupied and nervous.

"I'm not exactly sure what I want to say," he began, stretching his arms across her tabletop. "I don't doubt that I'm making a fool of myself. I seem to do that when it comes to dealing with women."

"I'm sure that's not true." Jody's guilt was mounting until it was a palatable thing. Glen was one of the nicest men she'd ever known.

"I guess the real reason I'm here is to ask you what I did wrong."

"You didn't do anything wrong."

"I realize I was rushing you and if I haven't already apologized for that, then I am now. I . . . it's just that I think the world of you and Timmy, and knowing I'd done something—"

"Glen," she said, interrupting him. "Believe me, please, it isn't anything you said or did. Timmy received a package from his grandmother, Jeff's mother, with things that had been Jeff's as a boy, and now . . ."

"And now," Glen finished for her, "Timmy feels another man in his life would be betraying his father's memory." Glen grew silent for a moment, then slowly he leveled his gaze on her. "More important, so would you. I know how much you loved Jeff," he continued, his voice gaining conviction, "that was one of the things that attracted me to you the most. You're not the kind of woman who'd give her heart lightly, and when you do, it means something."

The compliment made her uncomfortable.

"That appeals to me, Jody, because I'm that kind of person myself. I didn't fall in love until recently and it's been hell getting over that relationship. Love means more to me than being sexually compatible. It means being an important part of your life as you'll be in mine. It means encouraging you to be everything you've ever wanted to be, sharing in your triumphs and comforting you in your failures. It means giving you the courage to try again. That's what love is all about."

Jody didn't know what to say. She wasn't likely to meet anyone like Glen in a good long time. A man who looked outside himself was a rarity. He'd spoken of his broken relationship and the pain it had brought him, and yet he was willing to trust again, willing to love again.

"I've been thinking about marriage for a long time," Glen went on. "And because of that I've put unnecessary pressure on you and Timmy. I want you to know how sorry I am."

"Please," she said, "don't apologize again. It isn't anything you've done."

He stood as if sitting had become intolerable. "I want you to know I don't plan on taking Jeff away from you and Timmy. It would be impossible. All I'm asking is that you give me a chance to prove myself to you. All I'm asking is that you make room in your life for me."

Jody recalled the way her son's eyes had lit up when she mentioned the outing with Glen and how that expression had gradually faded as he looked at the trophies that had once belonged to his father. Like her, Timmy had assumed having dinner with another man would betray Jeff's memory.

Glen plowed his hand through his hair. "I realize men aren't supposed to react to rejection like this. We're supposed be flippant and to take it on the chin and all that. Forgive me, Jody, if I've made you uncomfortable. I hope I haven't embarrassed you, but I wanted to speak my piece. I figured I'd better do it while I had the courage." He turned and walked out of her kitchen.

He was at the front door before she stopped him. "Glen?"

"Yes?"

"Thank you for stopping by. You've given me something to think about. I'll . . . probably see you at the copy machine soon."

He nodded and his soft, dark eyes held hers captive. "I can be patient, Jody, I just haven't proved it yet, but I promise you I will." With that, he turned and let himself out the door.

"Here they come." Bonnie Stewart stuck her head in the labor room door where Leah was stripping the sheets from the bed. Her patient had recently delivered a healthy eight-pound baby girl, her third child. The labor and delivery had gone smoothly and mother and father were delighted with their latest addition.

Leah's shift had been over half an hour earlier and she'd hoped to be long gone before the birthing-class tour group arrived. There was something about ten pregnant woman parading through the labor and delivery rooms that left a sour taste in her mouth.

She was being unfair, Leah realized, but meeting with these groups had always been a painful experience for her. Dealing with the mothers-to-be, one and often two or three at a time, was challenge enough. A roomful tested the very limits of her patience.

"I'll be out of here in nothing flat," Leah tossed over her shoulder. Bonnie didn't know the extent of Leah's dislike for these predelivery tours, but she was aware enough to warn her the little darlings were on their way.

"Leah, hello."

Once Leah had been asked to be a guest speaker for one of the birthing classes and she'd talked briefly about labor and delivery and answered an hour or more of questions. As luck would have it, the tour guide was Jo Ann Rossini who'd been the instructor for the class Leah had visited. Jo Ann walked into the room with ten or more women, all in varying stages of pregnancy.

"Ladies, this is the nurse I mentioned earlier. I sincerely hope one of you is lucky enough to go into labor during Leah's shift. Leah Lundberg is one of the most wonderful labor coaches you're likely to meet."

Leah appreciated Jo Ann's kind words, but she was eager to escape.

"I'll be out of your way in just a moment," Leah said, bundling up the sheets and stuffing them in the laundry basket.

"There's no need to hurry. You'd probably do a much better job of giving a tour around the labor room than me," Jo Ann insisted.

"Leah's shift was over a half hour ago," Bonnie said, coming in. Leah was so grateful she could have kissed her fellow nurse, not that staying beyond when they were scheduled was anything out of the ordinary. It was part and parcel of her job, which, despite everything, Leah loved.

"Would you mind if we asked you a couple of questions?" A timid voice rose from the back of the group. The girl didn't look to be any more than eighteen, with eyes the size of poker chips. Her hand rested on her protruding stomach, which she rubbed as if to reassure her unborn child.

"I've only got a few moments."

"My mother said only a woman who's been through labor and birth can fully appreciate what it's like for another woman," one of the other mothers-to-be added loudly. She was large and brusque and looked as if she wanted to punish her husband for getting her into this predicament. "Don't you think that's true?" she added on a brash note.

"Ah . . ." This definitely wasn't an area Leah wanted to address. "A doctor doesn't have to experience a festering cut to know how to treat one," she said, making sure no emotion bled into the words.

"How long can we expect the labor to last?" came another question. This one was less intrusive.

"It's different with every woman, as individual as we each are. I've seen women who suffer little more than a few twinges of pain, and others who feel like they're giving birth to a grand piano. Labor can last anywhere from a few minutes to days."

"That long?" It was the same timid voice that had spoken earlier.

"Just remember the vast majority are within the normal range."

"Thank you, Leah," Jo Ann said, stepping forward. "We appreciate your taking the time for this. I know you're on your way home so we won't keep you any longer. Remember Leah," Jo Ann said, speaking to her class. "Because once you've had her with you during labor you aren't likely to ever forget her."

"One last question." The same brassy woman who'd spoken earlier did so again. "Tell us how many children you've had yourself."

Leah looked at the other woman, her gaze connecting with hers. "None," she said, then turned and walked out of the room. Her steps gained speed as she hurried down the hallway, tears blurring her eyes.

"Bremerton," **Shirley** said, joining Mercy on the deserted flight deck of the aircraft carrier *Nimitz.* Bright stars dappled the crisp December night like beacons from home. "Why in the name of heaven did you decide we should meet here?"

"I like ships, especially navy ones."

Goodness shared a meaningful look with Shirley. "You haven't done anything, have you?"

Mercy's eyes widened as if she were offended by the suggestion. "Good grief, I know better than to move ships around."

"Gabriel wouldn't ignore that," Shirley said, folding her arms and glancing approvingly toward Mercy as if to say she appreciated the maturity Mercy revealed.

"Gabriel, nothing," Mercy said, "I don't plan on tangling with the U.S. Navy. They can be real sticklers about that sort of thing, although it would be fun just once to—"

"Mercy!" both Goodness and Shirley cried simultaneously.

"Come on, you guys, don't you know a joke when you hear one?" The petite angel drifted effortlessly upward, resting on the bridge.

Goodness wasn't sure of anything these earth days. Humans had frustrated her in the past, but she'd never had to deal with one as obstinate and foolish as Monica Fischer. There was a soft spot in her heart for preachers' children. Goodness was convinced Gabriel was aware of her feelings and that was what had prompted him to give her this particular assignment.

"I don't mean to change the subject, but are those submarines over there?" Shirley asked. She was dangling from the top of the communication tower and pointed to a series of seven fast-attack black boats docked in the murky, moonless waters at the Puget Sound Naval Shipyard. "I don't believe I'll ever understand how the human mind works. Imagine designing a boat that's supposed to sink."

"Can we get back to the matters at hand?" Mercy asked. "I don't mind telling you I'm at my wit's end when it comes to helping Leah and Andrew."

"You!" Goodness cried.

Shirley cleared her throat. "To be honest, I should tell you matters aren't going all that well for me either."

"But I thought—"

"Weren't you saying—"

Shirley held up her hand, stopping them both. "Timmy's grandmother ruined everything for me. It's as bad now as it ever was. Jody turned down Glen's dinner invitation and Timmy believes if he becomes friends with Glen that he'll dishonor the memory of his father."

Goodness felt sorry for her friend. They should have realized nothing is ever as easy as it seems, but then Shirley had been so smug about her assignment.

"What are you going to do?"

"I don't know," Shirley admitted. "Glen's patient, but I wonder just how long he'll continue to invite Jody if she shows no signs of wanting to go out with him. Until the package arrived from his grandmother, Timmy was working with me, and we all know what an advantage it is to have a child on our side."

"How long is it until Christmas?" Earth time always served to confuse Goodness.

"Three weeks," Shirley mumbled, her wings sagging with discouragement.

"You've got plenty of time, just be patient and do what you can," Mercy suggested. "You'll find a way, I know you will."

Goodness didn't have any better ideas herself. Her own lack of success with answering Monica's prayer request was getting downright depressing. The preacher's

daughter claimed she wanted a husband, yet she ignored the attention of the man most suitable. Instead
she was flirting with disaster secretly meeting a private
eye with an attitude problem.

"I'm doing worse than ever," Mercy admitted
grudgingly as if this were something new the others
hadn't figured out yet. "Shirley had a great idea. She
felt, and I'm in complete agreement, that if Leah could
sample joy, then she might find the steps leading to
serenity."

"What's the problem?"

"Everything," Mercy admitted, telling them about
the scene in the hospital with the birthing class earlier
that day. "I haven't figured out how to help her. Leah's
more miserable now than when I first arrived."

"I thought you told me she seemed more accepting."

Mercy folded her arms. "Perhaps. It's difficult
for me to tell. She's been overly burdened lately with
work, the holidays, and the guilt of knowing how badly
she's hurt her husband with her demands for a child.
If anything, her grip on her pain has tightened—she
holds it close to her heart so that it suffocates her
happiness."

"Poor Leah," Shirley whispered, then turned her
attention toward Goodness. "What about you? Are
matters any better with Monica Fischer?"

"I'm growing more and more concerned about Monica," Goodness said, sharing her own disappointment. "She hasn't given Michael the time of day and he's such a dear young man."

"You sound as if you're attracted to him yourself."

"I am. Well, who wouldn't be? He's dedicated and caring and a prince of a guy, not that Monica's noticed."

"What about the private eye?"

Goodness tossed her hands into the air. "She continues to meet him on the sly. My guess is she's more attracted to him than ever."

"What about him?"

Goodness cringed. "The more I know about Chet Costello the less impressed I am. He's lived hard and loved hard and it shows."

"What does he want from Monica?"

Goodness didn't have the answer to that any more than she did the other questions. "As far as I can guess, she's everything he isn't. He doesn't share her faith, her interests, her values, yet he's attracted to those qualities. He carries the misery of his past with him, and as far as I can see he hasn't cared about anything or anyone for the last four or five years, himself included."

"You know, there might be hope for him yet," Shirley said. "Monica must think so too, otherwise she wouldn't continue seeing him."

"How can you suggest such a thing?" Goodness demanded. To her way of thinking, any relationship between the two was doomed from the start. If anyone was capable of teaching Monica the lessons she needed to know, it would be Michael, not Chet.

"I don't have any suggestions for you," Mercy told her. "I'm having enough trouble dealing with my own problems with Leah. I'm sorry I can't be of more help."

"Don't fret," Goodness said as a means of encouragement to her friends.

"We've got three weeks yet," Shirley reminded them. "There's no need to panic. Anything can happen in that time, anything at all."

"Right," Mercy said, eyeing the aircraft carrier *Carl Vinjon*. Goodness recognized that gleam in her friend's eye. It spelled trouble. She had to be honest, she found the radar system downright attractive. And feeling as disgruntled as she did with humans and romance, Goodness didn't think she should be held responsible for what might happen.

"You're both right," Shirley agreed, glancing toward the submarines. "Anything's possible."

Crews from all three Seattle television stations were at the Bremerton shipyard the following morning. The sky was filled with navy helicopters that circled over-head, and a no-fly zone had been declared.

The top navy brass converged on the area and the activity on Sinclair Inlet was unprecedented. No less than ten navy vessels circled the area. Three of the fast-attack submarines patrolled the waters.

"Can you tell us exactly what's happening here?" Brian Lewis asked Marilyn Brock, a reporter from Seattle's ABC television affiliate.

Marilyn Brock pressed the earphone to her head. "As best we've been able to learn, the aircraft carrier *Nimitz* and the *Carl Vinson* have traded places. You heard me right, Brian and Carol, traded places. The *Nimitz* was docked at Pier 12 and is now in Pier 24, where the *Carl Vinson* was formerly docked.

"Also from what we've been able to find out, despite very tight security, an unidentified object showed on the radar screens this last evening. Reports are mixed. Some claim it was nothing more than a commercial flight off course, but others have said it was the silhou-ette of an angel."

"An angel?" Brian Lewis repeated.

"You heard me right. This is definitely one for the record books."

Chet had called himself every kind of fool. He'd waited around the area at the Westlake Mall for nearly thirty minutes and Monica had yet to show. After the tempestuous kisses they'd shared, she'd probably had her sensibilities so shaken she decided against seeing him again. It was just as well. Their relationship wasn't headed anywhere.

Monica Fischer was little more than a passing fancy to him, but even as he said the words, Chet wondered if they were true. What she was to him remained a deep, dark secret, even to himself.

Well, there wasn't any need to wait around here any longer. If she was going to meet him, she would have done so earlier. A cold beer would ease his disappointment, he decided, heading toward the Blue Goose.

"Chet, Chet Costello."

He caught the tail end of his name and whirled around, searching through a mob of empty faces, seeking Monica. His heart gladdened when he caught sight of her making her way through the crowds, weaving in and around those who were going too slow to suit her.

She wore her hair up and tightly pulled away from her face. The severe style sharpened her features, but Chet was too pleased to see her to worry about the way she wore her hair or the drab, lifeless colors that made up her wardrobe.

She was breathless by the time he reached her. He stopped himself just in time, otherwise he would have wrapped his arms around her and lifted her off the ground. As it was, his arms gripped hold of her elbows.

"I had trouble getting away," she explained, smiling up at him, her pretty eyes revealing her relief. "I wasn't sure you'd still be here."

"I was just about to give up," he admitted. They were causing something of a distraction and Chet turned, looping his arm over her shoulder and guiding her across the street. He hadn't a clue of how much time they'd have together, but he fully intended to make the most of it.

"Where are we going?" Monica asked.

Chet paused. "Do you have any particular place in mind?"

"No." She shook her head. "Do you?"

He wasn't sure she'd agree. "My apartment. You look half frozen and it's the only place I can think of where we'll have some privacy."

Her steps slowed. "I . . . don't think that's such a good idea."

"Why not?" he asked. He'd perfected his innocent look until it was practically an art form. "I was thinking we could talk, and get to know each other a little better." Sure he intended to talk, but there was a whole lot more on his agenda. Monica possessed a delectable body that she carefully disguised behind clothes that were at least one size too large for her. She needed to learn exactly what it meant to be a woman, and he was an able teacher. Ready and able. It had been a good long while since he'd been this strongly attracted to a woman. That worried him, but not enough to prevent him from seeing Monica. He'd sort through his feelings later once he'd coaxed her into his bed.

Generally Chet preferred to relieve his sexual frustrations with Trixie, a cocktail waitress who worked at the Blue Goose on weekends. They had a long-standing relationship, or better said, a long-standing understanding. They didn't pretend to be in love, pretense was beyond them both. A divorcée with two teenagers to raise on her own, the cocktail waitress wasn't looking for another long-term relationship, and God knew he wasn't either. They were comfortable with each other.

"I have to get back before nine, otherwise my father will ask a lot of questions and I refuse to lie to him."

"For the love of heaven, you're twenty-five years old."

"I know. You don't understand."

Pressuring her wasn't going to help his cause any. The way he figured it, after he'd made love to Monica he'd be over whatever it was that attracted him so strongly, and would exorcise her from his thoughts and his life.

"I was thinking we could have coffee and talk," she suggested.

"People might see us."

She blinked. Obviously that thought hadn't occurred to her, and being seen with him would surely be cause for talk. That might put her father and her in an embarrassing situation. Monica loved her father too much to do anything that would hurt him in any way.

"We could find a dark corner somewhere," she suggested next.

This wasn't going to be nearly as easy as he'd assumed. "All right," he agreed, "on one condition. I want you to take the pins out of your hair."

She looked at him as if he were daft. Her fingers tentatively investigated the back of her head. "You want me to let my hair down?"

It should have been clear, but he nodded.

"Why?"

"Do I need a reason?"

"I suppose not, it's just that it's such an unusual request." Already her fingers were working at the pins, unfolding the thick knot of hair, which streamed over her shoulders in a warm cascade of dark chestnut. She kept her gaze lowered as though she felt foolish.

He was right. Her looks were substantially softened by the effect. She was lovely, more so than he would have guessed. Her face was fresh and scrubbed clean. It didn't take much to imagine what a little makeup would do for her already appealing good looks.

"Great," he said, when it became apparent she was waiting for him to say something. "You don't look like you're waiting to be thrown to the lions now."

"I beg your pardon," she said, her eyes snapping.

Chet laughed boisterously and reached for her hand. "Come on, let's go have that coffee before we start arguing."

"I'll have you know I dress this way for a reason. I'm trying to promote a meek and humble spirit. With the world the way it is, with girls looking to Madonna as a role model, I feel I should do my part to promote purity."

"Sweetheart, listen, you shouldn't knock those scantily clad outfits until you've tried one. Just promise me you'll let me be there when you do."

"I wish you wouldn't say things like that."

He probably shouldn't have. She was as skittish as a colt, as well he could understand. This was probably the most daring thing she'd ever done in her life, meeting him this way without her father knowing what she was up to.

"Do you want me to tell you how sorry I am?" he asked, as they made their way down First Avenue.

A dingy café he frequented was about the only place he could think of where they'd have a bit of privacy.

"No."

Her response surprised him. He was thinking she'd demand an apology of him and then proceed to lecture him on the error of his ways. Perhaps there was hope for her after all.

The café was dreary, and he felt a bit embarrassed to be bringing Monica into such an establishment, but since she'd turned down the offer to visit his apartment, that didn't leave them with much choice.

He led her to a table in the back and called out his order for two coffees. The chef, Artie Williams, who was an old army cook, appeared from inside the kitchen. He wore a grease-smeared T-shirt and apron.

Artie glanced curiously toward Monica when he delivered two ceramic mugs. "You're out of your element with this girl, aren't you, Chet?" he said in his gravelly voice.

"Just pour the coffee and keep the commentary to yourself," Chet barked. He was having trouble enough breaking down Monica's barriers without his so-called friend's help.

Monica held the cup between both hands as if she were looking to warm her palms. "What would you like to talk about?" she asked, her eyes nervously avoiding his.

"Why'd you come?" he asked. He'd feel he was making progress if he could get her to admit to their attraction.

"I . . . don't know. Michael asked me to stop by his house this evening and I had to make up this excuse and the whole time I was on the bus I kept thinking I must be crazy."

"Then we're both crazy," he muttered, and sipped his coffee. It was hot, black, and thick. Just the way he liked it.

Monica sipped hers too, made a face, then reached for the sugar bowl. She added three heaping teaspoons before she sampled the liquid again.

"Where does that leave us?" she asked.

"I was thinking you could tell me."

"I can't." She raised her eyes to his, then quickly lowered them. "No one's ever kissed me the way you have."

That didn't come as any surprise to Chet. "That's only the beginning."

"What do you mean?"

"Kissing is the tip of the iceberg. There are a dozen different directions we could go from there."

She looked at him as if she hadn't a clue what he was talking about and he realized what should have been obvious from the beginning. Monica Fischer, preacher's daughter, was a virgin. He didn't know there were any left in the world and damned if he hadn't stumbled onto the last living one.

"What's wrong?" she asked. "You look as if you just swallowed a basketball whole."

"I feel that way." He stood so abruptly that the chair shot two feet away from the table. Slapping a fistful of change on the table he reached for her arm, practically lifting her out of the chair. "Come on, we're out of here."

His grip was so tight, Monica's toes barely touched the ground.

"Chet," she cried, "what are you doing?"

"Getting you out of here."

"Where are we going?" she asked. The way her voice struggled to stay even revealed the extent of her surprise.

"I'm taking you back to the bus stop."

"Why?" She shook herself free of his hold and whirled around to face him.

"Because, sweetheart, I just realized something. You're a virgin and I'm the last person you should be around."

"Why?" she asked. Apparently she still hadn't caught on.

"Because," he said, having trouble keeping the anger out of his voice, although it was directed at himself, and not her. He was a bigger fool than he'd realized.

"*Because* doesn't tell me anything."

She was having trouble keeping pace with him, but Chet didn't care. The sooner he was rid of her the better.

"Tell me what's so terrible about being a virgin. Good grief, you make it sound like I've got a communicable disease or something."

"All right, since you want to know I'll tell you, but you aren't going to like it." Chet stopped in the middle of the sidewalk. Although it was well past seven the streets were busy. Several people were forced to walk around them. "I wanted you to go to my apartment tonight for one reason and one reason only. I planned to seduce you."

Monica went pale. "I see."

"Apparently you don't. Good-bye, Monica." Having said that he turned and walked away, leaving her standing alone in the middle of the sidewalk.

Chapter 10

"Mom, I need another dollar." Timmy raced up to the table at the pizza parlor, his face bright and his eyes sparkling with excitement. "I'm blowing the brains out of the Laser Man."

"I don't think this is the kind of video game I want you playing."

"Mom," he protested, "I was just kidding. I'm winning, or I was until just now, but I need another dollar. Hurry, I gotta get back before someone else gets the machine."

Luckily the pizza parlor wasn't overly crowded, although a handful of kids had gathered around a row of video games against the back wall. Jody didn't know how they could play at all with the lights so dim.

"Just a little while longer," Jody said, rummaging through her purse for yet another dollar. Timmy's easy acceptance of this outing with Glen had come as a welcome relief.

"Here." Glen held out a fistful of change to her son. "Take what you need."

"All these?" Coins spilled over Timmy's small hands. His eyes were round with disbelief as he hurriedly pocketed the change. "Gee, thanks."

"I want you to enjoy yourself."

"I will. Thanks, Glen," he said, walking backward. He turned abruptly, eager to get back to his prize machine.

"I don't know if that's such a good idea," Jody felt obliged to say. She didn't want Glen to spoil Timmy, especially if they were to continue seeing each other. Her son might come to look upon Glen as his own personal Santa Claus.

"I have an ulterior motive," Glen told her, his eyes brimming with a smile. "If Timmy's busy with the video machines, we'll have a chance to talk."

Jody already guessed as much, but was uncomfortable having him say it out loud. Agreeing to this outing had been an enormous decision for her.

She'd been afraid to accept, but more afraid not to. Afraid of what she was becoming, afraid of what she already was. She'd stood in one place for so long she feared she'd rooted there like the flower garden she so carefully tended. Bit by bit, Glen was urging her forward. Each step was agony. Each step momentous.

"It hasn't been so bad, now, has it?" Glen asked, coaxing her into admitting the truth. Even that didn't come easy.

"It has been fun," she agreed. Timmy had certainly enjoyed himself, downing an amazing five pieces of sausage and pepperoni pizza and a huge cola. Jody didn't know where he managed to put it all. Generally when they ordered a medium-size pizza it was enough for two meals.

"Would you feel comfortable enough to go out with me again?" Glen asked, and his eyes held hers steadily until she couldn't bear it any longer and looked away.

Glen was pressing his advantage and deliberately pushing her, forcing her to stretch her boundaries. This was only the beginning, she realized with a hundred forming regrets. From here on out it would only get more difficult, more threatening.

It certainly wasn't going to get any easier. Soon Glen would want to hold her and kiss her, and if she continued to date him, he'd consider it a natural conclusion to their spending time together.

He hadn't made any secret of what he was after. He wanted a wife and a family, and he'd said so from the first. Part of her attraction was her son. Glen and Timmy got along like gang busters. Glen was literally the answer to her son's prayer. That was the crux of the problem. Jody wasn't dating Glen for herself, but for her son. Now she had to learn to do so for herself.

"I was able to get two tickets to *The Nutcracker*."

"*The Nutcracker?*" Jody repeated, her voice no more than a breath of sound. The ballet was performed each December by the Pacific Northwest Ballet, and was said to be both charming and brilliant. For years Jody had heard how captivating the costumes and music were. Everyone she'd ever known who'd attended had come away filled with the Christmas spirit. Since Jeff's death, Christmas had been a season to endure, not one to enjoy. Something told her this year it would be different.

"They're for this Thursday night. I realize it's a week night, but I was lucky to get those."

"I . . ." The temptation was strong, stronger than she expected. "I'm honored that you'd ask me," she said, hedging, trying to decide if she should continue this relationship.

"Then you'll come?"

A tension-filled minute passed before she agreed with a short nod of her head.

Jody watched the play of glad emotions on Glen's face, watched how he struggled to disguise his excitement, and in that moment she realized she'd crossed the line.

This was the beginning for them.

Everything else that had led up to this moment had been a prelude of what was to come. The time was right. It had been for a good long while, but she'd been too stubborn to accept it. As odd as it sounded, she was too comfortable in her grief to recognize what was happening.

There was no turning back now. Any qualms she experienced would need to be met head-on, one at a time.

Glen must have realized how momentous her decision was because he reached across the table for her hand, squeezing her fingers. "You won't regret this," he whispered. "I promise."

"I don't know why you want to go out with me," she said, her voice small and trembling. She bit into her bottom lip in an effort to keep it still.

"You don't understand?" Glen frowned as if dumbfounded by the question. "You're a beautiful woman, a woman of character and strength. Every time I'm with you I'm struck by your courage."

Jody laughed nervously. "Then why am I frightened out of my wits?"

"Because this is all so new, but I'm not going to push you into anything you don't want. Oh, I'll prod and poke and nudge you along from time to time, but you have my word, I won't rush you into anything you don't want."

"Mom." Timmy's voice echoed across the room sounding as though it came from the bottom of a tin drum. He raced back to the table, skidding to a stop. "When are we going to get our Christmas tree? I was talking to George, he's the kid who showed me how to beat Laser Man, and his family's already got theirs, and you know what? They went to this farm, but this isn't the kind with cows and pigs, this is a farm with Christmas trees. And guess what?" he asked, dragging in a deep breath. "They cut it down themselves. We could do that, couldn't we, Mom?"

"Ah . . ." Jody wasn't sure how she'd manage chopping down a tree, but she was up to the challenge. "I'll see if I can find out about the tree farm."

"I know where there's one," Glen volunteered. "It's a ways north, but if you wanted, the three of us could make a day of it. We'll leave early Saturday morning, get the tree, and then decorate it in the afternoon."

"That'd be great," Timmy said, so pleased he could barely stand still.

"How does that sound to you?" Glen asked, looking expectantly at her. What else could she say? Little by little Glen was easing his way into their lives. Jody was uneasy with that, and at the same time eager.

"It sounds like a lot of fun."

Glen's eyes met hers and a slow, satisfied smile started to form.

Monica's fingers bounced against the keyboard like clumps of hail hitting the sidewalk. Her hands kept pace with her thoughts, which sped at a record hundred words or more a minute.

She'd been stunned by what Chet had said to her. So shocked she hadn't had time to react. Not then. Reaction had set in later that evening as she rode the bus home. She'd tossed and turned most of the night, her indignation scaling previously unreached thresholds of fury.

Chet Costello was everything she'd originally assumed. He was much worse than she, in her innocence, had suspected. Egotistical, untrustworthy, why, the man was a blight on decency.

He'd planned to seduce her, to break down her defenses and use her body for his own selfish satisfaction. As if she'd have allowed such a thing! As soon as he realized she would have nothing more to do with him, he couldn't be rid of her fast enough. Without a qualm he'd cast her aside like so much dirty laundry.

The one glitch in his plan was that he hadn't expected her to be a virgin. As if she were the kind of woman who'd fall into bed with him! And to think she'd actually been—it pained her to admit this—attracted to that scoundrel.

Thank heaven her father was away for the morning. To think she'd actually toyed with the idea of introducing Chet to her father, of bringing him into their family home. That would have been a disaster. Her father had always been an excellent judge of character and he would have seen through Chet in an instant.

Monica drew in a deep, wobbly breath as her resentment flared bright and then slowly burned itself out. She covered her face with both hands and attempted to pull herself together, which was difficult when she was shaking so badly.

After several moments had passed, Monica straightened, grabbed the sheet from the printer, and crumpled it. Having vented her feelings, there was no need to mail the letter. Any further communication between them whatsoever was completely unnecessary. Her hand automatically reached for the mustard-seed necklace dangling from her neck, fingering it. She'd worn the piece every day since Chet had bought it for her, until it had become habit.

Chet had made his views on life plain. If anything she should be grateful that he'd put an end to this madness when he had. One small part of her, however, refused to conform. One small rebellious corner of her soul yearned for the discoveries he would have shown her.

The thought terrified Monica into accepting how far she'd slid toward sin.

Well, she was safe. He was out of her life now. Good riddance was all she could say.

A knock came softly from the outer door.

"Come in," she snapped, then realized she sounded like an old shrew, and said it again, softer this time. Church secretaries weren't supposed to be confrontational.

Michael opened the door and stepped inside. "Hello, Monica."

"Hello," she said, tossing the crumpled-up letter into the wastebasket.

"Your father said I'd find you here." He stepped into the office, his stance doubtful. His gaze hesitantly met hers as if he were unsure of himself.

"What can I do for you?" she asked, working hard to keep the impatience out of her voice. All she needed now was for him to load her down with extra work. Having wasted a good portion of the morning writing

Chet and telling him exactly what she thought of him left her with a backlog of unfinished church business.

"I realize it's short notice but I'd like to take you to lunch, that is, if you'd let me."

The invitation was so unexpected that she didn't know what to say. "Lunch?" She had to look at her watch to check the time. The morning had sped past on the wings of her aggravation. "I suppose that would be all right," she said without much enthusiasm.

"Great." His eyes lit up and she realized what nice eyes Michael had. He loved his music and had done wonders for the church choir. It was because of his efforts that the small band had formed. He'd volunteered several hours a week to church work.

Monica liked Michael. She'd always liked him—there wasn't anything to dislike about the young man. He was godly, principled, and sincere. Everything she should want in a man.

But didn't.

"If you have no objection I thought we'd go to the House of Pancakes. They serve a decent lunch."

"Sure." The House of Pancakes. That was the problem. Michael was a wonderful man, God's own servant. Humble, gentle, the perfect choice of a mate for a preacher's daughter, only . . . only she'd dined on pancakes most of her life and she was ready for some salsa.

There'd been a trace of hot sauce in Patrick. That was what attracted her to Chet, she realized now. He'd been daring and fun and he'd made her laugh. He'd also badly wounded her pride.

"I'll get your jacket for you," Michael offered. "I wouldn't want you to a catch a chill." He took her navy blue wool coat from the rack and held it open for her.

Michael was a gentleman and Chet was a rogue. If she had a lick of sense, she'd cultivate the relationship with Michael and thank God there were still men like him in this sick and decaying world.

Since the House of Pancakes was only two blocks away, they decided to walk. Monica buried her hands in her pockets and struggled to keep her attention on what Michael was saying. His voice was a low monotone and she had trouble concentrating.

A car drove past, the same sick green color of Chet's Impala, and she whirled around, wondering if it could possibly be him. Her heart leaped into double time at the prospect.

If it was Chet, it would do him good to see her with another man. If he'd come to apologize, as well he should, then she would accept nothing less than his pleading for forgiveness.

She held her head high, refusing to allow him to think he'd left her floundering in the wake of his crass behavior. But the sight of the car had been fleeting and she couldn't be entirely sure it was him. More than likely it wasn't. Men like Chet Costello didn't know how to apologize.

It was Andrew's night out with his friends, and Leah schlepped into the living room, carrying a book and a cup of coffee. The house was lonely without her husband. Empty. The contrast between her life and that of Pam, who struggled to squeeze in a few moments for herself, struck Leah once more.

What she needed was a hobby, Leah decided. Something that would take her mind off the fact that she didn't have a child. Something that would occupy her time so she didn't dwell on how hollow her life was. Perhaps she should do volunteer work. There were any number of worthy causes that would welcome her attention.

Maybe when the holidays were over, she decided.

She read the first chapter without much enthusiasm. Finally, she put the book down and wandered into the kitchen for a refill on her coffee and stopped abruptly in front of the sink. In the bay window she'd arranged a row of cacti she'd carefully nurtured over the years. Andrew teased her that if she forgot to water them, it wouldn't matter. Five thick pink-and-turquoise pots each held a different variety of cactus, and each one had sprouted a flower.

In the last hour.

A variety of pink, red, and white blossoms had appeared as if by some miracle from the time she'd finished the dishes and wandered into the living room, until now, no more than an hour later. It wasn't that she didn't notice. One might have gone undetected, but not five. She could have sworn not a single one had been blooming an hour earlier.

Unexpected tears pooled in her eyes, the moisture hot and unwelcome. She brushed them away from her cheeks with the back of her hand. "It seems everything in this house is fertile except me," she murmured aloud, and headed blindly toward the living room to await her husband's return.

Sitting on the kitchen counter, her knees crossed, her foot swaying like a too-fast pendulum, Mercy heaved a gigantic sigh. Getting those flowers to appear hadn't been an easy trick. She would have preferred African violets any day of the week over cacti!

Everything she'd done for Leah had backfired. The flowers were supposed to be a sign of hope. A way of telling her that all was not lost and that there was someone out there who'd heard her prayer and was working hard to see that it was answered. Well, it was back to the drawing board.

Perhaps what Shirley had suggested about Leah experiencing joy before she could find her peace was what it would take. First Mercy had to figure out a way to manage that, but if she could coax cacti into bloom, then anything was possible. Right?

"Shirley." Goodness shot across the darkened family room of Jody and Timmy Potter's house in a vapor of speed and excitement. "Give me five," she cried, holding up her right hand for the other angel to slap. What a difference a few earth hours could make. For the first time since Goodness had accepted this assignment she was making progress. Real progress. Monica and Michael had gone to lunch together. It wasn't much but it was a start in the right direction.

"Oh, do be quiet," Shirley whispered heatedly. "You know better than to be exuberant when there're children around. Timmy might very well hear you."

"But I've got great news. Monica and Michael had lunch together and I arranged the whole thing without them suspecting. I tell you it was a work of art the way I got Michael to show up at the church office."

"Please keep your voice down," Shirley pleaded a second time, placing her finger against her lips.

"All right. All right, I'll do my best, but this news is too good to keep to myself."

Shirley whirled around so unexpectedly that Goodness was caught by surprise. A sleepy Timmy Potter wandered into the room, rubbing his eyes. He was wearing flannel pajamas with silly-looking armed turtles.

Shirley moved behind him.

"Mom," Timmy called.

A moment later Jody Potter appeared in a long flannel nightgown that had seen better years. Shirley had her work cut out for her if she planned to find this woman a husband any time soon. Her charge looked downright frumpy.

"Timmy, what are you doing up?"

"I thought I heard something."

Jody turned on the light and searched the room. The minute her back was turned, Shirley and Goodness righted the floral arrangement and set the magazines in order. Both headed straight for the ceiling, hovering there.

Jody searched the room, finding nothing out of the ordinary. "There's no one here."

"I thought I heard something," Timmy said with a yawn. "But I guess not."

"I guess not, too," Jody said, placing her arm around her young son's shoulders and steering him back to his bedroom. "Unless, of course, it was God's own angels looking down and smiling on us."

"You think it might have been?" Timmy asked excitedly, looking up. He paused and blinked, rubbed his eyes again, then looked back.

"Who knows?" Jody said and turned out the light.

Monica's attitude toward Chet altered drastically over the next couple of days. He was still a scoundrel and a no-good rogue, but darned if she didn't miss him. There was no explaining it, no possible way of reasoning it out in her mind.

She tried to fill the emptiness that surrounded her with a flurry of activity. The night before she'd dragged out the Christmas decorations and gone about setting them around the house and office. Her father, impressed by her initiative, assumed this burst of energy was somehow connected with her long lunch with Michael. Monica didn't correct him.

Monica knew she wouldn't see Chet again and wondered if he missed her. She wondered how he looked upon their time together or if he'd given her as much as a fleeting thought in the days since they'd last been together.

She wore her hair down that morning and when she walked into the kitchen her father lowered the morning paper and smiled gently at her.

"Monica," he said softly, "how nice you look."

"Thank you."

"Will you be seeing Michael again this afternoon."

"I . . . I don't know." How keen her father was on the young musician. He'd pegged Michael early on as the perfect husband for her. He was right. Her father generally was. How she wished she felt the same way about the earnest choir director. There was no question of what a fine man Michael was. Several of the eligible women at church would have gladly welcomed his notice. For now those attentions were sadly wasted on her.

"It seems to me I said something to Michael about coming over for dinner one night soon. You don't mind, do you?"

"Of course not, Michael is welcome anytime." So this was to be the way of it. Her father would chart her romance for her, making excuses for the two of them to be together again.

"I'm sure he'll approve of the way you've done your hair," he added, looking pleased.

She smiled weakly. "I'll see you in a few minutes," she said, anxious to escape their conversation.

"You're leaving for the office so soon?"

"I . . . have several things I need to do first thing this morning."

"I won't be in until later. I'm visiting Mrs. McWilliams," he reminded her, downing the last of his milk and setting the glass in the sink.

The woman was an old and faithful church member who'd recently broken her hip. Lloyd visited her at least twice a week.

"I'll see you later, then," Monica said, eager to make her escape. She walked across the yard to the old church building and let herself in by the side door that opened onto the sanctuary area. She'd been raised in this building, lived the majority of her life in the same house with the same people.

Instead of heading directly to the office, which was situated in the room at the rear of the church off the foyer, Monica paused and looked toward the altar. An unspoken prayer rose in her throat and she found herself moving toward the altar rail.

Monica kelt there and slowly bowed her head. "Guide his life, Father," she whispered. The tears that filled her eyes came as a surprise and the remainder of the words were choked off in her throat. She wasn't sure how to pray for Chet. But God knew and she'd leave the man and the matter in His capable hands.

Several moments passed before she stood.

Her morning slipped past almost unnoticed. Typing was something of a chore with her hair continually falling in her face. It irritated her so much that she found two bobby pins in a desk drawer and clipped both sides behind her ears.

She was busy working on the bulletin for Sunday morning worship service when the door opened. Monica looked up from the computer and her pulse quickened. Quickened was a mild way of explaining what happened to her. Her heart was banging against her ribs with such force she wasn't able to do anything more than breathe.

"I see you took my advice about your hairstyle," Chet said, and sauntered into the office as if he were right at home.

"What are you doing here?" She glanced anxiously toward her father's office, forgetting he wasn't there.

"Don't worry, he's off visiting Mrs. McWilliams."

"How . . . how do you know that?"

Chet laughed lightly and rearranged the figurines that made up the nativity scene she'd set in a froth of angel hair, switching the camels and the mules. "I know just about everything there is to know about you."

Playing a game of cat and mouse with him was beyond her. Chet was much too clever for her. "Why are you here?"

"To see you. Why else? I'm not exactly the type of guy who frequents churches."

She was on her feet without knowing how she got there. Clenching her hands together in front of her, she drew in a steadying breath. "Why do you want to see me?"

"I figured I owed you an apology."

His willingness to admit it surprised her. "Then I accept your regrets," she informed him, sitting back down. "You don't need to trouble yourself further."

"I came for another reason," he said, easing himself onto the corner of her desk as if he had every right to do so.

"What's that?" Monica placed her hands on the keyboard, ready to resume her task although heaven knew she couldn't have typed had her life depended on it.

"You planning on seeing that milquetoast choir director again?"

"I . . . I don't believe that's any concern of yours."

"Perhaps not, but if you do, you're cheating him and you're hurting yourself."

Monica had taken about as much of his advice as she could tolerate. "What gives you the right to say those kinds of things to me?" she demanded.

"I know you, sweetheart."

She hated it when he called her that and he knew it. He was purposely trying to irritate her.

"You've got fire in your blood, not milk. You've sampled desire. Now that you know what it is to be weak with wanting a man, you won't be able to accept second best. Not anymore—it's too late for that."

"You have your nerve."

"You're right," he agreed readily enough, "I do." He stood and walked around to her side of the desk.

Monica watched him, not knowing what to expect. Every nerve was at full attention. A siren was blaring in her head, blocking out all sensible thought.

When he reached for her, she didn't offer the least bit of resistance. As it never failed to do, his touch rippled through her, snapping her senses to life. He roughly lowered his mouth to hers where he planted desperate, hungry kisses.

She resisted him at first, attempting to jerk her mouth from his, but he wouldn't allow it, trapping her face. Her stand against him was pitifully weak, and soon she was as much a participant in the exchange as he was.

Slowly he eased himself away from her. "Heaven help me," he whispered and Monica was convinced he didn't mean this as a prayer.

Something attracted his attention and he jerked his head around. "Someone's coming," he whispered.

Monica was too startled to do anything.

"Whoever it is, get rid of them," he instructed, slipping behind the door that led to her father's office.

Get rid of them, Monica thought in panic. She wasn't accustomed to playing these ridiculous cops-and-robbers games. She hadn't a clue of what to say or do.

The door opened just then and Michael strolled inside. He smiled at her warmly. "I hope I'm not catching you at a bad time."

"Bad time," she repeated with a phony laugh. "Of course not. Come on in, Michael."

Chapter 11

"You're sure you don't mind?" Pam asked, leading Scotty by the hand into Leah's house. "After all the trouble I've gone through for this silly Christmas party of Doug's, who'd believe my baby-sitter would come down with the flu? At the last minute, no less. It was the oddest thing. One minute she was fine and the next she was sick."

"You should have brought over Diane and Jason too," Leah said.

Pam laughed outright at that. "Even my mother won't take all three at once." Flustered and in a rush, she set everything down on the sofa and started unpacking the items she'd brought along for her middle son. Sorting through the brown paper sack, Pam removed Scotty's pajamas, an extra set of clothes for the morning, his stuffed dinosaur and a tattered yellow blanket. "He's mostly given up his blanky, but he might need a bit of security to sleep in an unfamiliar bed."

"I'll make sure he has it with him."

"I brought along some extra training pants," Pam said, setting out a stack of them.

"I don't wet," Scotty said, his fists braced against his small hips. "I'm a big boy."

"I forgot his potty seat," Pam cried. "Oh, well, you'll just have to hold him over the toilet."

"Don't worry, Scotty and I'll figure everything out as we go. Isn't that right, bud?"

"Right." She held out her hand for him to slap, which he did with enthusiasm, his arm making a high arch into the air.

Pam straightened and held back her hair with both hands. "I hope to heaven that's everything. Here's the number where Doug and I'll be," she said, pulling a slip of paper from her coat pocket. Getting down on her knees, she wrapped her arms around her three-year-old. "Promise me you'll be an extra good boy for Auntie Leah?"

Scotty clung to her neck and planted a wet kiss on her cheek.

"We're going to have a great time, aren't we, Scotty?" Leah urged, knowing how bad Pam felt to be leaving him in an unfamiliar setting.

Scotty nodded, but looked uncertain when his mother left. Pam was halfway out the front door when she turned back. "He probably needs to go now."

"Pam," Leah said, ushering her friend out of the house, "scoot, otherwise you'll miss your hair appointment."

"I'm hurrying—"

"Stop looking so worried. Everything's going to be just fine."

Scotty was standing at the window, his mouth pressed to the cold glass as he watched his mother pull out of the driveway. He looked at Leah and his bottom lip started to tremble.

"Scotty, how about helping me with lunch?" she asked, holding out her hand. "You can decide what to fix for Uncle Andrew, all right?"

The boy shook his head, smearing his lip prints from one pane to the next.

"Are you hungry?"

Once more Scotty shook his head. "I want my mommy."

"She's going out to dinner with your daddy and his friends from work."

"I want to go too."

"This dinner is only for mommies and daddies."

Apparently this wasn't what Scotty wanted to hear because the tears started in earnest. He was breaking her heart, standing with his back to the window, rubbing his eyes and sobbing softly. She couldn't bear to see her godson weeping so pitifully, so she lifted him into her arms to comfort him. Scotty buried his face in her shoulder, snuffling into her expensive cashmere sweater. Leah smiled to herself and shook her head. This was what it meant to be a mother, to be loved and needed. She'd treasure every moment of the time with this precious little boy.

It took Leah only a few moments to get Scotty interested in helping her assemble sandwiches. Andrew arrived about the time the boy was licking the jelly off the knife and sticking it back inside the jar.

"So we have company," he said, removing his jacket and hanging it on the peg just inside the door.

Scotty looked at her husband as an unknown entity, his big dark eyes following Andrew's movements around the kitchen as Leah explained Pam's sorry predicament.

"Peanut butter and jelly?" Andrew grumbled under his breath, eyeing their lunch.

"That was what Scotty wanted us to have."

"You sure he didn't suggest pastrami on rye?" Andrew mumbled out of the corner of his mouth.

"Scotty made the peanut butter and jelly all by himself," Leah said, urging her husband to compliment the boy on his efforts. There was more peanut butter on the countertop than the bread, but Scotty had done it himself and beamed with pride.

"So I noticed." Andrew skeptically lifted one corner of the bread. The peanut butter was spread so thin the white bread showed through. He looked at Leah and they both burst into laughter. It wasn't especially funny, but they seemed to find it so.

Scotty studied them as if he didn't know what to make of the two. Leah kissed his chubby cheek and set the sandwich and a small glass of milk down on the table. Moving out the chair, Scotty climbed onto the seat. He knelt on the cushion and leaned against the glass tabletop, his small hands circling the glass.

"Apparently lunch is served," Andrew said, bowing and gallantly gesturing for Leah to take her place at the table. He held out the chair for her, then seated himself.

After sampling the sandwich, Andrew eyed Leah. "Is Scotty choosing the dinner menu as well?"

"Hot dogs and macaroni and cheese," Scotty said with his mouth full of food.

Andrew looked at Leah and there was something so crestfallen in his eyes that she couldn't help it, she burst out laughing. Andrew didn't know what she found so funny, but soon he was laughing too. Scotty, who hadn't a clue of what was going on, joined in, milk dribbling out of the corner of his mouth.

Mercy looked down upon the scene from where she was lounging on top of the double-wide refrigerator. Her scheme had worked beautifully, although she did feel mildly guilty about inflicting Pam's baby-sitter with the virus.

Scotty's visit with Leah and Andrew was going much better than she'd anticipated. So well that it was all Mercy could do not to stand up and cheer. The sound of Leah and Andrew's laughter brightened the room like floodlights on an empty stage.

The kitchen radiated with the warmth of their happiness. The dim, dark pall of melancholy faded as the joy was slowly released, circling the room with tails of light. The gloom, discouragement, and despair that marked this house lifted like dissipating fog over the Golden Gate Bridge revealing the sound structure of this marriage, and the deep, profound love Leah and Andrew shared.

This was what Mercy had waited for so impatiently. Joy.

Her gaze wandered closely over Leah and the emotion she read in the young woman's face deeply stirred her soul. At last they were making progress. The light was on, the mist had lifted.

It was a beginning.

The lunch was over and Leah lifted Scotty from the chair, washed his hands and face, and carried him into the guest bedroom. Knowing his penchant for amusing himself instead of napping, she sat in the rocking chair and held him in her lap. Scotty chose a book and she read to him until he dozed off.

For a long time after Scotty was asleep, Leah continued to hold him, enjoying these rare moments of peace and the ecstasy of having a child in her arms.

Kissing the top of his curly head, she was amazed at all Pam managed to do with a houseful of preschoolers. Scotty had only been with her a couple of hours and already she was emotionally and physically exhausted.

Andrew arrived just then, leaning indolently against the door frame, his face wide with a saucy grin. "It looks like you could use a nap yourself."

"No one ever told me toddlers could be so exhausting," Leah admitted.

"Here," Andrew whispered, gently lifting Scotty from her arms. "Let's put him to bed."

Moving around her husband, Leah turned back the sheets and Andrew carefully laid the sleeping child onto the mattress. Covering him with the quilt, Leah bent down and kissed her godson's forehead.

Neither Andrew nor Leah were in any hurry to leave the room. Standing next to her husband, she nestled in the warm security of Andrew's arms, her head resting against the solid wall of his chest.

"He's really something, isn't he?" Andrew said softly, so as not to disturb Scotty's sleep.

"He's a ball of energy."

Andrew kissed the side of her neck. "Come on, I think we could do with a nap ourselves."

From the way he made the suggestion, Leah knew resting was the last thing on her husband's mind. She caught his eye, and whispered regretfully, "Andrew, we can't."

"Why not?"

"Scotty might wake and—"

"Do you think Doug and Pam worry about that? Besides, I can be real quiet, and with some effort so can you," he whispered, steering her toward their bedroom.

Sometime later, Leah woke to the sounds of someone hopping up and down at the foot of her bed. She rolled onto her back to find Scotty doing a marvelous impression of a kangaroo.

"Hi, Scotty."

He was holding onto his front with both hands, his eyes wide and appealing.

"Scotty?" she asked, sitting up, clenching the sheets to her breasts. "Do you need to go potty?"

"That would be my guess," Andrew said, yawning. "Come on, fellow, I'll show you the way." Lifting the boy into his arms, Andrew carried him to the bathroom.

Leah grabbed her sweater and finished dressing. "How's everything going in there?" she called out.

"Not good. He seems to need something."

"What?"

Scotty apparently didn't trust Andrew to properly relay the message. "I need my blanky . . . I need my blanky . . . I need my blanky."

Leah retrieved the yellow monstrosity in record time and rushed back into the bathroom where Andrew was holding Scotty over the toilet seat. The boy grabbed the blanket, and held it against his face. As soon as the blanket was in position, he released a long, grateful sigh and relaxed.

When Scotty finished, Andrew sagged onto the side of the bathtub. "What was that all about?"

"Pam said something about forgetting his toilet seat. He must have been terrified of being perched up there."

Andrew looked at Leah and she looked at him and soon the two of them dissolved into giggles.

"I'm a big boy," Scotty insisted, looking downright proud of himself, his laughter mingling with theirs.

Monica was convinced Michael would guess that Chet was hiding behind the door in the other room. Why Chet felt he needed to disappear, she could only speculate.

The man was a fool to show up at the church this way. She'd wanted to shout at him, and throw the entire contents of her filing cabinet in his face. Heaven knew he deserved that and far worse. Why, she should have slapped him silly.

She would have, too, if she hadn't been so pleased to see him.

"Your hair looks especially nice today," Michael said with glowing approval.

"Thank you." Knowing Chet, it was probably all he could do to keep from leaping out from behind the door and commenting that he'd been the one to suggest the change.

"I'm playing the piano for the Methodists' church cantata this evening," Michael was saying. "Their regular pianist came down with the flu. I thought I'd stop by and see if you'd like to come along."

"Tonight?" Monica asked, stalling for time. In truth she was looking for an excuse, anything to get out of this date, but nothing readily presented itself.

"I mentioned this evening to your father and he said you didn't have anything planned," Michael pressed.

"No, I don't believe I do." So her father had put him up to this. She should have realized that sooner.

Michael hesitated, glancing at her as if he were waiting for her to say something more. Uncertain, Monica steadily met his look.

"Did Lloyd mention anything about dinner?"

"Dinner?" She knew she was beginning to sound like a parrot. "Why, yes. Dad did say something this morning about having you over for dinner some evening. We'd be more than happy to have you join us, if you'd like."

"Tonight?"

"Tonight . . . why, sure . . . tonight would be perfect, wouldn't it, since I'll be there for the Methodists' cantata."

"What time?"

"Six," she said automatically, willing to agree to anything that would convince him to leave faster. Knowing Chet was listening in on the conversation made matters ten times worse.

"Great," Michael said, looking well pleased with himself, "I'll see you around six, then. Would you like me to bring anything?"

"No. Everything's under control. Good-bye, Michael," she said, sitting back down at the computer, hoping he'd take the hint and kindly leave while her sanity was intact. She placed her hands on the key-board until she noticed how badly she was trembling and immediately lowered them to her lap.

"I'll look forward to this evening," he said, reluctantly moving toward the door. He was looking for an excuse to stay, but she refused to give him one.

Despite her obvious signs of distress, she tried to concentrate on the computer screen.

"Your father claims you're a fabulous cook."

"I do a fair job," she muttered. This was getting worse every minute and she didn't know how much more she could bear.

"Good-bye for now."

"Good-bye, Michael," she said, closing her eyes in relief.

Michael left then and the door closed with a soft clicking sound. The instant he was gone, Monica leaped out of her chair, raced around her desk and into her father's study. By the time she arrived she was both breathless and furious.

"Why'd you hide?" she demanded. "Of all the crazy things you've said and done in the last few weeks, this takes the cake."

"It would have required awkward explanations," was all he'd say.

"Well, he's gone now."

"So I see." A frown darkened Chet's face and he glared at her. "So you're going to continue seeing him despite what I said."

"What choice did I have?" she cried, throwing her arms into the air. "I said what I had to, to get him to leave. Besides, what business is it of yours who I do or do not date?" How could he say such things to her when he was the one who'd put her in this predicament!

It took him a long time to answer. "You're right, it's none of my damn business."

Monica was pleased that Chet did care, but she didn't want him to know it.

"Michael's not so bad," he said after a moment. "It's plain as day that he's crazy about you."

The man was full of surprises. First he demanded that she stay away from Michael and now he was urging her to see the other man.

Chet's eyes were clouded as if he carried the weight of the world on his shoulders. "I should never have come."

He strode past her and in her heart Monica knew if he walked out the door she'd never see him again. She had to do something.

He was all the way across the room, his hand on the doorknob, before she found the courage to speak.

"Don't go." She advanced a single step toward him and stopped.

Chet turned around slowly as if he wasn't sure he'd heard her correctly. Gradually a grin danced its way across his lips. "You don't want me to leave?"

Her tongue was trapped against the roof of her mouth and she shook her head, unable to say the words a second time. It had demanded every ounce of courage she possessed the first time.

His gaze narrowed into thin, disbelieving slits. "Why not?"

She shrugged.

"Come on, sweetheart, you can do better than that."

"Don't call me that." She backed away from him, as far as she could go, until her buttocks were pressed against the edge of her desk.

"What would you like me to call you?"

It was a mistake to have asked him to stay, a mistake to let him know how much of the time he dominated her thoughts. He made her weak where she'd once been strong, and she'd found no compensation for what she'd lost.

"I think you should go," she whispered.

He cocked his thick brows at that. "You don't seem to know what you want, do you? You want me to stay, yet you invite that mild-mannered choirboy for dinner."

"My father invited him."

"Ah, your father," Chet said thoughtfully. "Michael's the type of man he wants you to marry, isn't he? We both know what your daddy would think of the likes of me."

"That's not true. My father isn't like that."

"Sure," he scoffed. "He'd welcome me with open arms. Don't kid yourself, Monica, we both know better. Listen, sweetheart, forget I was ever here, all right?"

"No. No, I won't forget," she whispered heatedly. "I can't forget."

She read the questions etched in his eyes and realized they were a reflection of her own. She didn't have any of the answers and apparently neither did he.

Walking toward him was the boldest thing she'd ever done in her life. Flattening her palms against the hard expanse of his chest, she slowly, reluctantly raised her eyes to his.

He didn't give her a chance to speak. His mouth came down on hers in a kiss that was as hot as it was wild. Instinct dictated her actions as she raised her arms and looped them around his neck, giving herself completely to his kiss.

His arms folded around her waist, greedily holding her against him as his mouth plundered hers. Her feet dangled several inches off the ground.

The kiss ended only when they were both desperate to breathe.

Monica was left stunned, her heart in a panic. It had always been like this between them, this craziness. Her head felt as if it were in its own orbit, spinning madly out of control. Emotionally she was a wreck, close to tears and trembling.

Chet's lips returned to hers in a series of long, slow kisses and her world righted itself. Everything slipped neatly back into place. Only when she lifted her head from his did outside influences overtake her.

For the love of heaven, they were in a church building, and yet she couldn't have left his arms in that moment for all the gold in the world.

"I've got to get out of here," Chet whispered against her neck. He drew in a deep breath as if that would give him the necessary fortitude to ease her out of his arms.

"Not yet," she pleaded.

The sound of voices in the yard outside was all the incentive they needed. They broke apart as if they'd been burned.

"That's my father," Monica said, her gaze flying to Chet.

Chet jerked his head both ways. "I'll go out the window."

"That's crazy."

By the time she reached him in her father's office, he'd hoisted the window open and had one leg draped over the sill. "Meet me tonight," he said.

"When?" she pleaded, glancing over her shoulder. "Where?"

"Never mind."

"No," she whispered frantically. "Tell me when and where."

He smiled, and the look in his eyes was enough to cause spirals of heat to coil in her belly. He reached for her, kissed her once hard and fast and whispered, "I'll let you know." With that he vanished.

The door opened and her father casually strolled inside, humming softly to himself. He looked surprised to find her standing there.

"Monica."

"Yes, Dad?" she said, still trapped in a sensual daze.

"You might want to close the window. It's downright chilly in here."

"Oh, sorry," she said, lowering it as if it were nothing out of the ordinary to have it open in the middle of December.

"**I'll open** the door for you," Timmy cried, running toward the front porch, leaving Glen to untie the Christmas tree from the top of his car.

"Timmy has his own key," Jody explained, catching the rope that Glen tossed down to her as he untied the tree.

Glen looked toward the front of the house. "He enjoyed himself this afternoon, didn't he?"

Jody smiled and nodded. "I swear he was like a jackrabbit, leaping from one tree to the next, certain each time he'd found the perfect Christmas tree. It's a miracle we were able to convince him to choose just one."

"What about you, Jody?" Glen asked thoughtfully. "Did you have a good time too?"

It shouldn't be so difficult to admit to the truth, but it was.

"I had a very nice time," she said, keeping her eyes averted.

His laugh came unexpectedly. "Good girl," he praised. "I knew you could do it."

Jody laughed then too, because it was rather silly of her to hold out against the obvious.

Timmy returned breathless and excited. "The door's open," he announced, eager to help in any way he could.

Her son was a marvel, Jody mused. Rarely had she seen him more animated. He'd laughed and chatted incessantly, until she was convinced he was going to drive Glen nuts. For a man who wasn't accustomed to being around children, the attorney had been marvelous.

"Mom got the tree stand and all the decorations out last night," Timmy told Glen, for about the fifth time. Actually Jody had lost count of the number of times Timmy had felt it was necessary to clue Glen in to this information.

Together, the three of them carried the Christmas tree around to the backyard.

"We're going to need to cut off a couple of inches from the bottom," Glen said, once they'd got the tree to the patio and recovered. The trunk was too wide for the stand. "Think you might be able to help me saw it off?" he asked Timmy.

It was like asking the boy if he liked popcorn. Timmy beamed with pride as he solemnly nodded his head. "Sure, I can do it."

"I know you can," Glen said, affectionately patting his shoulder.

"While you're busy with that, I'll put on some hot chocolate," Jody said, pushing open the sliding glass door. The tears that stung her eyes were unexpected.

She wasn't entirely sure what prompted them, nor was she sure she wanted to know.

The changes in Timmy had been revealing. Yes, it was Christmastime and yes, he was excited, but it made her realize how rare those times were. Generally Timmy involved himself in his video games and didn't show much enthusiasm for anything else—with the one exception being baseball, which he dearly loved.

Between sniffles, she brought the milk out of the refrigerator and set a pan on the stove, furious with herself for the weakness of tears.

Glen appeared unexpectedly and she twisted her head away, praying he wouldn't notice. "That's quite a boy you've got there," Glen said. "I swear he's another Paul Bunyan."

"He's certainly had the time of his life." She was grateful that the hot chocolate gave her an excuse to keep her back to him.

Glen moved behind her and gently placed his hands on her shoulders. Jody froze, unaccustomed to a man's touch.

He bent forward and kissed the side of her neck.

"Where's Timmy?" she asked, her voice trembling.

"Putting the saw away." Glen turned her so that they faced each other. He frowned when he saw her tear-bright eyes and slid his thumb across the high arch of her cheek. "Bad thoughts?" he asked.

She shook her head.

"Let me help." Then, before she could protest, he lowered his mouth to hers. It was hardly enough pressure to call it a real kiss. Gradually he increased the intensity, deepening the contact. Jody felt like a rag doll, limp and unresponsive. The kiss was sweet and undemanding, but Glen was the first man to touch her since Jeff. Doubts blew against her with hurricane-force winds until she pressed her hands against his chest and broke the contact. Later she'd analyze her feelings toward Glen, but for now it was too new.

Glen sighed softly. "It would be very easy to fall in love with you." He continued to hold her until he heard Timmy's approach.

Once her son was back, Glen carried the tree into the house, and with a good deal of ceremony, set it in the living room. When it was in place in front of the large picture window, they sat back and sipped hot chocolate.

Unwilling to rest, Timmy sorted through the boxes of decorations. It seemed with every one, he found something he needed to show Glen. Each discovery involved a lengthy explanation.

Glen's patience surprised her, and she told him so.

"He's a great kid," Glen said. "Who wouldn't like him?"

"Can we decorate the tree now?" Timmy asked, standing in the middle of three strings of lights. Wires were wrapped around his feet and another strand was draped over his shoulder as he grinned broadly in their direction. "You aren't going to make me wait until Christmas morning to see my presents, are you? I'm much too old to pretend I believe in Santa Claus."

"It's tradition," Jody said, as means of an argument.

"Oh, phooey. I still have to pretend I believe in that silly kid stuff for my grandma, but it's downright embarrassing. I just hope none of my friends find out about it."

"Sometimes there are things a man has to do," Glen said, and Jody marveled that he kept a straight face.

"Can we decorate the tree now?"

"Sure," Glen agreed, setting aside his empty mug.

"It'll be our best tree yet, won't it, Mom?"

Jody was saved from answering by the phone. She left the pair to untangle the strings of lights and took the call in the kitchen.

"Hello."

"Jody, dear, it's so good to hear your voice."

"Hello, Gloria." It had been a year or longer since she'd last spoken to her former mother-in-law. "Did you get my letter?" Jody asked, glancing guiltily into the living room. There wasn't any reason for her to feel the least bit contrite for dating Glen or for kissing him, but she did, as if she'd been unfaithful to Jeff's memory.

"I have some very important news," Gloria said, ignoring the question.

"Who is it?" Timmy wanted to know.

"Just a minute, Gloria," Jody said, and placed her hand over the mouthpiece. "It's your Grandma Potter," she explained. "I'll let you talk to her when I'm finished. I'll call you in just a minute." When Timmy was gone, she replaced the receiver at her ear. "I'm sorry to interrupt you. You were telling me you had something important to tell me?"

"My dear, it's the most wonderful news. Brace yourself because what I'm about to tell you will come as a shock. Jeff's alive."

Chapter 12

M onica paced her bedroom, wondering what, if anything, she should do now that she was home. Her evening with Michael had been miserable. Michael couldn't be blamed for that; he'd been sweet and considerate, wanting to please her.

When he'd arrived for dinner, he'd presented her with a potted pink poinsettia, which riddled her with guilt. Throughout the meal he'd praised her efforts while her father looked on approvingly. Monica was a fair cook, but the pot roast and mashed potatoes and gravy were nothing to brag about.

The cantata, while inspirational, had seemed to drag. Every note was torture and Monica knew why.

She was looking for Chet, half expecting him to slip into the pew next to her at the Methodist church. It was just like something he'd do. Monica had sat through the entire program with her stomach in knots wondering when and where Chet would show up.

After she returned home, she wondered if he'd come for her, as he'd said he would, but as the night ripened, she was further burdened with uncertainty.

Fortunately, her father had gone to bed early. She hadn't been fooled. Lloyd Fischer was hoping she'd invite Michael in for a cup of coffee and had afforded them the necessary privacy to talk. Monica, however, had made her excuses, thanked Michael for a lovely evening, and then quickly slipped inside the house.

Waiting for Chet was intolerable. The not knowing. Twice now she'd ventured through the house, turning lights on and off as she tiptoed from one room to the next, fearing she'd wake her father.

At ten, she sat on the end of her bed, depressed and miserable. She picked at her fingernails, which she kept square and neatly trimmed. Although she'd often admired women with beautifully manicured nails, she personally thought of them as vain. The Bible has a good deal to say about vanity and a good many other things, including . . .

Her thoughts were interrupted by a soft knocking sound against her bedroom window. Monica flew off the bed and was breathless by the time she boosted open her window and stuck out her head.

"Chet?" she whispered as loud as she dared, leaning out. "Is that you?" She was eternally grateful that her father's room was at the front of the house, opposite her own.

"Are you expecting anyone else?"

She heard Chet, but couldn't see him. "Where are you?" she demanded, squinting into the inky black night. Shadows flickered here and there in what little light the moon offered. Still she couldn't locate him, and yet he sounded incredibly close.

He appeared then, like an apparition, and stood directly in front of her. For a moment they did nothing but stare at each other. Monica's heart was positioned somewhere between her chest and her throat and felt like a concrete ball.

Chet's look was unreadable. This private investigator was superbly talented at hiding his feelings.

Her own were as plain as a first-grade primer, she was sure of it. She was so pleased to see him it would have been impossible to disguise even a small part of her feelings.

His eyes darkened with intensity before he framed her face with his hands and gently pressed his mouth to hers. Monica sighed and wrapped her arms around his neck. The upper part of her body was thrust out the window so that her waist was pressed against the sill.

"I'm so pleased you came," she whispered again and again between frantic kisses. Her fingers were in his hair and her mouth was working against his, her need urgent.

The power Chet held over her was frightening. Each time they were together a little more of her restraint was stripped away. A little more of her control.

By the time they broke apart, Monica was gasping and trembling. She was aware of every part of her body his hands had touched. Her face, her shoulders, her neck. She felt a deep, physical hunger that shook her to the core.

"How was your date?" he asked.

She shook her head, not wanting to discuss Michael.

"Did you enjoy yourself?" he demanded, refusing to allow her to brush off the question. His hands held her face prisoner, and his eyes burned into hers.

"I was miserable."

His shoulders relaxed and he rewarded her with a shockingly thorough kiss. Before she had time to recover, he hoisted himself inside her bedroom.

Monica backed away from the window, and sank onto the edge of her mattress, her knees too weak to support her.

Chet glanced about the starkly furnished room and frowned. "Let's get out of here."

"Where would we go?"

"My place."

"I don't think that's such a good idea." Where she gathered the strength to refuse him she never knew. She folded her hands in her lap and concentrated on drawing in deep, even breaths. If ever she needed a clear head it was now.

Chet was pacing the room, restless and agitated. "We can't stay here."

"Why not?"

"Monica, be reasonable. Your father's—"

"On the other side of the house. He's a sound sleeper, he won't hear anything, and if he does, well, I'm twenty-five years old and if I care to invite a man into our house, then that's my business."

Chet's smile lacked amusement. "In case you haven't noticed, I'm in your bedroom, and inviting me to stay is a little like inviting the fox into the henhouse."

"Is your place any safer?"

He laughed softly at that. "No, but it'll ease my conscience. In the time it takes us to get there I just might find the strength to keep my hands off you. But I doubt it. You've got me so tied up in knots, it's a wonder I'm able to do my job."

Monica wasn't in any better condition herself. Brushing the hair from her face, she forced herself to think rationally. That, she soon realized, was a mistake. "As far as I can see we have absolutely nothing in common," she mumbled under her breath, discouraged and depressed.

"Except we're so damn hot for each other we're both about to break out in a heat rash."

"A relationship built on physical attraction is doomed from the beginning."

Chet nodded. "I couldn't agree with you more."

"So," she said, straightening her spine, searching for the necessary resolve to do the right thing. "Where do we go from here?"

"The logical choice is to bed. It'd help matters tremendously, don't you think? It's what any other couple would do in like circumstances. We just might be able to put this foolishness behind us and get on with our lives."

His words felt like a cold slap in the face. "That's the most ridiculous thing you've ever said to me," Monica managed despite her outrage. "I'm not some bimbo you can use to satisfy your carnal cravings and then toss aside. Dear heaven." She moaned, covering her face with both hands. "I can't believe we're having this conversation."

"All right, all right," Chet whispered, kneeling down in front of her. He pried her hands away from her face, clasped them in his own and kissed her knuckles. "You're right, it was a stupid thing to suggest. I shouldn't have spoken to you like that."

Leaning forward she rewarded his honesty with a lengthy kiss, one that gained in intensity and momentum until they were both sprawled across the top of her mattress, their arms and legs entwined.

"You shouldn't have done that," he whispered, his voice husky and low. He was struggling for control and for that matter so was she, but it felt so wonderfully good to be in his arms. Better than anything she'd experienced in all her twenty-five years.

"I better leave," he whispered.

"Not yet." She ran her tongue along the underside of his jaw, loving the taste of him; the scent of rum-and-spice aftershave enveloped her. She burrowed more completely into his embrace. For a moment she thought he intended to push her away, but instead he released a long, slow sigh and held her tightly against him.

"Monica . . . Stop," he muttered between clenched teeth, "otherwise I won't be held responsible for what happens."

Monica smiled to herself, knowing he'd never do anything to hurt her. Where the assurance came from she couldn't be sure, but she felt it as strongly as she did his arms around her.

"I knew it would be a mistake to come," he mumbled, seemingly to himself.

Monica continued to move her mouth over his throat. Her tongue made small circular movements against his jaw and over his ear.

"You're playing with fire," he said, his voice stiff with resolve.

"I know," she assured him.

"A man can only take so much of this." The words were barely audible.

"I know that too."

"I didn't mean for things to go so far," he whispered. He rolled away from her and changed their positions so that they were lying on their sides, facing each other.

Monica's head was cradled in his upper arm, their mouths separated by scant inches. Their breath merged and mingled. Her thigh met his. She was happier than she could remember being in a good long while. Monica would have been utterly content to stay exactly like this for the next hundred years.

Being here with Chet like this forced her to acknowledge how incredibly lonely she'd been in the last few years. Her mother had died and her friends, the only two she considered good friends, had both married and moved away. Funny she hadn't realized how empty and pointless her life had become. Nor had she realized what poor company she was to herself and others.

"What are you thinking?" he asked.

Their eyes met and she found him openly studying her. She quickly averted her gaze. "I didn't realize how downright good a man could feel."

He laughed softly and kissed the tip of her nose. "That's very honest of you."

"I couldn't very well deny it."

"You could, and have," he said. His fingertips grazed her temple, softly caressing her face. "I'll be honest too. You feel damn good in my arms. Tonight," he whispered, "while you were with Michael, I was like a caged animal."

"He doesn't mean anything to me," she rushed to explain.

He closed his eyes and nodded. "I know, but it didn't make any difference. There was this band around my chest that tightened every time I thought about the two of you together. Yet I know in my heart Michael's a better man than I'll ever be."

"Don't say that," she pleaded, feeling the panic rising in her voice. His next suggestion might be that they not see each other again and she couldn't bear that.

"Monica, listen—"

"No. No, don't say it. I have an idea." The words rushed out on top of each other.

"An idea for us?"

She nodded and bent forward and kissed him, using her tongue in all the ways he'd taught her until they were both panting and clinging to each other.

"As you said," she whispered, her chest heaving, "we seem to get along fabulously well on the physical level."

He chuckled. "That, my dear, is putting it mildly."

"It seems to me that we could learn to communicate on other levels as well."

He went still and raised his gaze to hers. She swallowed and forced herself to smile. His eyes narrowed.

"I was thinking that, well, if we feel so strongly about one another then we should . . ."

"Should what?" he prodded.

Monica gathered her courage and blurted it all out at once. "That we should get married."

"Leah," Andrew whispered in the darkened theater.

Leah's gaze reluctantly left the screen, where a Walt Disney animation film was playing.

Her husband pointed to Scotty, who was curled up in his lap. The toddler was sound asleep. Husband and wife shared a meaningful smile. Andrew reached over and stole a handful of popcorn from her box.

"Do you want to leave?"

She shook her head, surprised he'd ask. "This is the very best part. Besides, Scotty will want to know what he missed."

The older grandmotherly type in the row in front of them turned around and glared pointedly at Andrew.

"My husband apologizes for disrupting the show," Leah whispered.

"So does my wife," Andrew added.

The woman huffily turned around and Leah smothered her laughter as best she could. Her husband certainly wasn't helping matters any. He was making faces at the old biddy, which caused Leah to giggle all the more.

The woman turned around once again and Leah nearly choked in her effort to keep from laughing outright. Once she'd composed herself, she scooted down in her seat and leaned her head against Andrew's shoulder. She hadn't laughed this much in one day since . . . she couldn't remember when. It didn't matter, she was laughing now and it felt incredible. When had she allowed her life to become so cheerless? Time had slipped between her fingers with barely a notice.

Scotty was a delight, and she loved him until her heart felt as if it would burst. He would be about the same age as the baby they'd wanted to adopt. In some unexplainable way, Leah had transferred the love she had stored in her heart for the child taken from her. Pam must have understood that because she and Doug had asked Leah and her husband if they'd be Scotty's godparents.

In the last couple of years they'd done their duty and bought Scotty birthday and Christmas presents, but that had been the extent of their commitment. He held a special place in her heart, but Leah realized now that she'd cheated Andrew and herself out of the pleasure this child could bring into their lives.

Loving Scotty frightened her. She feared she might become overly attached to her friend's son. The pain of the lost adoption had cheated her out of enjoying Scotty the way she should. She'd feared that if she became overly attached, he'd be taken from her too.

The movie ended and the lights came up. Scotty yawned and, sitting up, rubbed his eyes.

"How you doing, big boy?" Andrew asked.

Scotty blinked several times, as if he'd forgotten where he was and who he was with. A look of panic came into his eyes as he glanced around the theater, and then to Leah.

"Remember, Mommy and Daddy went to dinner," Leah reminded him.

He nodded, but he didn't seem overly happy about it.

"I bet you're hungry," Andrew said, lifting him onto his shoulders. Andrew waited until the aisle was clear and then led the way out of the theater. It was dark by the time they reached the parking lot and the stars glittered like a splattering of diamond dust tossed across a bed of shiny black satin.

"Want to make a wish?" Leah asked.

Scotty looked to the heavens and nodded. He closed his eyes and drew in a deep breath, releasing it all at once. His eyes flew open and he grinned broadly.

"I bet he misses Diane and Jason," Andrew said, unlocking the car door.

"Nope," Scotty said. "I like you better."

"Don't get a big head," Leah warned her husband, under her breath. "He'd say the same thing to anyone who gave him horsy rides and took him to the movies."

"Maybe so," Andrew agreed, "but it's me he loves."

"Auntie Leah too."

Leah planted a kiss on his chubby cheek. "That's telling him, kiddo."

It wasn't until much later, hours after they'd finished the dinner dishes, long after they'd read Scotty a story and tucked him into the guest bed, that the emptiness surrounded her.

The night was dark and moonless as Leah slipped out of her bedroom and wandered into the room where

Scotty slept. Standing over his sleeping figure, she gazed down on this perfect child who belonged to her friend, and held the pain of her loss tight within her soul.

She finally moved and walked over to the closet. Standing on her tiptoes, she brought down the baby book she'd hidden there.

Sitting in the silence and the dark, she held the book in her lap and turned each empty page until she'd made her way through the entire satin-covered book. From newborn to the space for the high school graduation photo. When she'd finished, she pressed the book against her heart and rocked back and forth as if she were holding the long-awaited child in her arms.

Instead she clung to a hollow dream.

Jody gasped.

Jeff alive! It wasn't possible. She could hear her mother-in-law continue speaking but the words were unintelligible and seemed to come from a far-off distance. It was then that Jody realized she'd dropped the phone and had backed away.

"Jody." Glen was there and she turned and buried her face in his chest. "What is it?" he asked, his words as gentle as the arms that comforted her.

"Mom?" Timmy asked, picking up the receiver. Gloria continued talking, apparently not realizing anything was amiss. "Grandma says she needs to talk to you," her son said.

Jody shook her head. "No. No, I can't, not now."

"Tell your grandmother your mother will call her back later," Glen instructed. He encircled her shoulders and led her back to the living room. Gently he lowered her onto the sofa cushions. "What happened?"

Speaking was beyond her. Tears filled her eyes and spilled like burning acid against her cheeks, scalding her skin.

"Are you all right, Mom?" Timmy asked, racing to her side. "Grandma said she didn't mean to upset you. She told me to tell you to call her the minute you're feeling better."

"Did she say anything to you?" Jody demanded, gripping her son by the shoulders and making a careful study of his features. It was important that Gloria not say anything to Timmy. If her mother-in-law had made the outlandish claim to her son, Jody didn't know if she'd find it in her heart to forgive her.

"Say what?" Timmy wanted to know.

"I think your mother could do with a cold glass of water," Glen interrupted. "Would you get it for her?"

"Sure." Eager to help, Timmy hurried into the kitchen.

Glen's hands clasped Jody's. "What did Jeff's mother say to you?"

Speaking the words aloud was difficult. "She . . . claims Jeff's alive."

Glen released a troubled sigh. "Is there any chance it's true?"

Jody shook her head. "None. His body was positively identified by dental records. The same thing happened the first Christmas after we buried him. Gloria insisted Jeff wasn't dead. We argued and our relationship has been strained ever since. She's never understood that I had to divorce Jeff in order to sell the property, especially when she insisted she would continue to support Timmy and me, but I couldn't do that. I couldn't financially drain her or my own parents."

Glen sat next to her and gently patted her hand. "She sounds like a lonely old woman."

"I know. It shouldn't upset me when she does these things, but it does. I thought . . . I hoped she was making progress. I know she's trying, but it's hard for her. Jeff was her only child and she loved him very much."

"Here, Mom." Timmy vaulted into the room with a glass of water. The liquid sloshed over the rim as he presented it to her. "Is she all right?" Timmy asked Glen.

He nodded. "I think so."

"Grandma Potter's real nice," Timmy explained, "but she's a little weird sometimes. She visits old ladies who talk to the dead people and it doesn't have to be Halloween."

Jody, drinking the water, almost choked at Timmy's comment about Halloween. Leave it to a kid to put everything into the proper perspective.

"Your grandmother badly misses your father," Glen explained, kneeling down so his eyes were level with the nine-year-old. "And when you love someone so very much it eases the pain to pretend they're still with you."

"Grandma's been missing him a long time," Timmy said solemnly, then looked to Jody. "My mom has too. Until you came along all she ever thought about was my dad and her garden."

"How do you feel about that?" Glen asked.

"It bothered me a little because I'd like to have a dad who's alive and who can teach me the things a kid needs to know. I was kind of hoping you'd like me and my mom enough to stick around a while."

"I like you both a whole lot," Glen assured him.

"Enough to last through baseball season?"

Glen laughed and hugged the boy. "I'm sure I'll be around at least that long. Of course it's up to your mother if she wants to continue dating me."

"She does," Timmy said enthusiastically, "don't you, Mom?"

Jody knew she shouldn't allow her conversation with Jeff's mother to upset her, but it had. There'd been similar discussions over the years.

Jody remembered vividly every detail of every long-ago conversation. One had ruined her Christmas, but she refused to allow it to happen a second time. She'd met a good, kind man and she wasn't going to allow her ex-mother-in-law's grief to interfere in celebration of the holidays.

If that was the case, Jody reasoned, why couldn't she sleep? The house was dark and quiet, and she wandered from room to room, unable to quiet that deep inner part of herself.

The pain, she realized, was as fresh now as it had been when she'd been forced to accept that Jeff was dead.

Her father had phoned from Germany with the news. He explained that he'd be bringing Jeff's body home for burial. She had written down the flight details on a slip of paper and calmly thanked him for dealing with these agonizing details. It wasn't until after she'd hung up the phone that the full impact of what her father had said settled over her.

Jeff was dead. The years of not knowing had come to an end.

The intolerable waiting was over. The haunting questions had been answered, but the sharp edges of her grief were only beginning. The agony of the unknown felt almost comfortable compared to the brutal loss of hope she'd suffered in exchange.

Until Jeff's remains could be positively identified—until she could place her husband's body in the ground and stand at his tombstone, there had always been hope, however slim, that he was alive. Now that had been stripped away from her and she was left to bleed.

Jody remembered how she ripped the flight information from the pad and folded it over and over again until it was a tight square, clenching it in her fist. She needed something to hold on to. All there was for her was a folded slip of paper that listed the information on the flight that was bringing her husband's body home.

For a long time she'd done nothing but sit and stare into the silence. Her heart had felt as if it had stopped beating.

It was then, Jody realized, that a part of herself had died. No one could endure this kind of emotional torture and possibly survive.

She was dead to all the happy dreams they'd shared. Dead to whatever the future would hold, because she couldn't share her tomorrows with the man she'd loved so fiercely.

Helen Chandler had arrived shortly after the call came from Jody's father. She walked into the house and softly called Jody's name. Jody had stared up at her mother, her eyes dry, her heart shattered. At first she didn't acknowledge her presence. No one could comfort her. Not even her own mother.

"He's gone," Helen had whispered.

Jody nodded. She couldn't deny it any longer. The hope had been forever destroyed.

Her mother had attempted to console her, wrapping her arms around Jody's shoulders. But Jody held herself stiff and unyielding.

"Let him go," her mother pleaded. "Let him rest in peace."

"Peace?" Jody whispered. How could she possibly have peace now? She shook her head, refusing to release any part of her life with Jeff.

"He's been found, Jody. Jeff's coming home."

Perhaps Jeff's body had been located, Jody reasoned, but she was more lost now than ever. And she doubted that she would ever find her way again.

How much time had passed since that disastrous day, Jody wondered. Four years? Or was it five? Like so much else in her life, she'd lost track. She moved, one day into the next, dragging her pain with her, the weight almost more than she could bear.

It wasn't until Timmy had written the letter to God that she realized what she was doing to herself and to her boy. It had shocked her into taking action.

For the first time since Jeff's death, she was making a new life for herself and for her son, and she couldn't, wouldn't, let that be ruined. It had taken her this long to find her footing and she wasn't going to allow anyone to topple her again.

Chapter 13

Angels rarely wept. It happened so seldom, and only while they were on earth duty. Mercy had heard tales of angel tears, but never experienced the phenomenon herself. It was an unpleasant experience. Now they came as a surprise, misting her gaze. She brushed them aside, feeling Leah's pain as deeply as if it were her own as the young nurse clenched the empty baby book against her bosom.

Mercy had done everything possible, but she hadn't been able to help. It was the most frustrating case she had ever encountered.

If only Mercy could sit down and talk to Leah, face to face. If only Mercy could explain to this woman of the earth that she must find serenity within herself before her prayer could be answered. But that was impossible.

And so they both wept.

Leah cried silent tears standing guard over her friend's child while Mercy wept openly, unable to contain her sorrow at this feeling of helplessness.

"Married." The word went through Chet like a bullet, with much the same effect. He bolted off the bed and stood, the sour taste of panic filling his mouth.

"It seems the logical thing to do," Monica said, her voice as sweet as chocolate-dipped caramels.

Chet rubbed his hand down his face, hoping that would set matters straight in his mind. It didn't. If anything, his thoughts filled with pure terror. "Sweetheart, in case you haven't figured it out, I'm not the marrying kind."

"That's the point," Monica continued softly, "I'm not either. It seems we're perfect for each other."

"You're not the marrying kind? Don't be ridiculous." She remained on the bed, so beautiful he had to force himself to look away. Otherwise he just might find himself considering her ridiculous suggestion. Much more of this sexual teasing they'd been exchanging and he'd find himself agreeing to just about anything.

"I'm twenty-five years old and have never been asked," she reminded him.

"Michael's chomping at the bit, waiting for the opportunity," Chet muttered. He couldn't believe he'd said that, not after the fretful evening he'd spent thinking about Monica cheek to cheek with the other man. He quickly glanced about the room, making sure he wasn't leaving anything behind, such as his heart and a good portion of common sense. He looped his leg over the windowsill, eager to make his escape before he found himself actually discussing the possibility of marriage. The mere thought sent cold chills down his spine.

"You're leaving?" Monica was kneeling on top of the mattress. Her eyes were wide and pleading. "Don't go. Please."

The "please" had cost her a good deal, but Chet knew that if he didn't make his escape then and there, it would be too late. Before he knew what he was doing, he'd find himself agreeing to this asinine scheme of hers.

As it was, their ongoing relationship continued to confound him. He'd never meant to see her again after she'd lectured him on the misery brought on by the evils of alcohol. Little by little he'd knowingly allowed himself to be drawn to this preacher's daughter. They'd been a hair's breadth from making love only moments earlier. She didn't seem to realize how close they'd come.

"I should have realized," she said in a small, pitiful voice, "that you wouldn't want to marry me."

Chet groaned inwardly. He was prepared to slip into the night as unnoticed as when he'd first arrived, but she'd managed to do it again. This woman knew exactly which cords to pull to reach him. It happened like this each and every time they met. Much more of this and she'd have the threads wrapped so securely around his heart there'd be no escape.

"It isn't that," he said, his back to her. Looking at her was dangerous, especially now with her lips swollen from his kisses and her hair all mussed up. He'd never known a woman who looked more beautiful when her hair wasn't combed.

"Then what is it?" she asked. From the nearness of her voice he knew she'd moved off the bed and was standing almost directly behind him.

Nothing but the truth would satisfy her, Chet realized, yet he hesitated, knowing she'd argue with the devil himself.

"Tell me exactly what it is then," she demanded, and he noticed she was regaining some of her natural pluck.

"Listen, sweetheart," he said, knowing she disliked the affectionate term, "I'm not good enough for you."

Until he'd met Monica his life had been reduced to wild weekends, blown paychecks, and cheap thrills with a cocktail waitress. He'd been shot, beaten, and chased down by a jealous husband. Not exactly pick-of-the-litter husband material for a minister's daughter, but there was no telling Monica anything. He'd learned that the hard way.

"Don't say that." Her arms came up under his and she looped her hands on his shoulders, then flattened the side of her face against his back. She felt so good and warm pressed to him that for an instant he was nearly swayed.

"Nothing could be further from the truth," she insisted. "Don't you realize how much you've taught me? I was a prude until we met and now I know what it means to be in love. You've made me proud to be a woman."

"Lessons rarely come cheap."

"What's that supposed to mean?" Her arms slipped away from him and Chet was eternally grateful. He slipped out of the window, landing with a thud on the hard ground below.

Turning around to face her was a mistake in what was proving to be a long line of tactical errors. Her eyes were bright with tears and her lower lip was trembling. Something sharp and painful twisted in his gut. He could deal far easier with her anger than he could her tears.

"I'm not going to marry you, Monica," he told her harshly. "So get that idea out of your head right now. It's just not going to happen."

She was silent for a moment, then nodded. "You can't get much clearer than that. Good night, Chet." Her voice was soft and a little broken.

She had her hooks in him good and deep. The best thing for him to do was to get out while the getting was good. Working as a private investigator, Chet had developed a sixth sense for these things. The time to leave was about five minutes ago.

"I'll see you around," he tossed over his shoulder. He waited for her to close the window, but she didn't and he was left to wonder exactly how long she stood there watching him.

Fighting himself he made it all the way to his car, which he'd parked two streets over. He didn't want anyone to see his vehicle and connect Monica with him.

He unlocked the door and sat in the front seat and battled with himself until he accepted that he wasn't going to be able to leave matters unfinished between them.

He slammed his fist against the steering wheel, climbed out of the car, and retraced the same route he had taken only moments earlier. He came by the side of the darkened church and toward the back side of the house where Monica's bedroom was situated.

Her room was dark. He hesitated, then carefully made his way to the window, tapping lightly against the glass pane. He heard her climb out of the bed and pull up the sash.

Neither of them spoke right away. It was as if they were both unsure of what to say. After coming all the way back, Chet hadn't any more of a clue than when he left the car. Apparently Monica didn't either.

"I volunteered to be a bell ringer," she whispered. He couldn't see her face as clearly as he would have liked, but he could tell from the soft catch in her voice that she'd been crying.

Damn fool woman. She should have known better than to fall in love with the likes of him.

"When?" he found himself asking, already anxious to see her again. They were playing a no-win game, but for the life of him Chet couldn't make himself walk away from her.

"Tomorrow afternoon between two and three."

"Same street as before?"

"Yes." The last part was barely discernible. "Chet," she said more clearly, but he heard the hesitation in her voice. He heard the pain too, but ignored it as best he could, which was near impossible.

"Yeah?" he prompted when she didn't immediately continue.

She was kneeling, he noticed, her face only a short distance from his own. "Do you . . . are you in love with me?"

It didn't take him long to respond. "I don't know." It was the honest-to-God truth. What did someone like him know about love? Damn little to be sure.

"You can't be any more articulate than that?" The righteous ring was back in her voice and he found himself smiling.

"I like you," he said, realizing what an inadequate phrase that was.

"In other words I turn you on?"

He wasn't sure he liked her vernacular, but he wasn't in any position to be arguing since he was the one who'd taught her everything she knew about the sexual part of her nature. He never figured she'd be such a fast learner.

"It's more than that," was about all he was willing to admit.

"How much more?"

He should have known she wouldn't leave that alone. "I don't know," he said, raising his voice more than he'd intended. His words seemed to echo like thunder in the silence of the night. All they needed now was to wake her old man. "I just don't know," he repeated, softer this time. "Listen, Monica, it doesn't help to phrase the same question in different ways, the answer's going to be the same. I don't know about love. I've never been in love before, so how am I supposed to know if what I feel for you is any different than what I've felt in the past?"

"But surely you've had some experience with love."

His laugh was low and husky. "Experience I've got, lots of that, but mainly it's of the physical nature."

"In other words if . . . if we'd made love, then you might be able to tell me exactly what your feelings are towards me." The stiff indignation was back as inflexible as always.

"Not exactly." It did his heart good to hear the outrage in her voice, although he'd never known a woman who could irritate him faster. By the same token he'd never known a woman who did the other things to him she did either. The problem was, he still hadn't figured out whether he liked it or not. Mostly he liked it, he reasoned, otherwise he wouldn't keep coming back for more.

"I have my principles, Chet Costello, and I can tell you right now that I refuse to sleep with any man until after we're married."

Laughing was a gross error and he knew it, but he couldn't help himself. He could have had her any number of times. The only thing that had stopped him was knowing that neither one of them would be the same afterward.

Monica was innocent in the ways of men and he refused to take from her what rightly belonged to another. His thoughts were abruptly ended when Monica slammed the window shut, practically in his face.

Her eyes glared out at him accusingly.

He shouldn't have laughed and knew it even as the amusement escaped his throat. As means of an apology, he pressed his fingertips to his lips and then set his open hand against the cold windowpane.

Monica's angry gaze held his in what little light the moon afforded. After a moment, she pantomimed his action and poised her hand on the other side of the glass against his.

Reluctantly, he dropped his hand and turned away from her while he had the strength. He didn't know where the relationship was leading and as far as he could see they were striding down a dead-end street, but for the life of him he couldn't make himself terminate it. Maybe he did love her; he didn't ever want to think about the consequences of that.

"Young man."

The voice startled Chet. He was getting sloppy in his old age, otherwise he'd never have been heard cutting through her side yard. Chet whirled around to find a thin man standing on the front lawn, dressed in a robe and slippers, holding a flashlight. It could only be Monica's father.

Chet drew in his breath and waited.

"I'd like to know exactly what you're doing on my property this time of night?" Lloyd Fisher demanded, aiming the flashlight into his eyes, blinding him.

It was happening, Leah thought. She woke to the buzzing of the alarm and even before she opened her eyes she realized how queasy her stomach was. Was it possible? Could she be pregnant?

Mentally she tried to calculate the dates of her last menstrual cycle, and couldn't. Sometime the first part of November, she guessed. It would help if she hadn't tossed her notebook in the garbage.

It was wishful thinking, she finally decided. Or the flu. Probably a nasty virus, she mused, yawning.

"Morning," Andrew said, cuddling her. His hand automatically slipped over her abdomen as he scooted closer to her side. Leah savored his warmth. "Did you sleep well?"

"Hmmm."

"Me too."

Leah smiled. Their routine was the same every morning. It was these small things, these everyday habits that had become a part of the structure of their marriage.

After Andrew had gone to make the coffee, Leah decided to take her temperature for old times' sake, not that it would tell her anything.

Two minutes later she was studying the normal reading and calling herself a silly goose, grateful Andrew hadn't caught her with the thermometer in her mouth.

"I think I'll just have yogurt this morning," Leah said when she entered the kitchen.

Andrew studied her. "Are you feeling all right?"

"I'm fine," she assured him, taking a carton of blueberry-flavored non-fat yogurt out of the refrigerator. The bread popped up from the toaster and Andrew spread a thin layer of butter over the warm surface.

"You look a little pale," he commented, removing the lid from the strawberry jam. He smeared a thick coat over the toast and carried his plate and cup of coffee to the table.

"I do?" Her voice rose with a dash of excitement she couldn't hide. She brought her yogurt with her and joined him.

The toast was poised in front of Andrew's mouth and he slowly lowered it to his plate. He didn't say anything for several moments. "How late are you?"

"I don't know. I threw away my notebook, remember?"

"Surely you can figure it out."

"Can you?"

He shook his head. "I guess not. It doesn't matter though, does it? If you're pregnant we'll both be happy."

"And if I'm not?" she asked, watching him expectantly.

"Then you're not," he concluded, munching on the toast. He made it sound as if it didn't matter to him one way or another. Leah knew that wasn't true, not after having had Scotty with them for two days. Andrew was wonderful with children. He deserved to be a father. The familiar ache returned but the intensity wasn't as strong as it had been. The pain that had been so much a part of her all these years seemed to peel away and disappear.

She'd experienced this sensation only once before—the night she'd met Andrew.

She remembered the first time she saw him. They were both college students attending the University of Washington. Some friends had introduced them and the minute they'd exchanged greetings Leah felt a powerful emotional punch. She wished there was a word to describe the feeling that came over her. It was as if fate had given her a swift kick where she'd feel it.

From that moment on she knew this man was going to be an important part of her life. Afterward she discounted the feeling, chalking it up to the beer she'd had earlier. Andrew was steadily dating someone else at the time and she'd heard rumors that he was close to becoming engaged.

They ran into each other soon after that at the library. Leah was struggling with a chemistry class, certain she was going to fail. The library was the only place she could study and so she made the nightly trek across campus to hit the books.

Andrew had been grappling over a term paper and they'd sat at the same table for nearly two hours without speaking a word. Leah had wanted to get to know him better, but hadn't exchanged more than a preliminary hello, good-to-see-you-again sort of chitchat.

Andrew left first, whispered something about being glad to see her again, and was gone. But when she'd walked out of the library he was waiting for her. A couple of friends had delayed him, he explained, and besides he didn't think it was a good idea for her to walk across the campus alone in the dark. So he escorted her back to her dorm.

They continued to meet nightly at the library long after his term paper had been turned in and graded. Later Andrew told her she was the only girl he'd ever dated who helped improve his GPA. He'd done more studying with her than any other woman he'd ever dated.

Leah didn't know when she realized she was in love with him. The night they'd met seemed a good choice. She just knew.

Just as she knew now, in the deepest most sheltered part of her heart, that she was going to have a child.

Leah didn't question where this knowledge came from. It wasn't intuition, or instinct, or anything psychic, but a deep abiding belief that her time of waiting had come to an end.

"I suppose you're going to buy one of those home pregnancy test kits," Andrew said, frowning, as he carried his empty plate to the sink. He rinsed it off and stuck it in the dishwasher.

They'd been through this procedure no less than a dozen times over the years. The minute she was a day late, Leah typically ran to the drugstore, needing to know the answer as soon as possible. For all the test kits she'd purchased over the years, she should be entitled to a discount.

"Not this time," she said.

"Why not?"

"Like you said, if I'm pregnant, great, and if not, well, then I'm not." She looped her arms around his neck and kissed him. "I love you."

He didn't answer her right away. Instead he carefully studied her upturned face. "Something's different."

"It is?" she asked, beaming him a smile.

"I don't know what, but it's there in your eyes."

Leah knew what it was. She was pregnant. Oh, heaven help her, she was diving into the deep end again and she hadn't meant for that to happen.

She knew she was pregnant. Felt it to the very marrow of her bones, but she'd believed the same thing a hundred times before.

Now was different. The feeling she had now was as powerful as the night she met Andrew, but she couldn't allow her sanity to rest on something as immeasurable as a feeling.

"You're sure you're all right?" he asked, looking concerned.

"I feel wonderful," she said, tightly hugging her husband's waist. She closed her eyes, praying with all her heart that this wasn't a sick joke her mind was playing on her.

From the moment she'd received the call claiming Jeff was alive, Jody had dreaded contacting her mother-in-law. She carefully bided her time and waited until Timmy was down for the night. Even then it had taken Jody another half hour to fortify her courage enough to reach for the phone. She didn't know where she'd find the grit to face Jeff's mother when she was in one of these moods.

"Hello, Gloria," Jody said calmly, knowing she'd probably woken her mother-in-law from a sound sleep.

"Jody," she said groggily, "is that you?" Not giving her time to answer, she immediately continued. "I'm so pleased you called me back. I know this news is as much of a shock to you as it is me, but—"

"Gloria," Jody cut in calmly, unwilling to listen to any more. Her only chance of reaching Jeff's mother was when she sounded composed and confident. "Jeff is dead."

Someone had played the cruelest of hoaxes on them. "Who phoned you?" Jody demanded, and a telltale wobble came into her voice, betraying her slipping poise.

"I didn't get his name," Gloria explained. "You see, I was so excited that I wasn't thinking clearly, but he sounded very professional. He gave me details."

"What sort of details?" It was clear this line of questioning was flustering Jeff's mother all the more, but for the sake of them all Jody had to get to the bottom of this.

"I can't really tell you right this minute."

"Did he say where he was calling from?" Jody asked more calmly this time.

"Oh, yes, he was in Germany. Such a nice young man. You see, the call woke me in the middle of the night. I didn't believe him at first and then the more he talked the more I realized he was telling the truth. Jeff is alive. In my heart I always knew he was and now it's coming to pass."

"But wouldn't the authorities have contacted me?" Jody asked.

"I . . . don't know, dear. Maybe it has something to do with the divorce."

"But surely they'd want me to know. After all, Timmy is Jeff's son."

"I can't answer your questions, Jody. All I know is what they said."

"And what was that?"

"I should have written everything down, but I was too excited, and I'm on this new heart medication that makes my mind go all fuzzy at times."

Jody's grip on the phone relaxed. "Was this one of those times, Mom?" she asked softly.

"Oh, no, this was all very real. I thought to call you right away, but—"

"But you didn't," Jody concluded when the older woman hesitated.

"No," she admitted reluctantly.

"And why didn't you?"

"Because," Gloria said, following a heartfelt sigh, "I knew you wouldn't believe me, and I was afraid we would end up arguing and I do so hate the thought of us disagreeing. You and Timmy are the only family I have left."

Left. The details were quickly tallying in Jody's mind. Her mother-in-law was taking a new heart medication, one that, at times, confused her and she'd been woken abruptly from a sound sleep. The episode was probably a very lifelike dream. Not entirely sure the phone call had happened herself, Gloria had delayed contacting Jody until the following evening.

Because she'd been so desperate to believe her son was alive, Jeff's mother had clung to the dream, building it in her mind, until she'd convinced herself it was authentic.

"Have you heard from anyone since?" Jody asked softly.

"No. You think I should have, don't you?"

"It doesn't matter what I think. What do you believe?"

Speaking on the phone had always been an inadequate means of communication as far as Jody was concerned. She heard the faint intake of breath that came from her mother-in-law and knew Gloria was weeping softly. How Jody wished she could be there to wrap her arms around her and comfort her.

Jody had needed consolation herself the night before when Gloria had first phoned and there'd been a strong pair of arms to hold her. It had helped tremendously.

"How's Timmy?" her mother-in-law asked in an apparent effort to change the subject. "I bet he's getting excited for Christmas."

"Timmy's great." Jody couldn't talk about her rambunctious son and not smile. "We chopped down a Christmas tree this weekend."

"All by yourselves?"

Jody hesitated, unsure if she should mention Glen or not. This didn't seem to be the appropriate time to drop the news that she was dating again, although heaven knew it was well past the time she should.

"A friend went along and helped," she answered, being as diplomatic as she could.

"A friend," Gloria repeated slowly, thoughtfully. "Male or female?"

"Male." She couldn't leave it at that. She'd need to explain now. "Glen's an attorney who works at the same law firm I do."

"I see." Funny how much was visible in those two brief words. "Just how long have you been dating this . . . other man?"

"Mom, it isn't like that. We've only been out a couple of times, but it isn't anything . . ." She stopped herself in time from saying "serious." Glen was serious. He'd said as much from the first. He wanted a wife and family. Timmy wanted and needed a father figure. She needed a husband. One who would laugh with her, one who would hold her when she needed to be held. One who would fill the empty spaces of her heart.

"Everything's becoming clear to me now," Gloria said stiffly. "No wonder you don't want to hear about Jeff. You're involved with another man."

"Mother, that's not true." This was an impossible conversation, and growing more so every minute. The immediate sense of guilt she experienced was nearly crippling.

"The man who called from Germany knew that you'd divorced my son."

"Mother, we've been through this a thousand times or more. I didn't divorce Jeff because I didn't love him any longer. It was for financial reasons."

"I was never satisfied with that excuse and you know it. Both your parents and I were more than willing to support you."

"Mom, please—"

"The man who called asked me about you and Timmy."

"Mom, don't, please," Jody whispered, her small voice trembling. "It was a dream. It never happened."

"He did call." Gloria's high voice rattled from the telephone receiver. "Jeff's alive."

"I realize it's difficult for you to accept that I'm dating again, but it's time I got on with my life. Don't you think I've grieved long enough? Don't you think it's time?" Despite her resolve not to break down, she was crying. It happened like this nearly every time they spoke.

"I imagine you plan to marry this other man?" Gloria continued, her voice filled with disdain.

"I never said that."

"You can remarry, you know, there's nothing I can do to stop you."

"I don't know what I'm going to do," Jody said, bewildered and miserable, looking for a means of ending the conversation.

"That would make for a fine thing for my son to come home to, his wife married to another man."

"Mom, please don't say that."

"You know what I think?" Gloria said accusingly, knowing she had the upper hand. "You don't want Jeff to be alive. You've made such a fine life for yourself that it would be inconvenient for you if he did turn up alive."

"You know that's not true," Jody sobbed.

"Do I, now? You have your new boyfriend, you don't need Jeff anymore."

"Glen is a friend," she insisted.

"That isn't what you said earlier."

"I think it's time we ended this," Jody said, struggling for what little composure remained.

"That's just fine with me. But I think you should know, I'm going to tell Jeff myself just what kind of wife you turned out to be. He's going to call me soon, and then I'll tell him. Then he'll know the truth about you."

Chapter 14

L eah walked into her house and was greeted with the fresh, pungent scent of evergreen. The decorator had arrived and set up the Christmas tree, and it was breathtakingly beautiful.

The flocked tree looked as if it belonged in the foyer of a classy hotel. Glossy gold bows were strung in one continuous ribbon from top to bottom. Bright red porcelain poinsettia flowers were symmetrically placed. And then there were the angels. Leah counted twelve. In gold gowns with massive white wings, each one playing a musical instrument. A guitar, a harp, a saxophone, a tuba, and flute. A horn and trombone. It became a game to find each one hidden among the heavy white limbs.

"You're home," Andrew said, ambling into the living room from the kitchen. "Well," he said, his gaze following hers toward the Christmas tree, "what do you think?"

"It's beautiful."

"I thought so too."

She hung her coat in the closet.

"Debbi outdid herself this year," Andrew said, bending over and turning on the tree lights. Ten strings of miniature red globes glowed, casting warm shadows about the room.

The decorator was a friend of Andrew's mother. As part of her Christmas gift to Andrew and Leah, Shirley Lundberg had their Christmas tree decorated.

"I love the angels," Leah said, slipping her arm around her husband's waist and pressing her head to his shoulder.

"How'd your day go?"

There was far more to the question than what he was asking. What Andrew wanted to know was if she was feeling the same queasy sensation she had the last few days both in the mornings and late in the afternoons. He was asking if her period had started. In sum he wanted to know if she was pregnant.

"My day was great, how about yours?" she asked, smiling up at him.

His gaze skirted past hers. "Let's sit down," he suggested. With a flip of the switch, the gas fireplace roared to life and tongues of fire licked at the imitation logs.

Together they sank into the soft comfort of the leather sofa. Andrew's arm was tucked around her shoulders and he rested his chin on the crown of her head. "I've been thinking," he began.

"This sounds ominous."

He chuckled, but she noticed his laughter contained a dash of concern. "I'd feel a whole lot more comfortable if we got one of those pregnancy test kits," he continued.

"Why does it matter?" she asked, laughing off his request. "We'll know sooner or later, won't we?"

"You've been on this emotional high all week and I'm afraid if it continues much longer—"

"But I am pregnant," she said with supreme confidence. "I know it's finally happening for us. There's never been any physical reason why we can't have children. Dr. Benoit assured us of that countless times. How many times has he claimed all we need do is relax and that it'll happen when we least expect it? I don't know about you, Andrew, but I'm floored by this."

"Leah, please, listen to reason."

"Our time of waiting has passed," she insisted, unwilling to listen to his arguments.

"If you're so certain, then it won't matter if you take the test now or later, will it?" Andrew pressed.

"I'm not going to buy another one of those awful test kits. I hate them." She eased herself away from him and stiffly folded her arms. They'd been through this routine countless times and the result had always been devastatingly the same.

Negative.

No matter how long she studied the results she couldn't make them read what she yearned for so desperately. No, she wouldn't subject herself to that again.

"Leah, please. I just don't want you to get yourself worked up over this. You're a few days late and already—"

"I don't know that I'm late. You don't either. To my way of thinking, you're making more of this than necessary. As you said before, if I'm pregnant, great, if not, well, then I'm not pregnant."

He was uncharacteristically silent, but Leah knew her husband well enough to recognize how deceptive this calm could be.

"Let me do this my way," she asked, reaching for his hand and kissing his knuckles.

He didn't respond immediately. "I can't stand by and watch you do this to yourself. How many times have you gone through this?" he demanded. "It's always the same and each time your hopes go a little higher and you fall a little harder. Each time it takes you longer to recover."

Leah knew what he was saying was true, but this was different. This time she'd throw back her head and shout for joy. This time her heart and her soul would be left intact. How she wished there was some way to reassure Andrew.

"I don't want you to worry about me," she said.

"I am worried."

She leaned against him. "Don't, please."

"Does this mean you won't take the home pregnancy test?" The fire crackled in the distance adding punctuation to his request.

She hated to refuse him anything, but it was necessary. Those tests dredged up far too many unpleasant memories. That was all in the past, and her future, their future, was spilling over with promise.

"No, Andrew, I won't. Not this time." She threw her arms into the air and fell backward so that she was sprawled across his lap, smiling up into his face. "Now kiss me, you fool."

He closed his eyes as though to blot her out. "Leah, for the love of—"

She didn't allow him to finish, but gripped hold of his neck and levered herself upward until her mouth met his. As familiar as she was with her husband's body, Leah knew exactly what she needed to do to evoke a strong and positive response.

"Leah." Her name became a helpless plea.

"I have this incredible urge to ravish you," she whispered, opening the buttons of his neatly pressed dress shirt. He groaned when her hands met his warm skin.

"Dinner," he managed, between slow, deep kisses.

"What about it?" she asked, rotating her hands around to his back. His heart was pounding hard and fast, but then so was her own.

"Can wait," he told her brokenly.

Leah smiled softly to herself. "That's what I thought."

It wasn't until she was dressing for work the following morning that Leah found the pregnancy test kit. How long it had been sitting on the bathroom counter she could only speculate. Probably from the night before.

The night before. A small, satisfied smile lit up her eyes. They might be an old married couple, but the lovemaking couldn't get more incredible or more romantic than beneath a glowing Christmas tree in front of a flickering fire.

She carried the test kit into the kitchen with her and set it down on the kitchen table in front of her husband. "Is this a hint?"

"As broad as I can make it," he said, and finished his glass of orange juice. "For the love of heaven, let's get this agony over with."

It was then that Leah knew.

In the beginning she was afraid he was worried about her building her hopes upon a foundation of sand. But it was more than that. Andrew was suffering the torment of the unknown himself.

For years, Andrew had disguised his feelings, not allowing her to guess how very much he wanted children.

He was studying her now, his features sharp and anxious. "How much longer will you wait?"

She wanted to make some flippant reply, some casual remark that they could both laugh away, but it wouldn't work.

"If it'll ease your mind," she said, disliking even this small compromise, "I'll make an appointment with Dr. Benoit right away." The physician, however dear, produced a flood of unhappy memories. She couldn't think of him and not remember the months of hormone shots, the ultrasound, and everything else they'd attempted over the last seven years.

"All right, call your doctor friend," Andrew said, but he didn't sound especially pleased. He wanted to know. The sooner the better.

Not so with Leah. She'd already received all the confirmation she needed.

Monica had been standing in the cold, sounding the bell for charitable donations, for nearly forty-five minutes. She was cold, her feet hurt, and she was almost convinced Chet wouldn't show.

Not after her father had caught him walking out of their yard in the dead of night. Worse, she'd been left to speculate what had happened. Her father had remained uncharacteristically tight-lipped about the incident. She'd tried once to pry information from him, but to no avail. Any further questions and he'd guess that her interest was more than normal curiosity.

Monica felt Chet's presence several seconds before he came into view. Her body was developing a kind of sonar when it came to locating him. Her spirits lifted immediately and she drew in a deep breath and whispered a soft prayer of thankfulness.

"Hello," she whispered, when he strolled up to the bright red pot and slipped a twenty-dollar bill inside.

"We need to talk," he murmured, not looking at her.

"I know."

"Can you meet me afterwards?"

"Of course." She was in love and a woman in love would do whatever was necessary to be with her man. "Your apartment?" she asked, loving to tease him.

"No." The word was sharp and instant.

Monica couldn't help it, she laughed. "Where?"

"Pier Fifty-six. I'll be waiting for you at the restaurant. There's a table way in the back, closest to the water."

She nodded eagerly. "I shouldn't be much longer."

"I'll see you there," he murmured, and before she could say another word, he was gone. The man was like a magician. He could appear and disappear at the drop of a hat, or so it seemed.

Twenty minutes later, Monica was hurrying downhill, toward the Seattle waterfront. She raced across the street, promising herself she'd stop on her way to the bus stop and look at the Christmas display in Nordstrom's window. She'd heard it was angels this year, perched atop a train set that circled a frothy cloud. Stars shone bright from above. Another window was the traditional Santa's elves at the North Pole and Mrs. Claus baking sugar cookies.

Chet was sitting at the table, waiting for her. Puget Sound showed through the huge plate-glass window behind him. The sky was blue and clear and the ferry had just pulled away from the dock. The scene was lovely and for a moment she studied the tranquil waters.

"I'm so glad to see you," she said. She slipped out of her coat and waited a moment, wondering how long it would take Chet to notice her new dress, but he seemed preoccupied and said nothing. Monica was a bit hurt, but let it pass.

"I'm dying for a cup of coffee," she said.

Chet waved for the waitress, who carried the glass pot over to the table. "Do you want something to eat?" he asked Monica.

She shook her head. "Just coffee for me, thanks."

"Me too." The waitress refilled his cup and poured hers.

Chet smiled over at her and the same intense look was back, the one she'd noticed earlier. His frown deepened as if he'd become aware of a change.

"Something's different," he said, studying her.

Monica beamed proudly. He had noticed. "I'm wearing a little makeup," she whispered, leaning toward him. "Out of the blue I got a call from Donna Watkins, a lady from church. She invited me to lunch. Donna's wonderful with clothes and scarves and pretty pins. . . . I didn't always think so, but that doesn't matter now. She claimed she was getting dressed that morning and had the irrepressible urge to call me and invite me out.

"After lunch she took me shopping. I bought the dress and"—she tossed back her head to expose her earlobes—"these. They're lovely, aren't they?"

Chet's eyebrows shot toward his hair line at the sight of the small gold earrings. "I thought you claimed jewelry was a tool of the devil."

She might have thought that at one time, but would never have said so, at least not publicly. "Don't be ridiculous. I said that if a woman opted to wear jewels, then whatever she chose should enhance a meek and gentle spirit."

"Earrings do all that?"

He was teasing her, but she didn't mind. "I think so. Donna did too, but then she had on these huge Christmas tree decorations. They're wild. As far as I can see, each woman is left to her own interpretation of this."

She took a sip of coffee, grateful for the warmth it offered her. "Do you like the dress?" She tried to make light of it, but her heart was dangling precariously on her sleeve. Everything she'd bought that afternoon had been with Chet in mind. Each time she stepped before the mirror, her first thought had been what he would think when he saw her.

"It's very pretty."

It wasn't much as compliments went, but enough. "It's the first thing I've had in years that isn't black, gray, or navy blue. Donna says I'm a summer, if you know what that means. I didn't until she explained, but basically I should be wearing pastels, pinks, pale blues, and the like."

Chet nodded, but looked distracted, as if this summer business were beyond him.

"I'm sorry," she said, setting her cup down hard in the saucer, "I didn't mean to get sidetracked. Tell me what happened with my dad." She was breathless with anticipation. "He didn't say a word to me."

"Nothing happened."

Chet certainly seemed to be uncommunicative this afternoon. "Nothing?" she demanded. There was more to this than met the eye.

"I explained I was a private investigator and had cut through his yard. I apologized for the intrusion. As far as I could tell he believed me. After he'd read over my license he went back into the house."

"That was it?" Surely there was something more. It wasn't her imagination, her father had been unnecessarily quiet all morning. He seemed preoccupied and absentminded. When she mentioned meeting Donna for an early lunch, he'd encouraged her, and even sounded pleased. He insisted she needn't come back to the office when she'd finished. Since she was volunteering downtown, she should go directly there.

"You seem so quiet," Monica said after several moments of silence. She'd never seen the serious side of Chet. She'd seen him angry and frustrated, aroused and flippant, but never serious.

He didn't seem to hear her. "I don't think I ever realized how truly beautiful you are."

Unaccustomed to compliments, Monica felt herself blush. Her heart was so full, it felt as if it were ready to burst. Love must do this to a woman, she decided, but she wouldn't change this incredible feeling for the world.

He leaned forward and reached for her hand, gripping her fingers hard with his own. "I've been doing some thinking."

"About us?" Her chest tightened as though she already knew what he was going to say. In that same moment she recognized that no amount of arguing would change his mind.

Chet nodded. "It has to end, Monica. I never intended matters to go this far. You're bright and beautiful and someday you'll meet a—"

She stopped him from saying anything more by pressing the tips of her fingers against his lips. She knew her eyes were wide and pleading. They stung with the effort to hold back a wall of tears.

"Don't say it," she pleaded softly.

His hand gripped her wrist and he closed his eyes as if this were causing him as much pain as he was inflicting upon her. He kissed her fingers and slowly moved her hand away.

She lowered her gaze. "There's this song," she whispered in fractured tones, having trouble speaking. "Michael plays it on the piano. It's from some musical. I don't know which one . . . it's about two people who must end their affair, and the girl who's singing asks only one thing."

"What's that?"

"All she wants is to choose the time and place where he tells her good-bye. She wants it to be on a Sunday at the zoo. I don't know why she chose there, but she did." She forced herself to smile and realized a toddler would have seen through the effort. "I always thought that was the most ridiculous song. The only reason Michael played it was that he knew it irritated me, and now . . . now I think I understand."

Chet didn't say anything for several minutes. Monica couldn't.

"The time is now," he said. "It's over."

She nodded. "At least let me choose the place. Not here in some fancy restaurant with half the world looking on. Let's go outside to the end of the pier. Tell me there you don't love me. Tell me there you never want to see me again."

She didn't wait for him to agree or disagree, but stood, taking her coat. With her head held high, she walked out of the restaurant and down the long pier, stopping when she'd reached the farthest corner.

The wind blew hard against her as she stood at the railing looking out over the green, murky waters. It amazed her that she could be so outwardly calm and still hurt this badly.

For a moment she feared Chet would choose to leave her there alone, but she was wrong. Soon he joined her. Standing beside her, he braced his elbows against the railing, and looked out over the water. Dusk was setting, and a soft shade of pink brightened the horizon. The wind whistled softly in the background.

"I can't say I don't love you, if that's what you're looking for." The words were almost accusing, tight with pain.

Monica's hands were buried deep in her coat pockets. She turned to study him. The wind slapped the loose tendrils of her hair about her face. "Why are you doing this?"

"Damn it, Monica, I don't want to argue. We both know all the reasons. We've been through all this. I'm not going to get involved in another debate with you.

One of us has got to keep his head on straight. Do you think I'm enjoying this?"

"No."

"Accept it, then. It's over before either of us has more cause for regret."

So this was what it felt like to die, Monica mused. She closed her eyes as the pain worked through her heart, then slowly nodded.

"Michael's a good man."

"I don't love Michael," she said evenly. "I love you."

He ignored her. "I ran a background check on him for you and he's squeaky clean. You couldn't ask for better husband material."

"Don't, please," she whispered fervently. She knew what he was doing, but it wasn't helping.

"If you're not attracted to Michael, fine. He's not the only fish in the sea. For that matter I'm not either. You'll fall in love again. Within a couple of weeks, maybe less."

Monica's short laugh was filled with more tears than amusement. "Oh, Chet, don't you know me at all? Do you honestly believe I'm the kind of woman to walk from one relationship to another? Do you really think I'd ever marry a man I don't love?"

His lack of response was answer enough. "Just don't do anything stupid," he warned.

"Like what?"

"Hell, I don't know, join a convent or something."

"That's for Catholics."

"I realize that, but knowing you, you'd convert just to spite me. There's too much passion in you for that, understand? You've kept it buried for too damn long as it is. You'll do fine," he said starkly, turned, and started to walk away.

"Chet."

He stopped, and his back and his shoulders stiffened, but he didn't turn around.

"Would you hold me, please. One last time."

It looked as if he intended to keep on walking. He took one step, and then another. Monica bit down so hard on her lip to keep from calling for him that she tasted blood. Whatever it was that caused him to change his mind, she would never know.

Before another moment passed she was in his arms. His hold on her was hard and tight. Sobbing, she clung to him.

"You're a fool," she told him, weeping so hard, she doubted he could understand her.

"I've always been one. Why change now?"

"Because I love you."

"Yeah, well, that and two bits will buy you a cup of coffee." He broke away from her so abruptly that she nearly stumbled backward. Gripping her hands with his, he raised her fingers to his mouth. "Dear God, I can't believe . . ."

"What can't you believe?"

"Nothing." He closed his eyes and folded his fingers over hers. "There's so much I owe you."

"But, Chet," she pleaded, "don't you understand? I'm so grateful for you."

"This is my gift to you."

"What?" she sobbed, "breaking my heart?"

"No, letting you go before I screw up your life as much as I have my own." He dropped her hands, and without another word, turned and walked away.

It was highly uncommon to get a summons from Gabriel while on prayer assignment, and Goodness was convinced she was about to be pulled off the case. She had her arguments all lined up. Good ones too. Matters were going much better than they appeared at first glance. She intended to explain everything, if only he'd give her the opportunity.

At last Goodness had something positive to report. Monica had come to her senses. It was no small task dealing with this human either. The preacher's daughter had been a challenge from the first, but Goodness had made progress. With some effort, she'd arranged the phone call from Donna Watkins, although she was disappointed that Monica had chosen to impress Chet instead of Michael with her new outfit.

"Goodness." Gabriel greeted her upon her arrival. He was pacing, his massive hands clenched behind his back. "I'd like a progress report on Monica Fischer's prayer request."

"I was hoping you'd ask," Goodness said, eager to tell her side of the strange happenings. "There's a fine young man in her church by the name of Michael Simpson—"

Gabriel cut her off with a look. "I understand she's currently involved with Chet Costello. And from what I hear, you're responsible for the two of them meeting."

"Was involved," Goodness said quickly, steering the archangel away from the unfortunate incident of Monica literally falling into Chet's arms. "That's all behind her now."

"You're sure about this?"

"You needn't worry about Monica and that shoddy detective any longer," Goodness concluded, folding her hands and proudly flaunting her wings. "Michael Simpson has a good deal going for him. He's talented and dedicated. I'm sure that within a matter of days, Monica will—"

"Days?" Gabriel repeated.

"Perhaps it will take a week, but I'm confident Monica will come to her senses soon."

Gabriel continued his pacing. "From what I can see of matters, Monica Fischer is deeply in love, and it isn't with Michael Simpson."

"I'm sure this private detective was nothing more than a passing fancy."

"You think so, do you?" Gabriel asked calmly. "Look at this and then tell me what you think." With a wave of his arm, the walls of heaven slowly parted, followed by a rush of warm, humid winds. Mists swirled and Goodness squinted, having trouble locating Monica through the thick fog.

Soon the vista cleared. It took her a moment to recognize the stark interior of the old church. It was the very sanctuary where Goodness had met her friends—where Reverend Fischer tended his flock of faithful believers.

Monica was kneeling at the altar, her face buried in her arms as she openly sobbed. It was her tears and her prayers that had created the humid fog. The sounds of her pain rose pitifully toward heaven as if echoing from a sound chamber.

"She's changed," Gabriel said gently. "Her hair is different."

"Chet, he's the private detective—"

"I know him well."

"You do?"

Gabriel nodded. "Is he responsible for the other things as well? I notice she's wearing an attractive dress and gold earrings."

"Ah, I believe so." Now didn't seem the time to mention Monica's lunch with Donna Watkins.

Gabriel's nod was thoughtful. "I suspected as much. As I recall, the last time I saw Monica, she was trapped in the web of her own righteousness. Am I wrong, or is she a little more willing to accept the differences in us all?"

"I couldn't really say, but I must explain, I did a bit of research on this private detective and I don't mind telling you, he's had a sordid past."

"I see," Gabriel commented with a decided lack of appreciation. This wasn't a good sign. "How far back did you investigate him?"

"The last couple of years."

"Did you learn about his gunshot wound?"

"Ah, I wasn't aware he'd been wounded."

"He nearly died. As I understand it, he stepped in front of a bullet to save his friend. He was willing to sacrifice his own life for that of someone he loved. Unfortunately it wasn't enough, his friend died."

"Oh, dear." The picture Gabriel painted of Chet was becoming clearer. Goodness's gaze slowly returned to Monica, kneeling at the altar railing, pouring her heart out in prayer. It rose like a sweet-smelling mist toward heaven. "What's she saying?"

Gabriel stood behind Goodness. "She's thanking God for teaching her about love, for giving her the short time she had with Chet. Her heart is filled with gratitude."

Goodness frowned. "Gratitude comes with tears?"

"Very often it does," Gabriel admitted with a be-leaguered sigh. "It seems to me you've taught Monica Fischer what she needed to learn."

"But I did nothing." Goodness was more confused than ever. Her efforts had all been geared toward Michael. "The changes are due to Chet Costello, not me."

"I know. Maybe we should look at him."

Goodness pressed her lips tightly together. "He's probably in a bar somewhere."

"He is." The picture of Monica faded and was replaced by one of Chet slouched atop a bar stool, nursing a shot glass. His shoulders were hunched forward and he ignored any attempts at conversation the bartender made.

"You notice he isn't in any church," Goodness felt obliged to point out.

"I realize that."

A cocktail waitress ambled to his side and whispered something. "That's Trixie." Goodness felt it was important that Gabriel know how well informed she was. She hadn't slouched in her duties.

"I know all about Trixie as well."

"Then you must be aware of their ongoing relationship," Goodness supplied.

"It's over and has been from the moment Chet met Monica," Gabriel said absently. "He's doing it again, you see."

"Drinking?"

Gabriel slowly shook his head. "No, he's sacrificing himself for another. He loves Monica, but he doesn't believe he's right for her. It seems to me that a man who's twice put the good of someone else before his own deserves something more than pain."

"He deserves love," Goodness whispered, watching Trixie.

Goodness thought she heard Gabriel groan. "Not Trixie," he said impatiently.

"Who, then?"

"Monica Fischer."

Goodness felt knocked off-balance. "You couldn't possibly mean that the good Lord intends to answer Monica's prayer for a husband with Chet Costello?"

Gabriel laughed, the rich and full sound echoing like a Chinese gong. "My dear Goodness, that's what He intended all along."

Chapter 15

Jody swore she didn't sleep except in ten- or fifteen-minute snatches the entire night. It had been like this when Jeff had first disappeared. Mentally and physically exhausted, she'd fall into bed, immediately slip into a druglike sleep only to jerk awake minutes later. The pattern was back.

Jeff was alive.

Jeff was dead and buried. Buried and mourned.

Resurrected.

The next morning, when the alarm rang, Jody was tempted to call into work sick. The only thing that kept her from doing so was the idea of facing the day at home alone with her doubts—a day alone with her fears. Alone. It held no appeal.

Sensing her mood, Timmy was extra quiet. He dressed for school while she cooked his breakfast and drove him to the bus stop.

"Have a good day," she told him as he climbed out of the car.

"You too, Mom." With that he was gone, hurrying to meet his friends.

The traffic into the city was heavy, but Jody barely noticed. She drove by rote, her mind wandering from one inane topic to another. When she pulled into her assigned spot in the parking garage, she was surprised to realize where she was and had no memory of the commute.

At least while she was at the office she could occupy her thoughts with matters other than Jeff's mother. Despite everything, a small part of her—no, she corrected, a very large part of her—had been wounded by the things Gloria had said.

Why should it matter that her mother-in-law would tell her dead son what a terrible wife Jody was?

Somehow it did.

It unsettled her that Gloria's opinion of her was so important. Jody had been a good wife. No woman could have possibly loved Jeff more. No woman could have grieved harder, or longer—except, possibly, his mother.

Because of Timmy it was impossible for Jody to isolate her life the way Gloria had. Because of Timmy she was forced to deal with the present. She'd done a good job, or at least she assumed she had until her son had written his letter to God. Timmy needed her, not to look back and weep with her pain, but to stand tall and proud and to point the direction of their future.

Jody had no more than settled down at her desk, her thoughts more confused than ever, when Glen Richardson arrived. She looked up at the attorney's warm, concerned face, and felt an immediate sense of serenity.

He had a calming affect on her and had from the first. It hadn't taken long for him to become a good friend, and she'd never needed one more.

"How'd it go with your mother-in-law?" he asked, sitting on the edge of her desk.

Jody averted her gaze. "Not good."

"She's a lonely old woman."

"I know," Jody said, "but somehow that doesn't make this any easier."

Glen's eyes were sympathetic. "I'm sure it doesn't. How's Timmy?"

"Great. He's checking the water in the tree stand every morning just the way you said. I swear, he's brought every kid in the neighborhood home to show them the Christmas tree he cut down by himself."

"Hey, don't I get any credit?"

"Apparently not. He's got the neighborhood believing he's a regular lumberjack. He wanted to wear his plaid shirt and boots to school this morning. It seems he's got an image to live up to now."

Glen chuckled, but then his eyes grew serious. "I hope you don't mind, but I bought Timmy a baseball mitt for Christmas. I realize it was presumptuous of me to do something like that without talking to you first."

Jody wasn't sure how she felt about Glen giving them presents. It was thoughtful, yes, but baseball mitts were expensive and it seemed to imply that there was something more than mere friendship.

"The mitt he showed me is too small for his hand," Glen explained. "I'm surprised his coach let him play with it. If Timmy's going to pitch, and he certainly seems to have his heart set on that, then he'll need a properly fitting mitt."

"It was very kind of you, Glen."

"But?" He scooted off her desk, and seemed to be waiting for her to chastise him.

"Timmy will think he's in heaven." Jody couldn't make herself berate Glen. She wouldn't have known Timmy's mitt was too small if Glen hadn't told her. If anything, he'd proved Timmy's point. Her son needed a father's loving guidance.

Glen looked at his watch. "I better get back to my office. I have to be in court later this morning."

"Thanks for stopping by."

"No problem. How about dinner one night this week?"

Before Jody even thought about what she was doing, she nodded.

This was a pivotal moment for her.

She'd welcomed another man into her life, calmly accepted his companionship. She had taken for granted that she would see Glen again and soon. More earth-shattering was how much she was looking forward to spending more time with him.

Some of what she was feeling must have leaked into her eyes, because Glen didn't leave. Slowly, he walked around to her side of the desk, claimed a second chair, and sat down next to her.

"What just happened?" he asked, leaning forward and bracing his elbows on his knees. "Something clicked in your mind just now. I could see it as plain as day. Tell me what it was."

"I realized how pleased I was that we're dating."

He laughed, and Jody was certain he didn't understand the significance of what she was saying. For the last seven years she'd lived her life in limbo. The still, shadow-filled existence had become a shelter to her. It had protected her from exposing her heart to any additional pain. What she had missed in all those years, wrapped in a cocoon of safety, didn't bear thinking about.

Now here, out of the blue, like a miracle, was a man who'd gently pushed and prodded his way past the barriers of her resolve. A man who hadn't asked her to stop loving Jeff. He hadn't attempted to push her dead husband out of her life. All he'd asked was that she make room for him.

"Glen?"

"Yes." He reached for her hand, holding it lightly in his own.

Where she found the courage, she didn't know. Didn't question. All at once it was there, like the warming rays of dawn at the end of a long, cold night. "Would you like to marry me?"

At first her words were met with a shock-filled silence. Glen looked at her as if he suspected he hadn't heard her correctly. "Did you just say what I think you did?"

Jody had never been more embarrassed in her life. She hadn't a clue what had prompted her to ask such a thing. All at once the thought was there, and the words had tumbled from her lips like awkward chunks of ice over the edge of a pitcher. She wanted to reach out and jerk back the question, but before she had a chance to do or say anything more, Glen spoke.

"I would consider it the greatest honor of my life to be your husband and Timmy's stepfather."

"I shouldn't have—"

"You should have," Glen interrupted with feeling. "I just never dreamed this would happen so soon." He looked at his watch once more and she could see the regret work its way into his eyes.

"We'll talk about it later," she promised.

"Set the date, Jody. We can shop for an engagement ring this weekend." How eager he sounded, how pleased.

Maybe it wasn't such a crazy idea after all. She'd waited so long and here was an opportunity of a lifetime. Here was a chance of finding happiness and she was grabbing hold of it with both hands.

Yes, it was happening so fast, but that was the way she wanted it. If she had too much time to think about remarrying, she might find an excuse to change her mind.

"Let's get married in January, after the holidays," she blurted out, as Glen headed for the door.

He turned around and flashed her a smile that rivaled the noonday sun. "January it is."

"Yes!" **Shirley** did a leap into the air off the filing cabinet, both hands raised in jubilation. A stack of papers went flying in all directions and Jody whirled around.

"What was that?" she asked as the papers fluttered to the ground.

Another woman in the office said, "It's that damn heating vent. It sends out a rush of hot air every now and again." She rolled her chair over to Jody. "Here, let me help you pick those up."

Jody looked up and frowned. The heating vent wasn't anywhere near the filing cabinet.

Shirley stayed plastered against the ceiling, her hands covering her mouth. "Oops," she whispered.

"Don't you think we should contact the maintenance man?"

"Naw," the other woman said. "It doesn't happen that often."

"Hey," Jody murmured, "look at this. It's a feather. How do you suppose a feather got in here?"

"I haven't got a clue," her friend said, handing her a stack of papers.

Shirley left before she caused any further damage and ascended directly toward the golden light of heaven, exhilarated with this unexpected turn of events.

To her delight Gabriel was waiting for her.

"Come in, come in," he greeted her. He was a magnificent angel, tall and regal looking, an impressive sight after a steady stream of men of the earth. For a fraction of a second Shirley admired the strength and power exuding from him.

"You're here to report about Timmy Potter?" Gabriel asked in a no-nonsense tone.

"That's right," Shirley said, nodding. "My mission's accomplished, Timmy's mother became engaged to Glen Richardson this morning."

"Glen Richardson," Gabriel repeated. He walked over to the desk where the cumbersome volume was stored and flipped open the thick book. He ran his finger down the page until he found Glen's name, then looked up at Shirley and frowned.

"He's a wonderful man and will make Timmy an excellent father," Shirley hurried to say. She strained her eyes to read what Gabriel seemed to question, but wasn't able to see anything beyond the archangel's massive hand.

"You need to return to earth right away," Gabriel continued. "There's been some misunderstanding. Jody and Timmy are going to need you. The winds of trouble are brewing."

"You can't tell me anything more than that?" Shirley asked. She should have known it wouldn't be this easy, especially since she was so new at this.

"There's nothing more I can tell you," Gabriel said, and she heard the regret in his voice.

"But . . ."

"Go," Gabriel said, spreading his massive wings. "You have work to do."

For years Leah had avoided the infant sections of department stores. Now she found herself drawn to them as if a magnet were luring her in their direction.

She was supposed to be Christmas shopping, instead she wandered about looking at beautifully crafted cribs, lovingly running her hand over the polished wood railings. The joy that blossomed in her heart was strong.

She was going to have a baby.

After all these years she was about to bear a child. Her waiting, her pain had come to pass.

Andrew's words of warning echoed harshly in the back of her mind. How she wished she could find some way to explain the deep certainty she experienced. She yearned to rub away his doubts and lend him the assurance she'd felt from that very first morning.

Soon she would be able to look him in the eye and tell him her body was nurturing his seed. For years she'd carried this dream with her, of watching her husband's expression when she told him he would soon be a father.

Nothing could have pleased her more than to purchase a complete layette right then and there, but she didn't want to risk another confrontation with Andrew. They had all the baby furniture they'd ever need in storage. Once Dr. Benoit had confirmed her pregnancy, there'd be plenty of time to set up a nursery.

Her appointment wasn't until the twenty-third, but she was fortunate to get one as quickly as that, so she wasn't complaining. Seeing the doctor that close to Christmas had its advantages. That way she wouldn't need to wait long to make the announcement to both sets of parents. If she saw Dr. Benoit any sooner, she'd never have been able to keep the happy news to herself.

Andrew's mother would be thrilled. Her own, too, of course, but her parents had plenty of grandchildren, while Shirley Lundberg impatiently waited for her first.

Leah had had names picked out for years. If they had a girl her name would be either Sarah, Hannah, or Elizabeth. A son would be named Isaac, Samuel, or John. Few understood the significance or what had prompted her decision.

The names were Biblical. Leah shared a good deal in common with the three women. Sarah, Hannah, and Elizabeth had been barren too, but God had heard their prayers and answered them with the birth of their firstborn child. As it happened, all three were boys, and those were the names she'd chosen for her own child, should she bear a son.

Deep in her heart, Leah felt this child was a miracle. He was a testament to faith. Over the years her hope had grown weak and faltered, but God had listened. He'd heard her cries. Even when it seemed all that was returned to her was the echo of her own sobs, God had been faithful.

Unable to leave the infant department without purchasing one small item, Leah opted for a beautiful sterling silver Christmas tree ornament for Andrew with Baby's First Christmas beautifully inscribed in the silver. Technically she was a year early, but she was eager for Andrew's reaction when he opened this gift. By then he'd know for certain she was pregnant.

As she suspected, her husband was waiting for her when she arrived home from her Christmas shopping spree. He trailed behind her from the garage all the way into the guest bedroom, where she stored the unwrapped gifts.

"How'd the shopping go?" he asked, following close on her heels.

Leah set her purchases on the bed and tossed him a saucy smile over her shoulder. "Very well, thank you."

"Did you buy me anything?" One thing she'd always loved about Andrew was his childlike attitude toward

Christmas. He was like a little kid about presents. He played silly guessing games with her, checked out the packages under the tree as often as he dared, and shook his gifts until they were in danger of being broken.

"I might have found you something," she answered cryptically, "and then again I might not."

"But you did," he said, sounding confident. He leaned against the doorway and cupped his hands behind his head, as if he had it all figured out. His pose suggested that she needn't wrap the gifts since he knew everything she'd bought anyway.

"You were gone a long time," he commented.

"Hmmm," she said, bringing the Christmas wrap out from the closet.

"Where'd you go?"

"Andrew, honestly!"

"Did you know the golf store was having a sale?"

"That does it," Leah said, throwing her arms in the air. "Scoot. I'm going to wrap these and I can't do it with you standing over my shoulder watching every move I make."

"Yes, but you have some great moves."

"Andrew, please, I'm serious. Scoot."

"Aha. So you did buy me something!"

"Good-bye, darling." She walked over to the door and closed it. The latch clicked softly into place.

Andrew stood stubbornly on the other side, refusing to leave. "You'll call me if you need anything, right?" he asked, sounding downright cordial.

"In a heartbeat."

A minute passed, perhaps two, but no longer. "Do you want something to drink?"

"No, thank you. Andrew, why don't you go in and watch television for a while?"

"Nothing good's on."

"What about football?"

"The game's over. How long is it going to take you to finish?"

"I can't rightly say." Was it any wonder family and friends made fun of her gift-wrapping efforts? She used more tape than any three people. She couldn't wrap a single gift without being hounded by her husband, who behaved more like a six-year-old than a mature adult.

A long, slow release of breath followed her announcement. "I'm going to make a cup of hot chocolate," he said, sounding as if he'd lost his last friend.

"Make two," she called out. She'd finish up later. By some miracle she'd managed to wrap everything she'd purchased for him, including a box of golf balls. The man had a sixth sense when it came to ferreting out his gifts.

Andrew was carrying steaming mugs of hot chocolate into the living room by the time she'd put everything away. They kicked off their shoes and snuggled up together on the sofa.

"When's your doctor's appointment?" Andrew asked, rubbing his chin along the side of her head. Leah was convinced she'd told him no less than three times. "The twenty-third."

He didn't say anything for a couple of moments. "How are you feeling?"

"Wonderful." Leah smiled to herself. He was becoming a believer. Bit by bit, little by little, as each day passed. Like her, he was afraid to believe. Like her, he couldn't make himself not do so.

"You know what I was thinking this afternoon?" she said, tilting back her head so their eyes could meet. "I'd like to start attending church services again."

"What brought this on?"

"I don't know. I realized it's been months since we last went to church. Far too long, and you know what? I miss it."

"I've always loved singing Christmas carols," Andrew said wistfully.

Leah nearly choked on her hot chocolate. "You can't sing."

"I know," he admitted readily, his eyes bright with silent laughter, "but that never stopped me."

"I noticed." She loved to tease him. It felt good to be together like this. "You wouldn't mind then if we went back to church?"

His eyes met hers. "Why should I? I think it's a good idea."

Leah nestled back into the warm security of his arms.

"It seems we have a good deal to be grateful for lately."

"Yes, it does," she agreed.

The moment was peaceful and serene and Leah happily traipsed along the meandering path of her thoughts. They led her on the same well-traveled road she'd traversed so often, trying to picture what Andrew's and her child would be like. She hoped, boy or girl, that their baby would inherit her husband's love of life, his excitement and joy for the little things.

"Leah," he said after a moment, "do you still believe you're pregnant?"

"I know I am. It's there—that confident feeling inside me. We're going to have a child, Andrew."

"You realize you've got me believing it now too, don't you?"

"Yes, and that's even better."

"This could be dangerous thinking for us both. We might be setting ourselves up for another major disappointment, and I don't think either one of us can take many more."

"We aren't," she assured him, not doubting, not even for an instant. "Here, feel," she said, taking the hot chocolate and setting it aside. Then, reaching for his hand, she pressed his palm against her stomach, holding it there, her fingers pressed over his. "Now tell me what you believe."

He was silent for what seemed like an eternity before he wrapped his arms around her and brought her tight against him, holding her as if he were suddenly afraid and needed someone to cling to.

"I love you," she whispered.

"I know," he whispered, and when they kissed she realized he was trembling.

"Monica," her father said, walking into the living room, his look contemplative. "Michael called again."

The needle was poised in her fingers, ready to pierce the linen fabric. "I don't feel much like talking, Dad. Would you make my excuses?"

"I explained you were a little under the weather."

She pulled the thread through the material. "Thank you." The needlepoint was a means of occupying her mind, but she doubted that she'd ever finish this project. The Ten Commandments were filled with Thou Shalt Not and that was the way she'd viewed life. Her views had subtly changed, thanks to knowing Chet.

Her father claimed his favorite chair across from her and reached for his Bible. He opened it and silently read for several moments before he gently closed the yellowed pages and set the leather-bound book aside.

"I've waited now for three days for you to tell me why you're so low. I don't know that I have the patience to hold out much longer."

Monica set aside the needlepoint, not knowing where to begin or how. The pain was too fresh yet, too raw. She lowered her gaze to her lap and clenched her hands together. Her father was a patient man, and she prayed he'd understand her hesitation.

He gave her a few moments, then leaned toward her and gently patted her knee. "It's at times like these that I wish your mother were alive. She'd be much better at understanding what's wrong than I am. Funny, isn't it," he said with a sad sort of laugh, "I counsel people from all walks of life and I can't help my own daughter."

"Dad, it's not that."

"I know, love. If it will make it easier, you don't need to tell me there's a man involved in all this. I have eyes in my head. In the beginning I believed it was Michael, but it's obvious he's not the one." He reached for his handkerchief and methodically cleaned his glasses. "I apologize for playing the role of the matchmaker with you two. I should have known better. I'm an old man who would like grandchildren someday."

Monica closed her eyes to a fresh wave of pain. Now there would be no children, because there was no Chet. It was melodramatic to think she would never fall in love again, never marry. But right then that was exactly how she felt.

"Whoever this young man is I'd like to thank him," her father continued after a lengthy silence.

"You don't know him, Dad."

"It doesn't matter."

She was forever grateful he didn't play a game of cat and mouse, attempting to guess Chet's identity.

"For the first time since you entered your twenties you've taken your eyes off yourself. You've worked so hard to do the right thing, to be the perfect example of God's love to others. Soon you focused all your efforts on yourself and how good you were. It was then that you started to notice the flaws in others. It became a vicious circle and I couldn't seem to reach you with the truth."

Monica raised her gaze to his. "I don't understand."

"Forgive me for sounding like the preacher I am. You're my only child and I love you more than words can say, but there've been times I wanted to take you by the shoulders and shake you good and hard."

"For what?" Although she asked the question, Monica was well aware of the answer.

"For standing in judgment of others instead of trying to look at them through God's eyes," her father continued.

"The man, his . . . his name is Chet," she whispered, feeling she owed her father some explanation. "I met him downtown, the first time the ensemble sang. He was going into a tavern and I tried to stop him by telling him how wrong it was for him to drink."

Her father smiled at that and settled back in his chair. "I suspect he didn't listen to you."

"No, quite the opposite. He laughed." She did too then, at the memory. Softly, sadly. "We met again by accident later and several times more by design.

"I couldn't understand what it was I found so intriguing about him. He's not like anyone I've ever known."

"You've been raised in the church. Your experience with the world has been limited."

She reached for a tissue and twisted it between her fingers. "He's a former policeman and has lived a hard life. He's done things neither of us would ever dream of doing. He's been shot and sometimes carries a gun, although he doesn't realize I know that."

"A gun?"

"At first glance he looks rough and mean," she hurried to explain, "but on the inside . . . I don't think I could have found a better man to love. He was honest when he didn't need to be, and gentle. There were any number of times he could have seduced me and didn't."

"I see."

The strain in her father's voice produced a small smile. She shouldn't have told him that part. Any father would have reacted the same.

"He's so damn noble I could cry . . . and have," she said, clenching her fists.

"I take it he's the one who insisted you not see each other again?"

Monica nodded. "He never said he loved me, but I know he does. He loves me so much he was willing to send me away rather than take the chance of hurting me."

"Monica," her father pleaded, "why didn't you bring him to meet me?"

It was a question that had plagued her as well. One she'd repeatedly asked herself the last few days. Chet had claimed he wanted it to end before there were more regrets, but she'd stewed in them for days. She feared Chet had assumed she was ashamed of him and that simply wasn't the case.

"I don't know why I didn't introduce you. I guess I was afraid you'd think ill of him, or me."

"But, Monica, you love this man. That would have been enough of a character endorsement for me. Your mother and I raised you and if you can't judge a man's worth by now then you wouldn't be our daughter."

"Oh, Dad, I wish I'd done so many things differently and now it's too late. Forgive me for not trusting you. I've been wrong about so much."

Her father patted her knee once more. "There's a special man for you. Remember how hurt you were when you learned Patrick was engaged."

Patrick. She'd nearly forgotten about him. It was laughable to think she'd been anything close to loving her former boyfriend. Her pride had been hurt at Patrick's surprise announcement. Far more than her ego was involved this time, and Monica sincerely doubted that she'd ever be the same again.

Chapter 16

"Hey, man, you don't look so good," Lou, the Blue Goose bartender said as he poured Chet another shot glass of Kentucky bourbon.

"If you're looking for a pretty face," Chet muttered, "call Trixie."

"You got the flu?"

"Yeah," Chet said, thinking that would get Lou off his back. He wasn't interested in company or conversation.

"Then get the hell out of here," Lou continued. "No one wants to be sick for Christmas."

Christmas. It was just another day like all the others as far as Chet was concerned. Christmas was for families and he didn't have one. No one bought him gifts, and there certainly wasn't anyone he cared enough to buy one for other than . . . His thoughts came to a grinding halt.

Funny how a woman could mess up a man's mind. He'd known Monica what . . . two, three weeks? He'd lost count and within that short amount of time she'd managed to worm her way into his heart until she was like a virus that had spread to every part of his body.

He couldn't eat or sleep for want of her. He couldn't close his eyes without his head filling up with thoughts of her. Nor could he get the image of her out of his mind. The one of her standing at the end of the pier, the wind ruffling her hair, her beautiful eyes bright with tears . . . and love. A love so damn strong it was like a torchlight beaming directly at him.

That final picture of her would haunt him to the grave. He didn't know how he was going to get through the rest of his life without her.

The rest of his life. Chet nearly laughed out loud. What life? That was the real question. He was sick to death of the endless lies, the constant need for charades, flirting with disaster.

That's how it'd started with Monica. A game, because she irritated him. One diversion too many and this time he was paying the piper in spades.

The empty days stretched out before him, followed by cruel nights staked out in some dark alley or a cheap hotel room crawling with loneliness.

The rest of his life was reserved in hell. He was born there and had spent a good majority of his carelessly lived existence there, except for one brief furlough with a preacher's daughter. Just long enough for him to taste what could have been his, so he'd know exactly what it was he'd thrown away.

He emptied his drink, slapped the money down on the bar, and stood. The room spun and he shook his head, hoping that would help. It was too damn early in the afternoon to be drunk.

When he left the Blue Goose the cold hit him like a sharp claw. He squinted in the sunlight, cursing it as much as he cursed himself. The only person he had to blame for this was himself.

This was what he got for involving himself with a missionary. He'd known from the first time he kissed Monica that something like this would happen. It hadn't stopped him from seeing her again. It hadn't stopped him from caring. Nor had it stopped him from nearly screwing up her life.

The walk back to his office did him good. He was beginning to think he might be able to pull himself together and accomplish something by the end of the day, when he strolled past the department store window. Santa was there, and a long line of kids were waiting for him to listen to their wish lists. A little boy was squirming in his lap.

Something about the kid reached out and grabbed Chet by the gut. Perhaps it was the boy's eyes, maybe it was the color of the kid's hair, which was close to his own. It came to Chet then as unwelcome pain. If his life had been different, he might have had a son.

That fantasy along with everything else had been destroyed years ago when he'd been brash and naive enough to believe in justice and truth. Years ago before Tom was murdered, before he hadn't been able to save his partner.

He forced himself to keep walking until he reached his building. His office lacked welcome, but Chet had wasted enough time already. He had work to do.

He sorted through his mail and tossed it unopened into the garbage. Reaching over the top of his desk, he pushed the button for his answering machine. A series of impersonal beeps followed. No one wanted him, not even his clients.

What he needed, Chet decided, was a change of scene. He should have left this stinking city years ago. Now that he thought about it, he wasn't sure what it was that had prompted him to stay.

His mind made up, he pulled the phone from its jack, stuck it in the bottom desk drawer, and then searched through his filing cabinet for his lease, wishing he could remember the terms.

A knock sounded at his door.

"It's open," he shouted, shuffling though his papers. He made decent money, but had never gotten around to hiring himself a secretary. He wished now that he had.

"I'm looking for Chet Costello."

"You found him." He looked up and damn near swallowed his tongue. It was Monica's father.

Lloyd Fischer grinned in recognition. "So it was you? I was guessing, you see. Monica didn't give me your surname. Then again, I didn't ask."

"What can I do for you, Reverend Fischer?" Chet asked crisply. He wasn't going to put up with an interrogation. Fact was, he wasn't up to much more of anything.

"We're working at the Mission House," the older man explained, looking around the room. His eyes revealed neither approval nor disapproval, just mild curiosity.

"What can I do for you?" Chet pressed a second time.

The question seemed to take the reverend by surprise and he reverted his attention to Chet. "I'm not exactly sure. Would you mind if I sat down?"

"I was just on my way out." The last thing Chet wanted was a lengthy conversation with Monica's father.

"This won't take more than a couple of minutes," he said, and helped himself to a chair.

The reverend was being deliberately obtuse, and Chet gritted his teeth with impatience.

"When was the last time you saw my daughter?"

"Tuesday." Chet made a point of looking at his watch as if he needed to be someplace important soon. "If Monica didn't give you my name, how'd you find me?"

"I read your license, remember?"

He was losing it, Chet mused. He'd forgotten the old coot had caught him coming out of the side yard that night and had asked to see his identification.

"My daughter's badly hurt, you know."

For one wild second Chet assumed Monica had been injured and the fear that seared through him burned hotter than the bullet he'd taken years earlier.

"Life's tough and then you die," Chet stated unemotionally.

The man grinned as if he easily saw through Chet's ploy. The grin irritated Chet. "Listen, I have work to do."

"Monica claims you love her. Is that true?"

"No." The pain of the lie pricked his heart, but he ignored it. "Listen, if you're worried about what happened between us, let me assure you nothing did. Now, if you don't mind I've got an appointment."

"Yes, I suppose you do," the reverend said, slowly getting to his feet. He extended his hand. "It was a pleasure meeting you, young man. It's plain to see why Monica thinks so highly of you."

Chet's chest tightened with a crippling ache as they exchanged hand shakes. "You should be beating the hell out of me for having ever touched your daughter."

The other man's eyes gentled as he slowly shook his head. "I was young once myself, you know, and deeply in love. Monica's a woman and old enough to know her own heart. I'm not here to judge you or my daughter. I came out of curiosity to meet you. And thank you."

"Thank me?" Lloyd Fischer was offering him gratitude when Chet had expected condemnation.

"Oh, yes, you've helped Monica tremendously." The minister looked older now than he had when Chet first saw him the fateful day he'd met Monica. Weary and burdened. "If there's ever anything I can do for you," he continued, "please don't hesitate to come see me."

"Sure," Chet said, but a man who'd lived the life he'd lived, and done the things he had, didn't make social calls to preachers.

He walked Monica's father to the door, and opened it for him, anxious for him to leave. If Lloyd Fischer stayed much longer, Chet just might start to believe in the impossible.

"She'll get over me," he said.

The older man nodded. "I suspect you're right. In due time. She loves you, and Monica's a good deal like her mother when it comes to love."

Chet hadn't a clue what that meant and furthermore he didn't want to know. His ladle of guilt was filled to capacity and overflowing.

"Good-bye, Chet. I appreciate you taking the time to talk to me." He patted Chet's upper arm as if he were little more than a schoolboy and then ambled out of the room.

Standing in the doorway, Chet watched as Monica's father absently walked down the hallway, strolling past the elevator. He turned around, looking confused, when he reached the end of the hall.

Chet shut the door, leaned against the thick white glass, and closed his eyes. He smelled of stale beer, hadn't shaved in two days, and as a general rule looked like crap, and this man of God had thanked him for damn near deflowering his daughter.

There was something screwy somewhere, and the hell if Chet could figure out where.

He was dizzy again and decided it was probably due to the fact that he hadn't eaten since the day before. The alcohol hadn't helped.

After showering and fixing himself something to eat he felt better. He'd finished his scrambled eggs when the thought subtly presented itself to him. Monica was at the Mission House. Hadn't her father said so himself?

"No," Chet said out loud. "I will not go down there." He reached for his television controller, his finger poised over the Power button.

"You're a fool," Chet muttered, already knowing there was no force on this earth that could keep him away.

He had no intention of talking to her. None. The picture windows in the place gave ample opportunity to view the inside without being noticed. He'd go down, check out what her father had said, and slip away without anyone being the wiser. It was something he'd done a thousand times before as part of his job. He was good at this sort of thing.

With purpose directing him, Chet locked up his office, and when the elevator didn't arrive fast enough to suit him, he took the stairs.

The mission was only a few doors away from his own building. It amazed Chet how easily he was able to find Monica in the crowd of workers. There seemed to be some sort of Christmas party going on. He spied Lloyd Fischer serving turkey with all the trimmings to a long line of derelicts.

Monica was in another part of the room with the children. Apparently she was telling them a story. A handful of kids were sitting on the floor looking up at the book she was holding. A toddler was fidgeting in her lap, reaching for her dangly earrings.

This was what hell must be like, Chet decided. To stand hidden in some corner and view the woman he loved so much it defied reason, and know he would never have her. Hell was watching her hold a child in her arms, and realizing she would never hold *their* child.

She was pale, Chet realized with regret, and dark circles shadowed her eyes. No wonder her father was concerned. Monica wasn't faring any better than Chet was himself. He wanted to shake some reason into her, but that was part of his hell too. He would never touch her again.

Coming here had not been one of his most brilliant ideas. He took a step back, and then another, and was ready to turn and walk away when Monica's gaze suddenly, unexplainably, locked with his.

Chet read her shock and watched the book she was holding tumble unnoticed from her fingers and fall to the floor.

Chet's heart faltered. He couldn't turn and walk away. Then she'd know his game. Then she'd know he'd purposely been spying on her. He had to do something and do it fast.

His shoes made harsh sounds against the sidewalk as he slammed into the Mission House door. He walked past the soup kitchen and moved directly to where Monica was sitting with the children. He braced his feet and glared down at her, sneering.

"Tell your father to stay away from me," he ordered coolly.

Monica's eyes widened with shock.

Not giving her a chance to recover, he turned and walked out, leaving the door to slam in his wake.

Jody let herself into the house that evening, same time as always. Timmy was sitting on the carpet in the family room, occupied with his video game.

"I'm home," she told him, walking into the kitchen.

"Hi, Mom," he called out. "Grandma called."

Jody's blood ran cold. "Grandma Potter?"

"Yes. She wants you to call her right away. She said—oh, darn—"

"What did she say?" Jody asked, hoping to hide her anxiety. It was times such as this that she regretted ever having purchased Timmy the video game system.

"Grandma said if you didn't call her right away that she would call you."

Jody wasn't up to another confrontation with Gloria.

"Glen's coming over for dinner," Jody announced, watching for her son's reaction, hoping to gain confidence in his enthusiasm to spend more time with the attorney. "I thought I'd make spaghetti."

"Sure. He'll like that." Timmy's gaze didn't waver from the television screen, his attention rapt.

Inviting Glen to dinner so they could talk to Timmy together about their engagement had been Glen's idea. Jody had immediately seen the wisdom of it, although now she wished she'd discussed the matter of her remarrying with her son much sooner.

Jody didn't doubt that Timmy would be thrilled. After all, this was what he wanted. His nine-year-old heart had yearned for a father, and his desire was what opened her eyes to the way she'd isolated her life.

"You want to help me set the table?" she asked, although it was an hour or longer before they'd eat.

"In a minute."

Jody rolled her eyes. She'd heard that phrase often enough to have it etched into the patio walkway.

Seeing that she wasn't going to get much conversation from her son, she fried the ground turkey and set the sauce to simmer. Once she'd finished, she reached for the phone and dialed her mother's number. If ever she needed emotional support it was now.

"Hi, Mom."

"Jody, how are you?"

"All right, I guess." She didn't want to unburden her soul, nor could she very well announce that she'd decided to marry Glen within earshot of Timmy. But she could tell her about Gloria's call.

"My guess is that Gloria wants to apologize, dear," her mother said, after Jody finished. "She was hurt and angry and said something she didn't mean, and now she's looking to make amends."

Jody was sure her mother was right, but needed confirmation before returning the call, and said as much.

"You need to remember," Helen continued, "you and Timmy are the only relatives she has left. I'm sure she regrets everything and would like to mend fences. The Christmas gifts you mailed probably arrived and they were the perfect excuse for her to contact you. She means well, sweetheart."

The doorbell sounded and Jody glanced at her watch. "That must be Glen," she explained.

"I do like that young man," her mother announced, and after a quick word in parting, Jody hung up the phone.

Her guess proved correct. Glen stood on the other side of the door, a bottle of wine in his hand and a bouquet of red rosebuds in the other. He kissed her on the cheek and handed her both.

"How's Timmy?" Glen asked as she arranged the roses in a crystal vase.

"Preoccupied," Jody whispered.

Glen's arm circled her waist as they returned to the kitchen. When Timmy noticed Glen had arrived, he turned off the game.

"Hi, Glen."

"How's it going, scout?"

"All right, I guess. Mom said you were coming over for dinner."

"Yeah, you don't mind, do you?"

"Oh, no," Timmy said, "I think it's great, but she made spaghetti and she makes me eat it with a spoon. She'll probably make you do the same thing."

"I think I can live with that, if you can."

"Yeah, I guess so," Timmy said.

"Son, Glen and I would like to have a talk with you before dinner." Rubbing her palms together as if warding off a chill, Jody looked at Glen for assistance. They hadn't talked about when they'd break the news to Timmy, and Jody worried their dinner would be a disaster with this hanging over their heads.

"Sure," Timmy said.

The three of them sat down together in the family room. Glen was next to Jody and Timmy sat across from them. Glen reached for Jody's hand.

"Your mother and I talked this afternoon and decided that we like each other very much," Glen explained.

"I kind of guessed that you did," Timmy said. "I saw you kissing her once."

"Did that trouble you?" Jody asked, watching her son for any telltale signs of jealousy. Although Timmy yearned for a father, he may not have understood that it would mean having to share his mother's attention with someone else.

"I don't know why people kiss on the lips," Timmy said. "It's seems silly when you're always warning me about germs, but adults seem to like it and even some kids. Rich told me he kissed a girl and it wasn't too bad."

"But how do you feel about me and your mother kissing?" Glen pressed.

Timmy frowned as if he didn't know how to answer. "All right, I guess."

Glen's hand tightened around Jody's. She noticed for the first time that he was nervous, which was something she suspected happened only rarely. Her gaze met his and he smiled weakly.

"Glen and I want to talk to you about us getting married," Jody said, surprised by how shallow her voice sounded. Saying the words aloud for the first time caused her heart to pound at a fast rate, as if she were walking up a steep hill. In many ways she was, and the anticipation of this new path she'd chosen suddenly felt momentous.

"Does this mean we'd be a family?"

Jody nodded.

"I'd be your stepfather," Glen explained.

Timmy frowned at that. "But we'd still be a family?"

"Of course we would. Isn't that what you wanted?" Jody sensed Timmy's uncertainty and wanted to reassure him that there was nothing on this earth that would ever change her love for him.

"Would you have more babies like Rich's mom?"

Jody released her breath and looked at Glen. They hadn't discussed the prospect of having children.

"I'd like that very much," Glen answered for her. "But we'll leave the decision up to your mother."

"What do you think, Timmy, would you like it if Glen and I married?" Jody experienced the strongest need to break down and cry. It felt like a band around her chest that tightened more with each second.

"Sure, that would be great. Glen could help me be a better pitcher and then you wouldn't miss my dad so much. It'd be nice to be part of a real family."

Jody bit back the words that claimed they were already a *real* family, he and she together.

"It's settled, then," Glen said, "your mother and I are officially engaged. You know what this means now, don't you, Timmy? Another set of grandparents and aunts and uncles that you'll need to meet." He placed his arm around Jody's shoulder and squeezed gently.

The phone pealed just then and Jody knew in her heart that it was her mother-in-law. Bracing herself, she stood and reached for the phone.

Her guess was accurate.

"I want to apologize for our conversation the other night," Gloria said, sounding calm and collected. It was almost as if the fog in her mind had cleared.

"We both said things we regret," Jody assured her. "This is a difficult time for us."

"Oh, no," Gloria corrected, "you're wrong, my dear. Life couldn't be more beautiful. Christmas has always been my favorite time of year, and more so now than ever before."

"Mine too. Remember the year you joined Timmy and me. We wish your health was better so you could travel more."

"Jeff always enjoyed the holidays," she said.

Discussing her dead husband just then, minutes after she'd announced her engagement to another man, was more than Jody could bear.

"Mom, there's something you should know," she said quickly. "Something wonderful has happened and other than Timmy you're the first one to hear." She didn't mean to announce her engagement like this, but she couldn't think of any other way to divert Gloria from speaking about Jeff.

"You do sound excited and rightly so."

"I told you earlier I'd met another man."

Jody waited for some acknowledgment but none came. "We decided we want to be married," Jody said, "and have set the date for January."

"Married!" Gloria shrieked. "But you can't, you can't! What about Jeff?"

"If Jeff were alive why wouldn't he contact me or Timmy?" she asked reasonably.

"He's been very sick and weak. I haven't talked to him myself yet, but the German official told me he's recovering and asking about you and Timmy."

"Mom, give me the phone number of the person you're talking to and I'll contact him myself."

"I'm sorry, dear, I don't have it. But everything he's said is true, I swear it's true, Jeff's alive. You've got to believe me. You've got to break your engagement before Jeff learns you're involved with another man."

"Mom, this is a cruel hoax. We buried Jeff, remember?" Jody gently reminded her.

It was as if Gloria hadn't heard her. "What am I supposed to tell my son when he phones? I demand that you tell this other man you've changed your mind. No, no, I'll tell him for you. He'll listen to me."

"Mom, please," Jody pleaded, her voice low and trembling.

Glen was standing next to her then, his arm around his shoulder. Gently he took the receiver from her hand, and explained that he was the man Jody was marrying. Naturally she couldn't hear her former mother-in-law's response.

Jody turned into his arm and buried her face in his shoulder.

"Grandma thinks my dad's alive?" Timmy asked, when Glen had hung up the receiver.

Jody was trembling too hard to respond. Glen continued to hold her, patting her back. "Your grandmother wants it to be true so badly that she's convinced herself your father is still alive," Glen explained, when it was apparent Jody was in no condition to do so.

Somehow they made it through dinner, although the three of them took turns attempting to make a festive occasion of it. Glen tried the hardest. Timmy made an effort as well, and Jody too, however feeble. She was grateful when Glen claimed he was working on the brief for an important case and left shortly after they'd finished clearing the table.

Jody walked him to the door. "I'm sorry about Gloria."

"Don't worry," he said, pressing his forehead to hers. "We'll get through this." He wrapped his arms around her and kissed her gently.

Jody let him out the door and watched until Glen's car was out of sight. He was a good man, a decent man, but she didn't feel any great passion for him. She smiled sadly and realized she'd been lucky enough to know about love from Jeff. Love wasn't the reason she and Glen had decided to marry. They cared deeply for each other, shared the same goals, and were comfortable with one another. A lot of marriages had far less.

"I'm done with my homework," Timmy said some time later. Jody had finished the dishes and was busy writing out Christmas cards. She was later than usual this year.

"Are you telling everyone about Glen?" Timmy surprised her by asking. He reached for the top card and read her brief note.

"No."

"Why not?"

"I thought we'd send out announcements later. I've already mailed out half my cards and it doesn't seem fair that half my friends know and half don't."

Timmy nodded as if her reasoning made perfect sense to him. He plopped his elbows on the table and tucked his chin in his hands as he watched her work.

"You know what I wish?"

"What?" she asked absently, thinking he was about to add another item to his detailed Christmas list.

"I wish what Grandma Potter said was true. I wish my dad was alive."

Jody's hand stilled as her fingers tightened around the pen. "I do too, sweetheart."

"Well, what do you think?" Shirley said, looking anxiously to Goodness. "Gabriel insists the winds of trouble are brewing, but I can't see it. Jody's engaged and from everything I can see Glen Richardson is a perfect match for her and Timmy."

Goodness, who was poised atop the Christmas tree, slowly shook her head. "You don't know very much about humans and love, do you?"

"Not really."

"After tracking Monica and Chet I could write a book."

"What's wrong with Jody and Glen?" Shirley asked impatiently. "They're great friends."

"I noticed, and that's a great place to *start* a relationship."

"If you're going to tell me Jody's still in love with Jeff, I'll agree with you. Good grief, I never dreamed this assignment would be so difficult. I do everything Gabriel wants and then he sends me hightailing it back to earth, claiming trouble's afoot. But he won't tell me where."

"It's obvious," Goodness said. "Glen doesn't love her either."

"Now, I sincerely doubt that. Glen's crazy about Jody."

"It's the little boy," Goodness said gently. "Glen's impatient for a family, and Jody has one ready-made for him."

"I disagree." Shirley might have been new at this business, but she didn't doubt Glen's honorable intentions for an instant.

"Why don't we check him out and see for ourselves," Goodness suggested. "I'll help you and then maybe you can help me. I'm having troubles of my own."

They left Timmy's house and had no problem locating Glen's. "He told her he was working on a brief," Shirley explained.

Glen was sitting at his desk, a pen poised in his hands, but he seemed to be having trouble. They watched for several moments while he did nothing more than stare into space.

"What's he doing?" Goodness whispered.

"I don't know. He seems to be thinking."

"Doesn't he know that will only get him into trouble?"

Shirley smiled. "I guess not. Look, he's opening a drawer."

Glen's shoulders heaved with a deep sigh as he removed a photograph from the bottom drawer. Goodness and Shirley looked over his shoulder. The photograph was that of a beautiful young woman with long black hair that cascaded over her shoulders.

"There's your trouble," Goodness whispered. "Glen's in love with another woman."

Chapter 17

This wasn't going to be easy. Monica had carefully steeled herself for the coming confrontation with Chet. She stood outside his office door, her heart pounding hard and fast.

Fervently she prayed she was doing the right thing. All she knew was that she couldn't leave matters between them the way they were.

She could hear movement and knew Chet was there. She drew in a deep breath, knocked, turned the door handle, and stepped inside.

Chet was standing in front of his file cabinet, tossing one file after the other into a large cardboard container. Boxes were piled high on every bit of available space. His desk was clear, and the infamous calendar was down.

He was moving. Leaving Seattle. Leaving her.

"I won't be taking on any new—" He stopped abruptly when he saw it was Monica. For one all-too-brief moment tenderness flashed in his eyes, but that was quickly replaced with practiced hardness. His gaze became sharp and dangerous like that of a cornered animal that was prepared to lash out in order to protect itself.

"What are you doing here?" he said.

"My father wanted me to apologize," she began haltingly. "He never intended to offend you."

"You've apologized, now go."

What gave her to courage to stay, Monica would never know. "Why are you moving?"

He didn't answer, but continued working at a furious pace, lifting several thick folders at a time, carelessly tossing them into the box.

"Where are you going?" she asked, trying a different vein.

"Away. Monica," her name was little more than a frustrated sigh, "please, just go. Don't make this any more difficult than it already is."

"All right," she agreed and he visibly relaxed at her words. "If you answer one question."

"It's over," he said with sharp impatience. "Leave it at that."

"I can't." Monica had honestly tried to accept that he wanted her out of his life. But no matter how hard she struggled to find acceptance none would come.

"I'm not going to debate the issue with you."

"Just tell me why you don't want my love," she said forcefully. "Tell me what it is about me—"

"It has nothing to do with you. The problem is mine."

"Then tell me. I need to know." Despite her efforts to the contrary, her voice cracked with the strain of emotion.

Chet moved as if he were in pain, slowly and with difficulty. His back was to her as he stared out the window. Monica stayed where she was by the door, trembling and hating herself for subjecting them to this torment a second time.

The room seemed to spark with tension.

"I know you love me," she whispered. "You can't make me believe you don't. There has to be something more."

"I'm not good enough for you," he shouted. "Now for the love of God get out of here."

"No," she said softly. "Not until you tell me why you aren't good enough."

"Monica, please."

She walked over and stood next to him. He was so close she could feel his frustration. It seemed to come off him in waves.

"Why aren't you good enough?" she asked again.

Chet's hands were braced against the windowsill, his knuckles white. A war was being waged within him and the battle seemed to be a fierce one. When he turned to face her, his eyes were dull with pain.

"I murdered a man," he shouted. "There, you know, now leave." He pointed toward the door, his face growing red and angry. "Get out of my life, understand, before I ruin yours too."

The force of his anger rocked her, but Monica stood her ground. "I don't know the circumstances," she said shakily, "but if you killed him, then he must have deserved to die."

Chet jerked back as if she'd slapped him.

"It doesn't matter what you've done, I'll always love you."

"No," Chet cried, and then reached for her, hauling her into his arms. The strength of his embrace all but crushed her, but Monica didn't care. There wasn't anyplace else she would rather be than with Chet. He seemed to be drinking in her softness, as if it were as vital to him in that moment as oxygen.

After a short while, he released a harsh shudder and relaxed his hold enough for her to breathe comfortably.

He brushed the hair from her temple and kissed her there. "I'll always love you, too," he whispered brokenly.

It felt like heaven to be in his arms. For the first time in days Monica felt whole, as if the part of her that had been missing had been found.

"You're right when you say he deserved to die. He was a drug lord and brought misery to thousands all for the sake of money and power. An easy death was too good for him. He deserved to suffer."

"Are you wanted by the police?"

He shook his head and laughed shortly. "No, I was too smart for that. I goaded him into a fight and I knew, being the weasel he was, he'd go for his weapon. He did, but I was ready. After an investigation, it was decided that I acted in self-defense, but I knew the truth. I murdered him just as if I'd waited in a dark alley and shot him in the back. He didn't have a chance."

"The gunshot wound," she said, flattening her hand over the scar on Chet's shoulder. She could feel it even through the material of his shirt. "That was when you were shot, wasn't it?"

"No," Chet told her. "Not then."

"He scared you, though, didn't he? Tell me what he did to you."

"None of that matters." He released her then abruptly as if he feared her touch, and backed away. "You got the answer you wanted, now go."

"But, Chet—"

"Go."

Monica flinched. "All right, but there's something you should know."

"How much more of this is there?"

"Not much, I promise you." Her voice wobbled a bit, but with the strength of her pride she managed to keep it under control. "There'll never be anyone who loves you more than I do."

"Monica." He groaned. "Stop, please. This isn't necessary."

"It is for me, so do me the courtesy of listening. Someday you're going to look back on your life and regret this moment."

"The only thing I regret is not moving sooner. Another twenty-four hours and I would have been out of here. You couldn't have waited one stinking day for this, could you?"

"No," she threw back at him. She didn't know when the tears came, but she felt their moisture against her face and brushed them aside. "I'll haunt you . . . or rather, my love will. I swear that's what will happen. It doesn't matter if you travel to the other side of the world, I'll be there. It's my face you'll see when you look at another woman. And . . . and when you sleep, I'll be there each and every night. You won't be able to

close your eyes without thinking of me, without knowing you walked away from the one woman in all this
world who loves you."

"Damn it," Chet stormed, his hands knotted into
tight fists. "Next you're going to tell me that you're
going to sacrifice your life for me. Listen, Monica, I
don't want you sitting here, believing that something's
going to happen that will change my mind. It's over,
understand? Over."

"Don't worry," she whispered and her shoulders
quivered. "That's what I came to tell you. I won't be
waiting for you, I can't, Chet. I've wasted too much of
my life already."

"Good," he snapped. "That's just the way I want it."

Jody had dreaded the office Christmas party for days.
She never had been one who enjoyed these types of social gatherings, and generally didn't stay beyond the
first few minutes. Glen, however, thought the party
the ideal time to announce their engagement to their
peers.

He'd presented her with a lovely engagement ring,
a solitaire diamond that was large enough to feel heavy
and awkward on her finger. She'd removed Jeff's wedding ring years earlier, not because of any desire to
put that part of her life behind her, but to satisfy her

parents. Both were worried about her and although she'd hated it, she'd placed the simple gold band in her jewelry box to appease them.

She could tell from the sounds drifting from the reception area that the party was underway. There were enough goodies to feed a small Third World country. Everyone had contributed something. Jody was guilty of overdoing it herself, bringing a large homemade cheese roll and several dozen gingerbread cookies Timmy had helped her bake the night before.

Her mother was watching Timmy, and insisted Jody stay late and enjoy herself. Because she was with Glen, she was obligated to remain as long as her fiancé wanted.

Glen came looking for her, his smile gentle. "You ready?" he asked.

"Give me a moment to freshen up first, all right?"

"Sure," he said agreeably.

It seemed for a couple engaged to be married, neither of them revealed a high degree of enthusiasm. Glen looked tired. Jody knew he was working hard on a difficult case and put a lot of time and effort into his client's defense, but she strongly suspected his fatigue was something more than his workload.

The restroom was several doors down the hall. Jody walked past a number of offices and wondered how many other Christmas parties were going on in the building that night.

She'd just stepped into a cubicle in the ladies' room when she heard two women.

"You're sure he's engaged?" the first voice asked.

"Yes. Lily took a good deal of delight in relaying the details to me." The second woman sounded shaken and very close to tears.

Jody bit down on her lower lip. Lily was an attorney who worked with Glen. Was it possible the two were referring to Glen and her? She wondered what she should do, or if she should say something.

"Honestly, Maryann, what did you expect Glen to do? You told him in no uncertain terms that you weren't interested in marriage."

Maryann. This was the woman Glen had mentioned, the one he'd once loved. Jody squeezed her eyes closed and tried to remember the particulars of his and Maryann's romance. All she could recall was that Glen was convinced Maryann didn't love him. Breaking off the relationship had devastated him. It was this common ground of loss in which their own relationship had been rooted.

"I . . . I assumed we could live together," Maryann told her friend. "Couples do that these days, you know, test the waters to see if they're compatible. It seemed to be a reasonable thing to do in light of all the divorce cases I've handled over the years. Oh, damn," she said, "I hate it when I cry. Look what it's doing to my makeup."

"What are you going to do?"

"About what?"

Maryann's voice faded and Jody assumed that was because she was studying her reflection in the mirror.

"You aren't going to let him go ahead with the wedding, are you?"

"How can I stop him?" Maryann asked.

"Tell him the truth."

Maryann hesitated, and when she spoke Jody could hear her tears. "I don't even know what the truth is anymore."

"Tell him you're in love with him."

"It's too late for that. Oh, Shelly, honestly, you're too much of a romantic to realize love doesn't automatically fix everything."

"It does if you're both willing to work at it," Maryann's friend insisted.

Afraid of eavesdropping any longer Jody walked out of the cubicle. It was then that the two women realized they weren't alone. Embarrassed, they both avoided looking in Jody's direction. Taking advantage of their surprise, Jody quietly slipped out of the restroom.

She returned to her office, walking past the merry-makers, needing some time alone to absorb what she'd learned. Sitting at her desk, she closed her eyes and tried to reason out what she should do.

The answer should have been far less complex than she was making it. Her sense of fairness said she needed to break off the engagement and explain what she'd heard to Glen. It was an ironic twist that in all the time she'd worked in the building she would meet Maryann now and overhear the conversation she had.

Yet there was a part of her that yearned to give her son the father he longed for, the man who would gently guide him through life. Timmy enjoyed Glen's company so very much. Her son had never been happier than the last few weeks when she'd been dating the attorney.

The real question was if Jody had it in her to grab hold of happiness, however limited, at the expense of another. Having placed the question in that frame, she knew instantly that she had no choice.

"I thought I saw you," Glen said, stepping into the small office. "What are you doing back here?"

Jody looked up from her desk and blinked, surprised to see him.

"What's wrong?" Glen asked. He was a gentle, sensitive man, Jody realized, and she was going to miss him dreadfully. But not nearly as much as Timmy would.

"Sit down," Jody said.

"Jody?" His eyes held hers as he sat.

She stared down at her hand and the beautiful diamond. Before she could find an excuse, she slipped the ring from her finger. "I should never have accepted this," she whispered.

"Why not?"

She held the ring out to Glen, but he didn't take it.

"We aren't in love," Jody said and her chest tightened with regret. "You're a special man and you deserve a woman who will love and treasure you with all her heart."

"You're that woman," Glen insisted.

"We both know that isn't true. If there was anything special about me, it was the fact that I have a son. Timmy was the real attraction. He represents the family you've always wanted. The son you long to have. I made a mistake too," she said, expelling her breath in a rush. "I hurried matters and all but proposed to you myself, long before either of us was ready for a committed relationship. I'm not exactly sure why I found it so urgent for us to marry so soon. Especially when I realized neither of us is anywhere near being ready."

"Let's not be hasty," Glen said, sounding very much like the attorney he was. "We can reason this out. There isn't anything that says we can't have a long engagement, get to know each other better. You're right, I am fond of Timmy, but don't discount what I feel toward you."

"There is a very good reason you shouldn't marry me," Jody whispered. "I'm deeply in love with another man."

"Jody, please, we've talked about this before. You don't need to worry about that. I'll never try to take Jeff's place in your life."

"And you," she continued undaunted, "are deeply in love with another woman." It wasn't until she said the words that she realized the depth of truth in them.

Glen didn't argue with her, and for that she was grateful. "I'd never be unfaithful to you," he assured her.

"But you're willing to do so with yourself."

Glen hesitated. "It's over, Jody, and has been for months. There isn't any hope of reviving the relationship. It's dead."

Jody smiled to herself and set the diamond ring on the desktop as she stood. "It may not be as dead as you think. I want you to wait here."

"Where are you going?"

"To find someone. I shouldn't be long."

Jody left him and hurried out the door. She wasn't entirely sure for which firm Maryann worked, but a quick inspection of the names on the outside of the doors on the floor helped. The receptionist directed her to Maryann's office.

"Hello," Jody said, letting herself inside. "I'm Jody Potter." She waited to see if the other woman recognized the name. "I was the one who overheard you speaking in the ladies' room a few minutes ago."

Maryann paled when she recognized Jody's name. "I had no idea you were there . . . we'd never met and . . ."

"Don't worry, I believe you. I'm here because I have an important question to ask you. Are you in love with Glen Richardson?"

The other woman folded her arms and looked out the window. "I don't mean to be rude, but this isn't any of your business. I understand you and Glen are engaged and—"

"It is my business now, don't you think?" Jody interrupted.

"I can imagine it was disconcerting for you to overhear my conversation with Shelly. It's just that . . . actually, I think it's best if I didn't say anything more." She drew in a steadying breath and then added graciously, "I want you to know that I wish you and Glen every happiness."

"Glen is a wonderful man."

"Yes, I know," Maryann whispered.

"It complicates matters considerably knowing how deeply he loves you," Jody said.

Maryann's head snapped up, her eyes wide with surprise. "I'm sure that's not true, not after the things that happened between us. I was such a fool. There's no hope, not anymore."

"Don't be so sure of that," Jody told her. "Glen's free."

"Free?"

"We're no longer engaged. He's waiting for you in my office now."

Jody had worked with attorneys for a number of years, but she rarely saw one speechless.

"Why . . . why are you doing this?"

Jody didn't feel particularly noble. "I've experienced that kind of love myself, and for a while was willing to take second best. Go to him, Maryann, and settle whatever it was that drove you two apart. But most of all, love him. He deserves to be happy and so do you."

Tears shone bright in the attorney's eyes. "Thank you," she whispered.

"Sure," Jody said, shrugging. "Anytime." She turned and walked out then, past the sounds of the Christmas party and into the cold, dark night the same way she had every evening since Jeff's death.

Alone.

Michelle Madison was alone and frightened, and desperately trying to disguise her fear. Leah had spent a good deal of the afternoon with her and the young woman's labor was progressing smoothly.

"How much longer?" Michelle asked, following an intense contraction. Her hands rested against her protruding stomach and she drew in a deep, calming breath.

"It shouldn't be much longer now," Leah assured her in gentle tones, although she was well aware it could be hours yet. She didn't want to discourage the young mother-to-be.

Michelle had come in earlier in the first stages of labor, before Leah had arrived for work. Because there was no one Michelle wanted to contact, she was alone. By the time Leah arrived for her shift, the labor had intensified and, frightened, Michelle had clung to Leah's hand, begging her to stay.

Since there weren't any other patients on the floor, Leah was able to linger at the young woman's bedside, guiding her step by step through the stages of labor and birth.

"I'm so pleased I'm having my baby with you," Michelle offered just before the next pain overtook her. She closed her eyes and drew in deep, even breaths while Leah softly encouraged her to relax and accept the pain.

"I was in the birthing class that visited the labor room when you were here."

Leah had thought the young woman looked vaguely familiar, but wasn't sure where she'd seen her.

"I don't expect you to remember me," Michelle continued. "Lots of people were asking you questions that day. Jo Ann Rossini claimed anyone who was lucky enough to have their babies on your shift should consider themselves blessed."

"As you might have guessed, Jo Ann's a longtime friend," Leah said, discounting the compliment. She wasn't a miracle worker and although she was gentle with the mothers, they were the ones who did the work. It was called labor for a reason.

"You said you don't have children yourself," Michelle murmured, her eyes closed as the lingering pain gradually faded.

There'd been a time when the careless comment would have felt like a body blow to Leah, but not now.

A child nestled beneath her heart, nurtured by her body, one conceived in love.

"Not yet," Leah concurred. She carefully studied the fetal monitor, pleased that matters were progressing normally for Michelle.

"You want children, though?"

"Very much," Leah confirmed.

A smile, fragile and ever so slight, turned up the edges of Michelle's mouth. Leah guessed the girl was barely twenty, if that, but she didn't want to burden her with unnecessary questions.

Michelle massaged her belly and took in several calming breaths, bracing herself for the next pain. "I didn't expect to love this baby. I imagine that sounds odd to someone like you."

"Of course not," Leah said, wanting to reassure her.

"Lonny didn't want to have anything to do with me after he found out I was pregnant. I believed he loved me, and in his own way, I'm sure he did, but he wasn't ready for the responsibility of a wife and family."

"You don't sound bitter."

"I'm not. At first I was. Not until later did I realize Lonny was right. Getting married now would have been wrong for us both."

"You're very wise for your years." Leah greatly admired Michelle for looking past her pain and finding her peace. Women much older would have difficulty recognizing such deep truths.

"For a while I seriously considered getting an abortion. I never thought I was that kind of person. That's what my mother wanted and later when my dad found out, he did too."

"But you didn't."

"I'm pleased now that I decided to go through with the pregnancy. It hasn't been easy, especially toward the end when I looked like a blimp. My parents have had a difficult time dealing with me having this baby. They said they loved me, but if I wanted to do this, then I'd do it alone. That's why no one is here."

"You're a strong woman, Michelle."

"It was the right choice for me. What surprises me is how much I love this baby."

"You're going to be a good mother."

"I want to be the very best."

With this kind of attitude, Michelle had a chance, Leah decided. She stepped around to the end of the bed. "It's time we check you again." The last series of pains had gained in intensity and she suspected Michelle would soon be entering the third stage of labor.

Once the task was completed, Michelle relaxed. "Will you be in the delivery room with me?"

"I'm not sure," Leah said. "Normally I'd stay but I have a doctor's appointment this afternoon myself. Let's play this by ear and see how matters go. You're doing just great so I don't think there'll be any problem."

"Good," Michelle, said faintly. "I want you to be there if you can. I need someone."

To have Michelle so alone at this important moment tore at Leah's heart. She longed to reassure her patient that she'd seen cases like hers often. "Your parents will come around soon enough," Leah said, gently patting her hand. "They're going to love this baby. They won't be able to help themselves."

"I think so too."

"Do you have any names picked out?"

Michelle shook her sweat-dampened head. "No, I didn't want to know if the baby was a girl or a boy. I thought I'd decide on a name later."

Another two hours passed before Michelle was ready for the delivery room. Leah went in with her, along with the anesthesiologist, Dr. Leon, and the gynecologist, Dr. Beecher. Leah had worked with the anesthesiologist on numerous occasions.

Michelle was a model patient and when the moment came for her baby to be born, she gave a shout of joy. "A girl, a girl." Leah weighed the squalling newborn, wrapped her in a warm blanket, and gently placed her in Michelle's arms.

"A girl," Michelle sobbed. "I'm so pleased I had a little girl. That was what I wanted, but I was so afraid to care."

"She's a beautiful baby," Leah said.

"Thank you. Thank you for your help."

After she carried the newborn into the nursery, Leah happened to glance up at the clock. She'd need to hurry if she was going to make it to Dr. Benoit's in time for her appointment. "I have to rush now, but I'll be by to see you in the morning," she told Michelle when she returned.

"Please don't forget," Michelle said.

"I won't," Leah promised. She started to leave, but Michelle grabbed hold of her hand. "I couldn't have done it without you. Thank you."

"I wasn't the one who worked so hard," Leah said, squeezing the young woman's hand. "Give yourself some credit."

Michelle beamed her a bright smile. "All right, I will." She closed her eyes and yawned. "I feel like I could sleep for a week."

" 'Bye for now." On her way out the door Leah realized Michelle was already asleep.

Leah felt wonderful. Her workday had been full and rewarding. She hurried into the parking lot and started her car, driving past the nativity scene on the hospital side yard. A sense of expectancy filled her. The way she felt, she didn't need Dr. Benoit to confirm what she already knew. There wasn't a doubt in her mind what he would tell her.

The housekeeper had instructions to place a bottle of fine champagne on ice, and there were two thick steaks in the refrigerator. This evening she and Andrew would celebrate. She'd call her parents and if possible wait until the following evening to let Andrew's mother know when they got together for Christmas Eve.

This would be the best Christmas ever, Leah was convinced of that.

Dr. Benoit was a kind, older physician with a quick wit and a gentle heart. He'd been a comfort to her in those bleak years, reassuring and confident when Leah felt having a child was hopeless. It was only fitting that he be the one to tell her she was pregnant.

"Leah," he said, coming into the cubicle. His smile was warm and tender. "It's so good to see you again."

"You were right," she said, holding onto his hand with both of hers. "It's happened. Andrew and I are pregnant."

He said nothing, but then Leah gave him no opportunity.

"Kathy is thrilled for me." Kathy was the nurse who'd collected the urine sample from her.

"Let's sit down and talk," he said, directing her to the chair. "Leah, you don't know how deeply this pains me."

"Pains you?" she asked. "I'm going to have a baby. How could such wonderful news pain you?"

The doctor's eyes softened. He took her hand in his. "Leah, the test is negative."

"There must be some mistake," she said, leaping to her feet.

"I'd give anything to tell you otherwise."

"But I'm late and experienced all the symptoms," she argued. "It isn't possible for me not to be pregnant."

"The mind is very powerful. I don't believe science has a clue of its potential. When a woman wants a child as fervently as you do, she's sometimes able to convince her body she's pregnant. That's what I believe happened in your case."

It wasn't true. Leah refused to believe it, and yet she had no choice. Reaching for her purse, she walked toward the door.

"Are you all right?"

"Sure," she said, but she wasn't and she doubted that she ever would be again.

Chapter 18

"You're back early," Helen Chandler commented when Jody walked into the house after leaving the office party. She took off her coat and hung it in the hall closet.

"Jody, whatever is the matter?" her mother pressed. "You look as if you've been crying." Helen followed her into the kitchen where Jody poured herself a cup of coffee. She wasn't the least bit thirsty, but she needed something to hold onto while she steadied her nerves.

"Where's Timmy?" she asked, surprised not to find her son in front of the television screen, battling it out with alien warlords.

"In his room," Helen answered with a slight frown. "He's wrapping his gift for you. He wouldn't even show me what it is. Now tell me what's wrong. I can't remember seeing you like this in a good long while. You're as pale as a ghost."

"I broke off the engagement with Glen," Jody whispered, not wanting Timmy to hear. Not yet. She'd tell her son as soon as she'd composed herself and could do so without emotion. Her heart wasn't entangled with Glen's and yet she ached for all the might-have-beens.

"But why?" her mother asked, sinking into the chair.

"I don't love Glen."

"Love," her mother cried. "How could you *not* love someone like Glen? He's perfect for you and Timmy. Why, that man walks on water. You couldn't ask for a better husband."

"I'm not going to argue with you, Mom. Everything you say is true, but it was more than not loving him. I know what it's like to be deeply in love, but when it came right down to it, I realized I couldn't accept second best."

Her mother's shoulders sagged with defeat. "You might have grown to feel that way about him. Jody, for the love of heaven, you've got to let go of the past."

"There was one other minor complication with Glen," she said, holding the coffee mug tightly. "He's in love with someone else and I learned that she's still in love with him too."

Helen braced her elbows against the tabletop and hung her head. "And so you did the noble thing and stepped aside. Oh, Jody, what am I going to do with you?"

Jody laughed and impulsively squeezed her mother's arm. "This entire experience has been a valuable lesson to me. In my heart, I know I did the right thing. I just didn't expect it to hurt so much."

"Life's lessons aren't cheap."

Jody nodded. "Ever since Jeff disappeared, I've clung to the misty memories of our years together. The circumstances surrounding his death and all that followed caused me to build a cocoon around Timmy and me. I was so terribly frightened of being hurt again. Jeff was a good husband and I loved him more than I thought it was possible to love another human, but I've built up those years in my mind into a picture of paradise."

Her mother's head came up. "I've waited a good long while for you to realize this. It sounds like you've done some heavy-duty thinking these last few weeks."

"I have," Jody admitted, and a good deal of it had been enlightening. "More than anything I realize I've clung to a half-filled glass, afraid to let go of that small bit of happiness I'd found and reach for the quart jar that was sitting right in front of me."

Helen's frown deepened. "I'm afraid you've lost me with all this talk of glasses and quart jars. I thought we were talking about you and Jeff."

"I'm ready to get back to my life now," Jody said pensively, "ready to reach out in faith and trust God for Timmy's and my future. I'm going to squeeze every bit of joy I can out of what's left of my life. For the first time since Jeff's death I feel like I have one.

"I don't want to spend the rest of it alone, either. There's a man for me out there—someone who'll be a good father to Timmy, and a good husband for me. A man who'll be a friend, a partner, and a lover."

Helen bit into her lower lip. "I've waited years for you to tell me this. I don't know what happened to open your eyes to the truth, but I'm eternally grateful." She stood and hugged Jody. "I'll leave you to talk to Timmy now."

"Thanks, Mom."

"Any time," her mother said. "I love watching Timmy. He's a delight."

"For that, yes," Jody said with tears in her eyes. "But for everything else too, for being there when I needed you, for listening to me, and most of all for standing with me, loving me, giving me the emotional support I needed. You're the best mom in the world."

"You were like this as a little girl," her mother said with a smile, "buttering me up before Christmas."

Jody laughed and the two hugged.

"Mom," Timmy said, standing in the doorway. "Why are you and Grandma crying?"

They both started laughing then, which was sure to confuse him all the more.

"Where's Glen?" Timmy wanted to know next.

"I'll see you tomorrow," Helen said, reaching for her coat and purse.

Timmy watched his grandmother leave. "What's going on around here?"

Jody smiled and patted the top of his head. "I need to talk to you."

"Did I do something wrong?" His eyes grew round with concern, or perhaps guilt, Jody didn't know which.

"No," she assured him, placing her hand on his shoulder and bringing him close to her side. "This isn't about anything you did, I need to tell you something important about Glen and me."

"Mom," Timmy muttered dejectedly, leaning against the doorway in the bathroom as if his weight were too heavy to support, "are you sure we have to go to church? It isn't even Sunday."

"We've been through this before," Jody said, adding the finishing touches to her makeup. "It's Christmas Eve. After church we'll go to Grandma's house and open our gifts with her."

"Will she have hot chocolate and goodies like she did last year?"

"I'm sure she will. Is the car loaded?" Jody asked.

"I did that a long time ago. I wish you'd hurry."

"We have plenty of time." She knew what Timmy really wanted was for the minutes to go by fast so he could get to the gift-opening part of the evening. The Christmas Eve church service was just unnecessary nonsense as far as he was concerned.

"I'll only take a little bit longer," Jody promised. "Don't let me forget the cheese roll and the crackers. They're in the refrigerator."

"Ah . . ."

There was something in Timmy's voice that clued her in to the fact that there was a problem with the cheese roll.

"What?" she said, lowering the mascara brush and turning her head away from the mirror to study her son.

"About the cheese roll."

"What about it?" Jody returned the brush to the holder and tightened the top. Setting the cosmetic bag aside, she faced her son.

"I had a little party with my friends the day Grandma was watching me."

"Yes?" Jody prompted.

"Everyone had something yummy to bring and you took almost all the gingerbread cookies and, besides, I like the cheese roll better than cookies anyway."

"In other words there isn't any left."

Timmy nodded and hung his head. "I have the feeling this isn't going to be a very good Christmas anyway."

"Because of Glen?"

Timmy lifted one shoulder halfheartedly. "I understand why you aren't going to marry him and everything. But I was kinda thinking maybe he wouldn't mind coming by and seeing me every once in a while."

"We'll wait until after Christmas and ask, okay?" The real attraction for Glen had always been Timmy and she sincerely hoped the attorney would maintain contact with her son.

The doorbell chimed.

"Who could that be on Christmas Eve?" Jody wondered out loud.

"I'll see," Timmy said, running toward the front door.

"Timmy," Jody called out after him. "Let me answer that."

She was too late. Her son enthusiastically threw open the door as if he expected Santa Claus to be on the other side.

"Hi," he was saying cheerfully by the time Jody reached the door.

"Hello," Jody said automatically, then gasped as she recognized the man standing on the other side of the screen door. In that moment, she swore her heart stopped dead. She flattened her palm over it and the room started to sway. Staggering two steps, she reached for the door to keep herself from collapsing.

"Mom, what's wrong?"

"Timmy," she said on the tail end of a strangled sob, pulling her son protectively toward her. "This is your father."

Leah had shed so many tears over the last seven years that she discovered that her fountain was dry. A numb feeling attached itself to her as she walked toward her car. She was barren. There was no child to swell and stretch her womb. There never would be. And yet . . . and yet she couldn't make her heart believe what surely was the truth.

The joy she'd felt these last two weeks, believing she was pregnant, was gone. All she could do was live day by day with the emptiness in her heart.

Now she must tell Andrew.

Naturally they'd both pretend it didn't matter, there was nothing else to do. They'd reassure each other and go on, one day into the next, through Christmas, pretending. All the family would be celebrating and she'd have no choice but to make believe all was well with her.

She drove home in a daze, parked her car in the driveway, and walked like a zombie into her house. She moved without direction or will, walking around the perfection of her home, stopping in front of their designer Christmas tree.

Her gaze rested on the beautifully wrapped gifts. Her one thought was to locate the Baby's First Christmas ornament she'd purchased for Andrew, remove it before he unwrapped it on Christmas morning.

Her search became frantic as she sorted through the presents. They'd both suffered enough.

Suddenly she was blinded by tears and couldn't locate the gift, couldn't recall which package contained the ornament. She tossed one gaily wrapped present after another aside, her chest heaving with sobs.

Collecting herself, her hands shaking almost uncontrollably, she methodically sorted the packages into two piles. Hers and Andrew's. Then one by one she tore open his presents until she'd located the silver ornament.

Taking it with her, she walked into the kitchen and threw it in the garbage. The champagne was on ice. She paused, picked it up, and with drops of water leaving a glistening trail across the floor, she carried that to the garbage as well.

The garage door sounded in the distance, signaling Andrew's return. His steps sounded eager as he approached the door leading to the house.

Leah was frozen, immobile.

Andrew walked into the kitchen and stopped when he saw her.

She didn't need to say a word. He came to her and wrapped her in his arms.

Leah woke the following morning, her throat dry and chest heavy. Her eyes stung. Andrew rolled over and tucked his arm over her side, scooting closer, cuddling her spoon fashion.

"Don't go to work today," he suggested. "I'll stay home with you."

"It's Christmas Eve. The hospital is already short-staffed."

"For once, think about yourself instead of that damned hospital."

The short fuse on his temper was the first indication he'd given her of his own bitter disappointment. In some ways having him release his frustration freed Leah.

"I'm all right now," she whispered.

"Call in sick," he pleaded.

"I need to work. It'll help." As if there was anything capable of easing this constant ache. It continued day after day, dull and constant, a steady, ever-present reminder that she was less of a wife, less of a woman.

Despite Andrew's protests, she dressed in her uniform, and even managed to down a cup of coffee before she left the house. Andrew walked her out to her car, looking weary and burdened. His hands were buried in his pockets.

"I'll meet you back at the house at four," he said. "I told Mother we'd be at her place around four-thirty."

She raised questioning eyes to her husband.

"We're spending the evening with her, remember?"

"Of course." She'd momentarily forgotten.

"Do you want to cancel?" Andrew asked, tenderly brushing the hair from her forehead.

"No, I wouldn't want to disappoint her."

Andrew nodded and hugged Leah. They clung to each other for a moment extra and then reluctantly separated.

Leah drove to the hospital and for reasons she didn't understand, she walked over to the side yard where the faded nativity scene was displayed.

The manger was empty. As empty as her heart. As empty as her arms. She hung her head and closed her eyes. If this was a battle, she was surrendering. A prayer sailed straight from her heart.

"I don't know why You don't want me to have a child," she whispered, "but I can't hold onto this pain any longer. It hurts too much. I can't trust even myself." She'd given up trusting God years earlier, preferring to rely upon herself. Now that foundation had crumbled and she was left standing on the sharp rocks of her self-inflicted pain. In essence she was holding up a white flag to God, accepting whatever it was He had planned for her life. She was through fighting, through insisting she knew best, through being miserable.

Her prayer complete, she lifted her head. As she looked upward her gaze continued toward the faded yellow angel that adorned the rickety stable. Leah gasped as a breathless emotion clenched at her heart.

The angel was magnificent, golden and bright, her wings spanned out in elaborate display. She was so bright that Leah couldn't continue to look directly at her. She blinked, thinking this was some type of optical illusion. The sun bouncing off a mirror, or some such phenomenon. But when she opened her eyes, the angel was still there.

Glancing around, she wanted to point out this miracle to whomever she could find.

"Look," she cried out, spying an older woman walking along the sidewalk. Her head was bent against the wind. "It's an angel," Leah cried, attracting the other woman's attention.

The woman stopped and looked toward the nativity scene where Leah was standing.

"That angel's been there for years. Hospital ought to do something about replacing that old set. It's about to fall over."

"This is a real angel," Leah insisted, looking back, but when she did she realized God's messenger had vanished. Leah stared good and hard, wondering if God was attempting to tell her something. If so, the meaning was directed at her alone.

"If she's real, then heaven's in sorrier shape than I realized," the woman said with a deep-throated chuckle.

Leah's heart felt as light as an angel's feather as she walked into the hospital. Since she was a few minutes early, she stopped in the nursery to take a look at the baby girl Michelle had delivered the day before.

The infant, wrapped in a soft pink blanket, was sound asleep. A small red Christmas bow was taped to the side of her crib. Leah rarely visited the nursery. It had been a painful experience in the past, longing for a child so hopelessly herself, but she experienced none of the sharp edges of regret this time. It was as if the burden on her soul had been lifted.

"So here you are," Bonnie said when Leah stepped out of the nursery. "Your husband phoned, looking for you. He sounded anxious."

"Andrew?" He rarely contacted her at the hospital.

"I assumed you only had one husband," Bonnie teased. "You might want to call him yourself. From the sounds of it he's pacing the floor, waiting to hear from you."

Leah headed for the phone, but after four rings the answering machine kicked in. If it was that important, Andrew would call again soon.

He didn't. No more than ten minutes later, Leah was reading over the nurse's report at their station when Andrew came rushing down the corridor.

"Leah," he called breathlessly. He wrapped his arms around her waist and lifted her off the ground. His eyes were bright and his voice sounded as if he were about to burst into peals of laughter.

"What is it?" she pleaded.

He released her and his hands framed her face. "I love you, Leah, never more than I do this moment."

She stared up at him, wondering at his craziness.

"You were right about us having a child. That feeling you claimed you had. It's happening, sweetheart, just the way you said it would."

"But Dr. Benoit said—"

"Mrs. Burchell phoned not more than two minutes after you left the house."

The name was vaguely familiar to Leah, but she couldn't remember from where.

"The lady from New Life Adoption Agency," he filled in. "They have a child for us. She'll be ready to leave the hospital first thing tomorrow morning. The mother's already signed the adoption papers."

"But we withdrew our names," Leah cried, covering her mouth, unwilling to believe it was true.

"I asked that she reactivate our file weeks ago. We have a baby, Leah. A precious baby girl."

Monica was right, Chet realized. She'd announced her decision to torment him and by heaven she'd done it. He'd close his eyes and he'd be damned if she wasn't there like some ghost, pestering him until he ended up spending half the night dulling his mind with late-night television rather than attempt sleeping. The minute he tried, Monica was there, all sweet and soft, wrapping the tendrils of her love around his heart, reminding him of all he'd rejected.

He'd been trying to get hold of a moving company for the better part of the afternoon. Every one he called insisted on knowing his destination. That was the problem. They didn't have rates for "any place that wasn't Seattle."

The bartender ambled over to where Chet was sitting. He was new, Chet noted, young and wet behind the ears. He'd introduced himself as Billy. Appropriate enough since he looked more like a kid than an adult. If Chet were the one serving up the liquor he'd have carded the youth.

"You want another cup of coffee?" Billy asked.

"Please." Chet had given up on booze. The desired effect caused too many problems. True, he could drown his sorrows, as the saying went, but there was a heavy price to pay. Hangovers had never appealed to him.

"What do you think of the new big-screen television?" Billy asked. "The boss had it brought in this morning."

"Nice," Chet said, without looking. He wasn't interested in making conversation. He wasn't entirely sure why he'd stopped in at the Blue Goose. It was a damn sight better than hanging around his place, he decided. Everything he'd managed to accumulate in the last thirty-odd years was packed and ready to go. He just didn't know where he was headed yet.

The bar was deserted, Chet noticed, which was unusual this time of night. A couple was off in a dark corner and the two only had eyes for each other. Hands too, apparently. Other than the lovebirds and Billy, Chet was the only other customer. "Where is everyone?" he asked.

"Home, I guess. It's Christmas Eve."

"It is?" He'd lost track of the days. In the back of his mind he knew Christmas was close, but it was a day like any other as far as he was concerned.

"I don't expect we'll get much of a crowd this evening. Places like this generally don't over the Christmas holidays," Billy commented as if this were something he'd garnered in his vast experience tending bar.

"Guess not," Chet mumbled, unwilling to be drawn into a conversation, but he could tell from the way the kid was hanging around that he wasn't going to have much of a choice.

"You'd think Lou would close up shop," Billy said next.

Chet sipped from his coffee. It was dark, thick, and potent enough to satisfy a Cajun.

"Apparently you don't know Lou," Chet commented.

"Not very well," Billy agreed.

Thinking he might divert the kid's attention, Chet swiveled around in his chair and concentrated on the television. The national evening news was on, forecasting gloom and doom. Chet had heard enough of that.

"Mind if I change the channel?" he asked.

"Be my guest," Billy said, handing him the controller.

Chet worked his way through the stations. Nothing appealed to him, not even a rerun of a play-off football game telecast earlier that week.

"Hey, go back, would you?" Billy asked. "I have a friend who was picked up by the pros. He's a defensive lineman for the Redskins."

Disgusted, Chet handed the remote control back to the bartender. So much for that idea. Oblivious to Chet's ugly mood, Billy punched the controller until he found the play-off game.

The kid focused his attention on the screen, which suited Chet just fine as long as he left him alone.

Before he realized it, Chet had turned around on his bar stool and was watching the game himself. So this was what his life had boiled down to—sitting in some bar on Christmas Eve, talking to a kid he didn't know and didn't want to know and watching reruns of old football games on television.

At halftime Billy disappeared into the back storeroom. Chet cradled the coffee mug in his hands and studied the television screen. The commentator was the well-known former coach of the Los Angeles Raiders, John Madden.

"You should be ashamed of yourself, Chet Costello," the TV commentator said.

Chet's head snapped up. He was losing it. The television was actually talking to him.

"Yes, I'm talking to you," John Madden said again. "You're the biggest fool I've ever seen."

By that time Chet was on his feet. He stared down at his drink, thinking the kid had played a cruel joke on him and laced it with some mind-bending drug.

"Quit looking at your drink," the former coach told him. "It's only coffee."

Other men claimed to see pink elephants, but not Chet. Oh, no, that would have been too easy. He had to have some voice come out of a television to chastise him.

"You're in love with Monica Fischer, and she's in love with you. So what's the problem? You think you're being noble, don't you? Wrong. You're a fool."

Chet had had enough. He didn't need this. Slamming his cup down on the bar, he started out the door.

"Go ahead and run," the voice said, sounding so close he swore he could feel the breath against the back of his neck. "It's what you've been doing for most of your life."

"Shut up," Chet shouted.

The couple in the back of the room glared over at him, and Billy, who was hauling a box of pretzels to the front, stopped in his tracks.

"Something wrong?" the kid asked.

Chet shook his head and slammed out of the bar. "Damn," he muttered, running his hand down his face. It was worse than he imagined. Monica had decided ruining his sleep wasn't bad enough, now she'd taken on his waking hours as well.

He was putting an end to that right now. With purpose directing his steps, he walked to the parking garage and drove to her house.

The streets were full of parked cars. The Blue Goose might be less than busy, but Lloyd Fischer's church was doing a bumper business. Light spilled out of the church, and the parsonage was dark, all but one small light in the front of the house. Music filled the night, traditional Christmas carols played on an old-time pipe organ.

Chet found a place to park on the street, half a block down from the church. Several people were walking toward the building. There was a family with two small children in tow, and an older couple, holding hands, smiling up at each other.

Chet stayed where he was, hidden in the shadows. One thing he knew, he wasn't walking into that church. He was deciding what he was going to do when he spied Monica coming out of the parsonage. The porch light went on as the light in the living room was extinguished. Her silhouette was framed in the warm glow of the single bulb on the porch.

She seemed to be in something of a hurry, Chet noted. Rushing across the street, he met up with her on the sidewalk.

She stopped when she saw him. Surprise worked its way across her features, starting with her eyes and then her mouth. She opened it as if to say something, then closed it again. She hugged sheet music against her breast and seemed to be waiting.

Chet didn't know what he intended to say. It was too damn hard not to bring her directly into his arms, hold her against him, and breathe in her softness.

"Whatever you've done has got to stop," he said between clenched teeth.

"Done?" she echoed, and blinked as if she didn't understand what he was saying.

"Leave me alone," he ordered.

She nodded once and waited, apparently for an explanation.

"I can't eat or sleep, and now I'm hearing voices as well."

"Voices?" The edges of her mouth quivered with amusement. "And what did these voices say?"

"That I was a fool for walking away from you." Chet rammed his fingers into his hair.

Monica smiled boldly at that and Chet swore he'd never seen a woman more beautiful. He shouldn't have come, and now that he was here, God help him, he didn't know how he was ever going to leave.

"I wish I could claim credit for that, but I can't," she said softly. "Dad told me he suspected you were drinking heavily. My guess is that it was the liquor talking."

"Not this time," he argued. "I haven't had a drop all day."

"I can't help you, Chet," she said sadly and raised her fingers as if to touch his face. He meant to jerk away, but found he couldn't. As it never failed to do, her touch rippled through him like an electrical current.

Her softness had branded his life and his heart. There was no escape. He could run to the far ends of the world and every breath he drew, every beat of his heart would be for her.

Capturing her wrist, he roughly drew her palm to his mouth where he planted a series of tender kisses.

"Dear God, Monica," he said, hauling her into his arms. He buried his face in the delicate curve of her neck and drew in several deep, uneven breaths. "I can't make myself leave you. I tried. God knows I tried."

The sheet music she'd been holding fell to the sidewalk as she clung to him. He felt her trembling, her tears moistening his face and her breath coming in soft gasps that fanned his throat.

He held her against him, his chin resting on the crown of her head. His eyes were tightly closed. "We'll get married, just the way you want, although I can't help but feel you're getting the bum end of this deal."

Chapter 19

"You're my real-life dad?" Timmy asked, staring up at Jeff with wide, disbelieving eyes.

"Yes, son, I'm your father." Although Jeff answered Timmy, his gaze was leveled on Jody, his look expectant and filled with nervous anticipation.

Her pulse had yet to right itself, and the dizziness from the frantic beat of her heart continued. He was terribly thin, she noticed. His cheeks were hollow and his eyes seemed to sink back into his head. This was a man she didn't know and barely recognized as the one she'd loved.

Jeff seemed greedy for the sight of Timmy and her, staring at the two of them as if he couldn't quite believe this moment was real.

Timmy opened the screen door and Jeff walked inside the house, pausing in front of Jody.

Her eyes begged him to convince her this was happening and that he was as real as he seemed. She'd been under a good deal of stress and she feared that this was all a figment of her imagination. Some dream she'd wake from with a start. When Jeff had first disappeared she'd repeatedly dreamed of a moment like this when they'd be reunited. Then she'd wake with a heavy heart and the loneliness would close in and swallow her.

Her hand trembled as she worked up the necessary courage to touch him. She laid her fingers against his forearm. He felt solid and real. Warm and alive.

Alive. Jeff was alive.

"Where were you?" she asked in a sobbing breath, pressing her hands to her throat. "Why did you leave us? Why?" The questions crowded on top of each other, damming her mind and her tongue. The only one to escape was the least important.

"Do you mind if I sit down?" he asked, and Jody realized how terribly shaky he was. "I'm a bit weak yet," Jeff explained.

It was all Jody could do to nod.

Timmy took Jeff by the hand and led him to the sofa. "You don't look like my dad," he commented, carefully studying his father. "You're too old."

"I feel like I'm about a hundred," Jeff said, examining his son. He cupped Timmy's face and his eyes filled with tears. "Not a day passed that I didn't think about and pray for you. I carried the picture of you with me through the months. I swear it was what kept me alive. I could endure anything as long as I remembered my wife and my son."

"Where were you?" Timmy asked, sinking onto the cushion next to his father.

Trembling almost uncontrollably, Jody sat in the chair across from them both, her legs too numb to continue to support her.

"I was in a Russian prison," Jeff explained. "It's a miracle I was released."

"You were in Russia?" Jody repeated in a breathless whisper.

"I'd gone to Germany on business and on a fluke decided to visit East Berlin. I was curious about the other side of the wall, but doubted that I'd be able to make it through the border with an American passport. It was surprisingly easy to obtain fake identification."

"You went through all that trouble because you were curious about East Berlin?" Jody found the entire story unbelievable and a fermenting kind of anger took hold of her. He'd risked everything for some crazy need to look at life on the other side of the wall?

"I was young and stupid, so incredibly stupid," Jeff said, the regret weighing down his voice. "My German was passable, and all I intended to do was wander into a few shops and get a look around. I was heading back to the border when I stumbled upon two soldiers beating a teenager. They would have killed him. I couldn't stand by and do nothing and so I intervened. That proved to be a costly mistake."

Jody's anger dissipated. He'd paid a terrible price for his curiosity, and consequently so had she and Timmy.

"I was taken in for questioning and soon arrested," Jeff continued.

"Why didn't you contact the embassy?" Jody demanded. He could have saved them both this agony.

"I wasn't allowed. And when they discovered I was an American with a false passport my fate was sealed. I was a spy, and tried as one. I wasn't able to talk to an attorney, and the trial, such as it was, lasted all of two minutes. Before I fully understood what was happening to me, I was shipped off to a prison camp in Russia."

Jody covered her mouth with both hands.

"I've been held there ever since."

"But how did you escape?"

"I didn't," Jeff explained. "I was freed. They dropped me off on a German street as if nothing had happened. The last two weeks I've been hospitalized and debriefed. From what I've been able to grasp this all has something to do with the breakup of the Soviet Union. There was a British man with an experience similar to mine who was released about the same time."

"Why wasn't I contacted right away?" Jody demanded.

"In the beginning I was too ill. Apparently the authorities communicated with my mother first. I learned that you'd divorced me."

"I had to do that for financial reasons," Jody told him. "It wasn't what I wanted."

A weak smile lit up his face.

"If you were well enough to travel, surely you could have made a phone call?" Jody wasn't satisfied, not yet.

"All I knew was that the woman I'd loved had divorced me. I talked to my mother only once and she insisted I get home right away because you were about to marry another man."

"Not anymore," Timmy told him. "They're only friends."

Once again, Jeff looked greatly relieved. "The doctors wanted to keep me longer, but I couldn't wait another minute. I had to reach you and talk to you face to face before it was too late.

"If getting out of Russia was miraculous, then finding an empty seat on a transatlantic flight was an even greater phenomenon. I was flying standby when some lady came running off the plane, claiming she was hearing voices over the headset that told her she shouldn't be on this flight. The funny thing was, she insisted it was Jay Leno, speaking directly to her. Whatever her reason, I got her seat."

"But you were dead. My father took your dental records with him to Germany and your remains were positively identified. We buried you. This isn't possible, it just isn't possible."

"It wasn't me, Jody. I don't know why your father would do such a thing."

"Oh, Daddy," Jody whispered and briefly closed her eyes. "It was three years after you'd disappeared and I refused to give up hope. My life was in limbo. For financial reasons I'd had to divorce you. Your mother didn't understand and I felt so incredibly guilty. Dad must have assumed that if we buried a body, I'd be able to put the past behind me and get on with my life."

"Your father has a lot of explaining to do," Jeff said without rancor.

"He died a little more than a year ago. Unexpectedly. I'd like to believe that if he'd known he only had a short time to live, he'd have told me the truth."

"I believe he would."

Jeff was more generous than he need be.

"Your mother was telling me the truth," Jody whispered, remembering the calls she'd received from Gloria Potter.

"I don't blame you for not believing her. I was terribly ill and hadn't spoken to her myself. I want you to know that I love you, Jody. I've always loved you and Timmy. It was the memory of the two of you that got me through this hellish nightmare. I also realize a lot of things can change in eight years, and I won't stand in the way of your happiness. All I ask is that you allow me to have contact with my son."

"Oh, Jeff."

"Mom and Glen aren't engaged anymore," Timmy explained excitedly. "He was in love with someone else and Mom's still in love with you."

Jeff's eyes slowly sought out hers as if he were afraid to trust what he was hearing. "Is that true?"

She nodded. "I never stopped, not for an instant. I couldn't breathe and not love you."

Jeff held out his arms to her, Jody flew off the chair and inside a heartbeat was at his side. Jeff wrapped both Timmy and her in his embrace.

Tears rained down Jody's cheeks as she spread soft kisses over Jeff's face. The three of them were laughing and crying all at once.

"God answered my letter," Timmy said excitedly. "He gave me back my very own dad."

A baby girl," Leah repeated, afraid there'd been some misunderstanding. "We should have been contacted by the adoption agency before now."

"Apparently the mother only made her decision yesterday afternoon. The crazy part is our daughter's right here in this very hospital. She's here, Leah. Here. Mrs. Burchell said she was born yesterday afternoon at Providence Hospital."

According to the records Leah had been reading when Andrew arrived, there'd only been one girl delivered on December twenty-third and that had been the birth she'd assisted. Michelle Madison's baby.

"Michelle," she whispered, closing her eyes. The frightened young woman who was so alone and had clung to Leah. The one Leah had spent her entire shift coaching through labor and birth.

"Andrew," she said, laughing and crying both at the same time. She took her husband by the hand. "Come, I'd like to introduce you to our daughter." Trembling, she led her husband toward the nursery. She had him remove his jacket and put on a sterile blue gown and set him in the rocking chair. Then with her heart so full it felt as though it would burst wide open, she gently lifted the sleeping infant from her crib and tenderly placed her in Andrew's arms.

"She's so tiny," her husband whispered, looking down on the plump pink face of their daughter.

"At eight pounds six ounces, her birth mother didn't think so," Leah said, smiling through her tears. "You two get acquainted and I'll be right back."

A look of panic came over Andrew. "Where are you going?"

"To talk to someone very special."

"What if she cries?"

"One of the nurses will help you, but don't look so worried. Everything will be all right." Including the rest of Leah's life.

Michelle was sitting up in bed when Leah came into the room. When she saw it was Leah, the young woman smiled and held out her hand, which Leah gripped. "Have you heard from the adoption agency yet?" Michelle asked.

Leah nodded. "My husband just told me." Now that she was here, Leah's heart was so full that she didn't know if it was possible to find the words to thank Michelle.

"When I decided against the abortion, I didn't know what I was going to do," Michelle started. "A friend suggested adoption and so I contacted New Life Adoption

Agency. Their counselors were great, they didn't pressure me one way or the other. I met with them several times and they listened. You see, I assumed that in order to give up my baby, I had to keep myself from loving her, and I couldn't seem to make myself do that. In the beginning when Lonny left me, all the baby represented to me was heartache, and later as she started to grow and move, I discovered how very attached I was getting. I couldn't help being curious about adoptive parents, though, and for the first time, just a few weeks ago, I read over several profiles. Your letter stood out in my mind."

"Why?" Leah wanted to know. The letter had been written years earlier, and she couldn't remember any of what she'd said.

"You wrote about being a delivery-room nurse and how you felt about helping young women through labor and birth. It seemed to me you must be someone very special. Then by some kind of fluke the birthing class I was attending toured Providence Hospital and we met you. Naturally I didn't know your last name, but I remembered what you'd written. When I asked Jo Ann about you she told me you didn't have any children yourself, I figured you must be the Leah whose letter I'd read."

"That was why you chose to have your baby here at Providence Hospital?" Leah asked.

Michelle nodded. "It was pure chance that you could be with me. I still hadn't decided if I could give my baby up for adoption. Then yesterday after she was born, you said something that helped me make up my mind."

"I said something to help you decide?" Leah was incredulous.

Michelle nodded. "You told me I would be a good mother to my baby. I'm not giving her up because I don't love her. It's because I love her so very much that I can.

"Mrs. Burchell explained that you'd had one birth mother change her mind at the last minute. You needn't worry, that won't happen this time. I feel very strongly that God led me to you and your husband and you're exactly the right couple for my baby."

"How can I thank you?" Leah whispered through her tears.

"By loving her, guiding her through the years for me. When she's older and has questions about me, tell her how God brought the two of us together, tell her that He handpicked her family for me."

"I will," Leah promised, rubbing the moisture from her cheek.

The two women hugged and after she'd dried her eyes Leah returned to the nursery. Andrew was gently rocking back and forth staring down at the face of his newborn daughter. One tiny fist was clenched around his index finger. The newborn was holding onto her daddy's hand.

"It looks like the two of you are getting along nicely," Leah commented.

"I still can't believe she's really our daughter," Andrew said.

"I don't have a single doubt she belongs to us," Leah assured him.

"Have you decided on a name?"

"Yes," Leah said, her response automatic. "Angel." Some day she'd tell her husband and her daughter about seeing the special Christmas angel, but not now. The angel had been His sign to her, His confirmation. She would carry that very special gift with her through the years.

"Angel?" Andrew repeated slowly, glancing up. "But I thought you had three names already chosen and I don't recall any of them being Angel."

"It seems fitting to me. Do you object?"

"Angel Lundberg," he said again as if testing it on his tongue. "It feels right. Angel Hannah Lundberg."

"My turn to hold her," Leah said.

Andrew stood and gently placed the sleeping baby in Leah's arms. Angel arched her back and stretched, yawning before she nestled comfortably in Leah's arms as if this were exactly where she was supposed to be. With that Angel Lundberg immediately returned to sleep.

"You're willing to marry me?" Monica asked, unsure if she should trust what Chet was saying. "But why now?"

"Because I know you're right. I'll regret letting you go the rest of my life. I love you, Monica. I heard a voice telling me what a fool I was and if it wasn't the booze speaking, then . . . hell, I didn't think anyone up there cared about me."

"I love you, Chet Costello. I can't explain that voice, but whoever or whatever it was, I'm thanking God."

He smiled and gently kissed her. "Next thing I know we'll have a couple of kids and I'll be a regular churchgoer."

That sounded like heaven to Monica. "Would you kindly shut up and kiss me again?"

He pulled her to him as if she were the most precious thing he would ever touch, as if he cherished every moment spent with her.

Monica inched her mouth from his and stared up into his face. His eyes met hers and it seemed they were filled with a thousand regrets.

"I love you so much," she whispered.

"You must."

"Stop." She pressed her finger over his lips. "I don't pretend to know everything there is about the Bible and God, but I do know that He said He would forgive us when we ask. If it's peace of mind you're seeking, it's available."

"In church."

"No." She pressed her hand over his heart. "You won't find what you're seeking in any building."

"I killed a man," Chet reminded her. "He murdered my partner and attempted to kill me. That's a little more serious than jaywalking."

"Do you think you're the only one who's ever done something he wishes he hadn't? You say this man you murdered attempted to kill you first. What you don't seem to realize is that in some ways he succeeded. He's reached out from the grave and gotten a stranglehold on your heart and your life." Monica saw Chet as a man whose life had been shredded to ribbons with the ax of revenge and regret. "Your time of hate is over. You can stop punishing yourself now."

"My time of love is about to begin."

"Oh, yes," she said, winding her fingers into the hair at the base of his neck. "Now, what was it you were saying about the two of us getting married?"

"Soon, Monica, I'm not going to be able to wait for you much longer."

She could feel the heat coming into her cheeks. "I'm not going to be able to wait for you much longer either. I don't think there's ever been a woman more eager to give up her virginity than I am."

They kissed and the heat of their love and need was like a spontaneous combustion. Monica didn't know what would have happened if her father hadn't happened upon them just then.

It was the sound of Lloyd clearing his throat that broke them apart. "Dad," Monica said breathlessly. "Oh, Dad, you'll never guess what—"

"Reverend Fischer," Chet said, taking charge. He looped his arm around Monica's waist and held out his free hand to her father to shake.

"I take it congratulations are in order?" the reverend asked.

Chet nodded. "If you don't object, I'd like to marry your daughter."

"Object," her father said, laughing. He slapped Chet across the back. "I'm thrilled for you both. You don't mind if I announce it at this evening's service, do you?"

Chet looked at Monica, then back at her father. "I'd be more than pleased."

Together the three of them walked toward the church where the music swelled and teased the golden silence of the night with its lyrical melody.

Shirley, Goodness, and Mercy stood in the choir loft looking down on the congregation that had crowded into the church for Christmas Eve services.

"You should all be pleased with your efforts," Gabriel announced from behind them in a voice as light as yesterday's dreams.

The three prayer ambassadors whirled around. Gabriel hadn't meant to surprise them, but he was well pleased with their accomplishments. His trips to earth were few and far between, but this was a special night, one created for exceptions.

"Timmy has his father for Christmas," Shirley said proudly, "thanks to a bit of manipulation with the airlines and a certain passenger."

"We need to talk about that," Gabriel said sternly. Shirley was new to prayer assignments, and had much to learn. He noticed she'd picked up a number of bad habits from her friends.

"What's going to happen to Jeff and his family?"

The future could be read by only a chosen few. Gabriel was pleased to offer a view to his young charges. "Jeff and Jody will go on to have another child, but not for two years. They'll have a little girl. As you can imagine they have a fair amount of readjusting to do first."

"What about Timmy?" Shirley pressed. "He seems to be a very special young boy."

"He is. Timmy Potter will grow up to become a top-notch pitcher with his goals set on the major leagues. He has a strong faith that will sustain him all his life."

"What about Monica and Chet?" Goodness wanted to know next, her eyes eager for a look into the future.

Gabriel was tempted to comment about this last bit of trouble Goodness had gotten herself into with the television screen. He decided against it, however. Goodness's methods had been unorthodox, but had worked wonderfully well. Chet had gone directly from the Blue Goose to Monica.

"Now, there's an interesting couple," Gabriel said, studying the pair who sat in a pew in the front of the church, holding hands. "Chet will go back into police work. It's what suits him best and he's good at it. Monica will present him with four daughters and all four will be holy terrors. Their lives together are going to take a fair amount of adjustment as well. They're both strong-willed people, but their love for each other is much stronger."

"Leah and Andrew were able to bring Angel home this evening," Mercy told him, although Gabriel was well aware the couple's daughter was doing so well she was able to leave the hospital early.

"You might be surprised with what the future holds for them," Gabriel said. He wasn't overly pleased with Mercy's appearance atop the nativity scene, but at least this time she wasn't racing forklifts along a pier and frightening night watchmen out of ten years of their lives.

"Are they able to adopt another child?"

"No, but three earth years from now Leah will become pregnant with identical twin boys."

"Twins," Mercy echoed with delight. "That's wonderful."

"I'm proud of you three," Gabriel felt obligated to comment. Their success had delighted him. "You worked well together."

" 'Surely goodness and mercy shall follow you all the days of your life,' " Goodness quoted the well-known Bible verse. "We make a great team."

"Can we do it again?" Shirley asked eagerly.

"Soon," Mercy insisted. "We help each other."

"I think we should all visit Los Angeles next," was Goodness's suggestion. "It seems to me that the City of Angels could do with our help."

The three looked expectantly toward Gabriel. "I'm not making any promises," he said, and with a sweep of his wings ushered the three ambassadors into the celestial realm of heaven where the Christmas celebration was just about to begin. All of heaven was awaiting their return.

THE NEW LUXURY IN READING

We hope you enjoyed reading
our new, comfortable print size and found it
an experience you would like to repeat.

Well – you're in luck!

HarperLuxe offers the finest in fiction and
nonfiction books in this same larger print size and
paperback format. Light and easy to read, HarperLuxe
paperbacks are for book lovers who want to see
what they are reading without the strain.

For a full listing of titles and
new releases to come, please visit our website:

www.HarperLuxe.com